The Mallaig Link

Also by this author

The Feast of the Antlion

Breathless

The Mallaig Link

A novel

Caro Ayre

Greenham Hall
TA21 0JJ

The Mallaig Link

Copyright © Caro Ayre 2016
All rights reserved

This is a work of fiction. Names, characters and incidents are the product of the author's imagination or are used fictitiously. Any resemblance to actual persons, living or dead is entirely coincidental.

The Author asserts the moral right under the Copyright Designs and Patents Act 1988 to be identified as the author of this work.

All rights reserved. No part of this material may be reproduced or transmitted in any form or stored in a retrieval system without the prior written consent of the author.

Greenham Hall
Greenham
Wellington
Somerset TA21 0JJ

The journey from start to finish of this book has been seemingly endless.

The number of people I have to thank for help and support on the way is too long to list. You know who you are, and I am truly grateful for all the assistance given over the years.

And an extra special thanks goes to my long suffering family who have endured my distracted attention throughout the process.

Chapter 1

Gavin McKay had been a Detective Inspector in Strathclyde long enough to recognize the smell of fear wafting towards him from the man huddled in the corner of the cell. The mud-splattered coat wrapped around his body was steeped in the stench of stale beer, vomit and cigarettes.

"Where's Gavin?" the man shouted. "I want to talk to Gavin."

"Your friend's been going on like this ever since he arrived," the duty sergeant said, as he pushed the heavy metal door wide open. "He was picked up for abusive behaviour. He appeared to be determined to get arrested, bringing him in was the safest option all round. With a bit of luck, now you're here, he'll shut up. I've asked Doctor Munro to come in and check him over."

Gavin stepped forward and touched the man's shoulder. The threadbare fabric of the scruffy coat was too thin to disguise the lack of flesh on the bones beneath. Lank wisps of hair, an untrimmed, speckled beard and the ravages of street life made Neil Gillespie look nearer sixty-eight than thirty-eight. Hell, it was only two weeks to their shared birthday. If Neil kept up his current lifestyle they wouldn't be sharing many more. Neil's deterioration pricked

Gavin's conscience. He could have been more supportive.

"I'm here, Neil." Gavin hoped there was no hint of pity in his voice. Since Neil's son died from an overdose two years ago, grief had taken over. Neil's head lifted, the movement gave Gavin a brief glimpse of his split lip and the plum-coloured bruises circling his eyes.

"About bloody time..." Neil muttered, as he pointed towards the door. "Tell him to push off."

Gavin signalled the sergeant to leave. "It's OK, he's gone."

"Did you bring some fags?" Neil asked with a nicotine-stained, gap-toothed grin.

Gavin dug into his pocket for the cigarettes and matches he'd bought on his way to the police station. He handed them over and waited, thinking how hard it was going to be once the no smoking laws were in place. Neil's hands shook as he removed the cellophane wrapping, eventually putting a cigarette between his swollen lips. He lit up, choking as the smoke hit his lungs. "You must go to the house," Neil mumbled, "near Mal... Mal... you know..."

"No, tell me."

"Mal...Mallaig, yeah, that's the place." Neil spluttered, "The place where they keep the stuff… it all happens there."

"What? Drugs?" Gavin asked, guessing Neil's drug crusade was still on-going. Neil didn't respond. "You haven't a clue have you? Why should I stick my neck out for you?"

"Find the bastards..."

"Who? The guys who beat you up?"

"You know..." he muttered.

"No, I don't." Gavin struggled to curb his impatience. Anger wouldn't help. He lowered his tone and said, "OK, you win. If you won't say who rearranged your face, tell me how to get to this place."

Neil seemed to consider this request, closed his eyes, took a deep breath and started reciting a precise set of directions. Gavin listened, picturing the route as Neil spoke, committing the details to memory.

Neil finished talking, slumped back against the wall and sighed. Gavin waited silently expecting him to add something. Nothing was forthcoming, so he asked, "What's the name of the house?"

Neil shrugged.

"Have you ever been there?"

Again Neil shook his head.

"Stop mucking about. Tell me what's so special about the place?"

With a sly grin Neil beckoned him closer and whispered. "You told me you'd like to help me nail our old pal, Hector Sinclair... this is your chance."

"Sinclair? He's just been promoted to Acting Chief Superintendent."

"I heard. Could've been your job, if you hadn't lost it."

"Lost what?"

"Your edge. Watch out, you don't want to end up a sad case like me. Maybe Hector becoming your boss will shake you up. I bet he's lapping up the power."

"Revelling in it, but what the hell has he to do with this house?"

"You find out. You're the copper." Neil pulled the coat up round his ears. "Get out of here, I need some sleep."

Gavin retreated from the custody suite, too late to go back home on the outskirts of Oban and too cold and wet to make a run enticing. He decided to catch up with paper work while the building was quiet. He made his way upstairs, passing the coffee machine on the way. A ribbon of light spilling out of the half closed door of his department puzzled him. None of his team would be at their desks this early. He had enough trouble getting them in on time when there was a big investigation on. He stuck his head round the door to check.

Paula Dawson, the sole occupant leapt behind a filing cabinet. Her hurried movement sent her handbag flying off the desk, scattering the contents.

"Paula, are you alright?" he asked, wondering why his newest recruit would want to hide from him, or anyone else.

The young DC had only been with the team for a couple of months. Her quirky hair style had nearly put him off choosing her, but her sharp wit and warm smile put her ahead of the other contenders. He bent to help retrieve her possessions while waiting for an answer.

Perhaps she was wearing something she was too embarrassed to be seen in. Unlikely, Paula was not the shy type, especially with regard to clothes. She liked to shock, one particularly short red suede skirt worn during her first week had every man in the station walking round with their eyes on stalks. Eventually one of the other women officers had a quiet word about the image needed for the job. Since then, to his relief, she had been more conservative and shown a remarkable chameleon-like ability to adapt to fit in.

"What got you in so early?" he asked, trying to put her at ease. He placed the retrieved pens and cosmetics on the desk, and spotted a large rucksack propped against the wall.

She stepped out from her hiding place, head lowered, holding a tissue to her nose, the front of her t-shirt covered in blood.

"Couldn't sleep," she mumbled, as she bent stiffly to pick up a lipstick he'd missed.

He stepped closer, lifted her chin with one finger to check where the blood was coming from. This was no simple nose-bleed. Her nose was battered, both eyes were bruised and her lip split, but he was more concerned about the possible injuries to her body.

"Have you seen anyone about this?"

She shook her head.

"Come with me, I think the doctor is downstairs, he can look you over."

"No. I'm fine," she mumbled.

"Who are you trying to kid?" he said. "Sorry, I insist." He didn't often pull rank, but on this occasion he had no hesitation. Her well-being was more important than his concern about being seen as a bully.

"I don't want anyone to see me like this."

This was the classic response of an abuse victim. He guessed the boyfriend was in the frame. Gossip was that she lived with a nutter. No doubt she'd refuse to press charges. He didn't care. What mattered was getting her checked over. "Fine, I'll get him to come up here."

Gavin didn't give her time to argue. He phoned the duty officer and asked him to send the doctor up to his office after he'd examined Neil Gillespie.

"Sit down," he said, pointing to her seat. He perched on the edge of the desk and pointed to her rucksack. "Been thrown out?"

"No, I walked out." There was a hint of pride in her response.

"Good. Any plans?"

"I could stay with my sister, but I don't want him harassing her."

"Better she doesn't know where you're staying," he said. "I have a spare room you could use until you get sorted."

The moment he said it he had regrets. Would she think he was trying to take advantage of her? Of course not, he was nearly twice her age. What would everyone else think? Did it matter? Did they need to know?

The fire door banged, Gavin went out to see if it was Dr. Munro. He led him into the office and introduced him to Paula.

"Can you check her over?" he asked. "I'll leave you to it, but I'd like a word about Neil Gillespie when you've finished.

There was a coffee machine down the corridor. He shoved in the necessary collection of coins and waited patiently for the hot water to fill the cardboard cup. He only managed a few sips before Munro emerged.

"She's been lucky. A couple of cracked ribs and a battered face, a few weeks rest should be all she needs. Shame she doesn't seem willing to charge the bastard that did it."

"I thought she'd say that," Gavin answered, "but I'd still like you to do a report as if she were. Hang onto it, you never know. I might be able to get her to change her mind."

"Persuade her to take a couple of photos, in case she needs them in the future. I didn't have any luck."

"What about Gillespie? Anything I need to be aware of there?"

"You mean apart from the beating? It didn't do anything life threatening. The liver damage caused by his booze consumption is another matter. But we've known that for a long time. He isn't interested in rehab so there's nothing I can do. He needs to get back into the hostel, rough sleeping is not doing him any favours."

"I'll do what I can," Gavin said and shook the doctor's hand.

He gulped down the rest of his coffee, threw the cup in the bin and went back to face Paula. She hadn't accepted his invitation to stay, but it was the best offer she'd get. He pushed open the door, and said, "Time to go."

She looked puzzled. "Where to?"

"My place... No arguments." He hoisted her rucksack onto his shoulder, pushed her bag into her hands and said, "We need to get a move on, unless you want to face the morning shift."

She glanced at the clock, and suddenly seemed more than willing to go along with his suggestion though she did put in a condition of her own. "Just until I find somewhere else."

He nodded. Now was not the right time to convince her to press charges. He'd work on that later.

Chapter 2

A flash of luminous orange bobbed into sight, distracting Jim Cullen from the breathtaking view of the distant Hebridean islands.

His first instinct was to ignore it, but curiosity won and he found himself scanning the water to find it again. The object had vanished.

The climb to the viewing point on the cliff had been tough. He struggled to get his breath back and then bent to touch his toes and stretch his muscles.

The blob reappeared. The distinctive, unnatural colour made him certain this was a life-jacket. It vanished again, bounced back, being pushed closer to the shore by the surging waves. The harder he looked, the more convinced he became he was looking at a life-jacket, and someone was wearing it.

His medical training told him the chance of survival in these conditions was negligible. But negligible didn't mean impossible. Automatic reaction kicked in. Jim scanned the cliff face, searching for a safe path. The first route he picked showed evidence of a recent landslide, so he scoured the scene once more trying to find a safer route without having to go right round the sweep of the bay.

"Come on, Digger," he called. His sister's black Labrador bounded towards him with a well chewed stick firmly clamped between his teeth.

If only there was someone on the island whom he could call for help. Even if he'd been carrying his mobile phone, it would have been useless, since there was no signal here, and the sparse island population didn't bother with phones. They had a radio transmitter for emergencies.

He'd worry about that later, first he had to get to the shore and reach the life-jacket.

Jim concentrated on his route, getting down wouldn't be easy, climbing back up would be a real challenge. He checked the water again. The vivid orange life-jacket was still moving nearer to the shoreline, he must hurry before the tide turned and towed it back out to sea.

Clambering up and down this cliff had been a regular childhood pastime, but he hadn't been down there for over ten years, and never in conditions like this. Recent rain had loosened the surface stones; the soil beneath was soft and slippery. Slithering and sliding, he reached a shallow ledge, halted to draw breath and took stock. 'Insanity,' he thought, but as long as there was a faint chance of saving a life he'd risk it. His foot slipped. He slid about ten feet, slowed and slid again, stopping on a little ledge with a sheer drop below onto the sand. Without warning, the soil beneath him crumbled, leaving him hanging onto a small protruding rock with his fingertips. He lost his grip and plummeted twenty feet to the seashore, somehow managing in the few seconds available to turn his fall into a roll to reduce the impact on landing.

Winded, but unhurt by his undignified descent, he got up and ran to the water's edge. The orange blob was still there.

Not wanting to be weighted down, he stripped off and abandoned his boots and clothes just above the tide mark and plunged into the icy water. The numbing waves hit his bare chest as he dived towards the life-jacket that bobbed tantalizingly beyond his reach. Each time he made a grab for it, a surge of water tore it away.

He swam on, gasping for breath as he lunged forward, catching hold of a tangle of trailing rope. He tugged hard, but it came free in his hand. He grabbed again at another strand, pulling it tight as the water surged around him, until the entangled mass was close enough to thump into his shoulder. A chunk of splintered timber was attached to the life-jacketed body keeping it afloat. Jim had no choice but to drag the whole lot with him to the shore.

Determination drove him through the pain of fighting the backwash until he felt sand beneath his feet. Once he could stand, he started to untangle the knots that held his victim to the makeshift raft. His fingers were too numb. Using his teeth he got one knot open, then found a second knot. He undid that one and pushed the mast away.

Now all that hampered his progress was the bulky life-jacket and water logged waterproofs. He got a firm stance on the sandy beach, ducked down, put his shoulder under the body, and straightened up. With the next retreating wave, he lifted the victim clear above the waves. Water swooshed out of the sleeves and legs of the waterproofs, lightening his load. What he'd earlier thought to be a hefty trawler-man actually weighed barely more than a child.

He stumbled through the shallows, until he reached dry sand and gently laid the inert body down. He sank to his knees, dreading the sight that lay hidden under the hood of the over-sized waterproofs. He stared at the stiff garish fabric for a moment before he pushed aside the hood. Long wet hair masked the features. His carefully pushed the hair out of the way, revealing a young woman's face. The paleness of her skin, and her blue tinged lips were in sharp contrast to the dark red and purple bruises on her cheeks. A streak of crimson blood still oozed from a gash on her temple. The fresh blood gave him hope that he wasn't too late.

Jim searched for a pulse. At first he could find nothing. The cold could be responsible for her body almost shutting down. He would not give up on her. He checked her airways again, they were clear. Then he felt the faint flicker of a pulse.

It was enough to galvanize him into action. Yanking off the life-jacket, he pulled open the waterproofs, revealing a tight black leather corset which was restricting her breathing. A voice in his head reminded him not to judge anyone by their appearance. Restoring air into her lungs was his priority.

He rolled her over to find double knotted silk cords lacing the garment from top to bottom down her back. Whoever tied them had not wanted them undone in a hurry. Jim tugged hard, ripping four of the eyelets out, giving enough slack to ease the worst pressure off her rib cage.

He rolled her onto her back, noting several round scars on her breasts which looked like cigarette burns. He leaned over her, held her nose and chin, and breathed life into her. He counted, breathed, counted, massaged, counted, breathed, on and on, until he was rewarded by a spluttering as her body took control again, expelling the water she had swallowed. Her eyes remained closed, and her limbs leaden, but she was alive.

A gust of wind on his semi-naked body reminded him of the dangers of hypothermia. He scrambled across the sand, gathered up his abandoned clothes and hurried back to where she lay. He pulled her up into a sitting position and started to dress her in them. He eased her lolling head through the neck of his shirt and jumper. Then pushing his arm up one sleeve, caught her hand, and pulled it through. The fabric stuck to her damp skin making his task harder. He repeated the operation, pulling the clothes down over her body, until they practically reached her knees. He laid her down and pulled his socks onto her feet.

He hastily tugged on his trousers and his coat, and shoved his bare feet into his boots. He shook her waterproofs hard, wrapped her in them, and lifted her onto his shoulder, anchoring her by partially zipping one of her legs inside his coat.

All he needed now was to find a scalable route to the top of the cliff.

Faced with a wall of crumbling sand, he had no option but to head for the far end of the cove. The abrasive effect of sand on damp skin trapped inside his boots, made him regret parting with his socks. But his concern for his patient was too great to let discomfort halt his progress.

The winter sun was rapidly sinking below the horizon. The fading light would soon be lost.

He started upwards, zig-zagging, back and forth and occasionally down again to find a better path. Half way up he reached a dead end. An overhanging rock blocked his path. He inched his way back and heard a whimpering noise just above his head. In his rush down the cliff he had forgotten all about Digger. If he could reach the dog then they'd be safe. Digger would guide them to safety.

Speed was the only thing that mattered, perhaps the difference between life and death.

Chapter 3

It had been three weeks since Neil Gillespie sparked Gavin's interest in the house at Mallaig. Mallaig was out of his normal beat area, but he couldn't ignore the information. He had almost given up hope of ever finding evidence that would prove Hector Sinclair was involved in something illegal.

He checked his speed. No good getting into trouble for nothing. Paula would not have left an urgent message for him to come all the way to Mallaig without good cause.

On his first exploratory trip, the day after Neil Gillespie confided to him in the cells, he'd followed the memorized instructions, passing the post office heading out of town, keeping an eye on the speedometer. After seven miles he almost gave up, thinking Neil was winding him up, when he saw a cluster of houses fitting Neil's description.

A few seconds deliberation had him driving past the gate lodge and on up the tree lined drive. The steep road was pitted and rough, gradually levelling off as it led into a dense plantation of conifers. The dark green walls gave a feeling of imprisonment. No light penetrated, sound was muffled. There was no birdsong, no insects buzzing, no relief to the oppressive and suffocating atmosphere, until he reached a sharp bend in the road where a narrow gap in the trees revealed a gleaming loch ahead. The road swung round plunging him back into dark shadow, finally emerging into an open glade which stretched down to the water's edge.

There was a house below him to the right. The sombre granite walls, dull battleship-grey shutters, and dark green of the overgrown yew hedges gave the place a sinister appearance. He drove towards it and parked his car. Braced against an icy blast of wind blowing in across the loch he strode across the empty sweep of gravel to the front door.

He tugged on the old-fashioned bell pull. There was no response to the distant clanking. He hammered on the sturdy door. Still no response. Slowly, he walked round the house. Damp mossy patches where water trickled down the walls below the overflowing gutters, gave the place an air of neglect. But the neglect didn't apply to security. All the shutters and doors were well secured. Only the boathouse, hidden by a vast rhododendron, was not locked. There was nothing of value inside.

Satisfied he'd seen enough, Gavin drove back down the drive. As he emerged onto the road he spotted the caravan site opposite the entrance. He made his way back to the little town, stopped at the nearest bar, ordered a pint and started chatting to the barman. One by one the other drinkers got drawn into the conversation, and for the price of a round, Gavin got a rundown on the area and some of the characters living in it. After another round, he mentioned driving through the forest and finding the loch, and the decaying house, then sat back and listened.

"Never been there since Gordon died," said one man.

"Some distant relative inherited the place, probably sold it on by now," said another.

"Sacked all the staff. No one goes near the place, I hear," said the third.

"That's not true," the barman informed them, "sometimes there are people up there. There's one big fellow who comes in occasionally and buys a few bottles of good scotch, and a couple of cases of beer. Not much of a talker though, he barely stops longer than it takes to down a pint."

The conversation veered off to discussions about the likelihood of the local rugby team winning at the weekend. Gavin pretended to be interested, but was busy making a plan while they talked. Then he pushed his unfinished pint aside, and slipped away quietly.

He hurried back to the caravan park. His luck was in, as he managed to take a good look round before he located the manager. The van nearest the road was old and tatty, but perfectly positioned for his purposes. He had to think of a plausible story for wanting that particular van. The manager was on his back, fixing the underside of a car, his hands covered in grease. He didn't seem too bothered by Gavin's request, though he tried to persuade him that one of the modern vans on the other side would be better. Gavin explained that his niece, who'd be using the place, was mad about vintage things, and might prefer a bit of privacy because she was coming out of a messy relationship. The man nodded to indicate he understood. After a short discussion about the rent, Gavin put money on the table and the manager pointed at the board where the keys were hanging before diving back under the vehicle he had been working on.

As soon as he was installed in the caravan, Gavin called his friend and colleague Tom Jackson.

"Tom, I need your help. Can you find out who owns a property just outside Mallaig?" He rattled off the details and added that he didn't want anyone else to know.

"Unlike you to be secretive," Tom answered.

"I know, but…" Gavin told him about Neil's information, leaving nothing out. The reaction he got from Tom was as expected.

"Let's hope we can nail him this time." Tom had more reason to distrust Hector than Gavin did. Hector had been involved in the incident that put Tom in a wheelchair.

Tom's courage and determination to stay working at the job he loved had kept him sane. His computing skills made him a valuable asset to the force. If there was information on the net to be found, Tom could extract it.

Gavin's next call was to Paula Dawson. This job was perfect for her. It would solve the problem of her staying at his place, and give her time to recover.

"I know you feel bad about taking time off work, I wondered if some surveillance work in a very quiet spot might appeal?" he asked.

"Am I so hard to live with?"

"No, you've been the perfect house guest. This has nothing to do with that, more that I urgently need someone to do a job for me without the world knowing about it."

"Count me in."

Gavin filled her in on his plan to keep watch on the entrance to the house at Mallaig. He apologized in advance for the van he'd lined up. And warned her he'd told the manager she loved retro things."

The only thing he didn't tell her was that the Acting Chief Super was his target.

Within an hour she was there, dressed in a truly memorable sixties outfit, boots, mini-skirt, and big floppy hat. She had a rucksack containing all her worldly possessions on one shoulder, and a holdall filled with cameras, cables and a laptop, which he had arranged for her to collect from Tom, weighing her down on the other side. Gavin left her to settle in.

Paula had been there for three weeks and so far all they had to work on was two vehicles, a blue Volvo, and a red one. The drivers identified from photos Paula took, were Ron Hill, who had a couple of previous convictions for violent assaults, and Dan Trench, with a record for handling stolen goods. The dark haired woman passenger travelling with Trench remained unnamed.

Tom's search for information on the vehicles showed that neither was registered to the current drivers, nor were they on file as stolen, and the registered owners did not appear on police records. There had been so little activity for Paula to report that Gavin had been on the verge of calling off surveillance. The only reason he hadn't was that it kept Paula safe from her ex-boyfriend.

Gavin reversed his car into the narrow gap behind the caravan to obscure it from the road.

"I'm glad you've come," Paula said as she opened the door of her temporary home. "Something has been going on, but I'm not sure what."

"Explain." Gavin said sharply as he followed her into the van.

"On Friday I got word my mother was ill and felt I had to go home. I remembered you were planning to go climbing over the weekend. I tried to get hold of Tom. Steven Fowler answered his phone and said

Tom had also gone away. I didn't know what to do and asked him to cover for me."

"Shit!" he said. "Sorry, how is your mother?"

"She's fine, it was a false alarm. My ex got her to text me."

"How did that go?"

"I gave him hell, I think he's got the message we're over. But I stayed with my Mum for the night because it was so late and Steven had offered to stay on if I needed him to."

"That's fine."

"No, it isn't, I'm sorry, but I thought I was doing the right thing by getting Steven to cover for me. Now I know it was a huge mistake."

"How come?"

"When I came back on Sunday evening, Steven seemed rather edgy. He said there was nothing to report, and I believed him." She fumbled with the kettle distractedly. "He quizzed me about what we were watching for. I told him, I thought you had made it all up to get me out of your house. After that, he took off in a hurry, which surprised me because he's usually trying to chat me up.

"But?"

"This afternoon the caravan park owner called by to ask how much longer we'd be staying. He'd worked out we were cops, and assumed that with all the activity going on over the weekend, we had raided the place."

"What activity?"

"That's just it, I don't know, there's nothing on Steven's report. According to the owner, at least five vehicles arrived late on Friday, and they didn't leave till the early hours on Sunday."

"And Steven supposedly saw nothing?"

"Worse than that, he managed to switch off the video camera I had linked to my computer. One mistake I could believe but to have missed so much isn't like him." She clicked the lid back on the kettle, placed it on its base, and turned back to Gavin. "If he'd said he'd seen one or two vehicles either coming or going I'd have thought nothing more about it. But for him of all people to fail to record any of them, well..."

"You think he wasn't here, or he's deliberately withheld information?"

She shrugged.

"Try the switch," he said, pointing at the kettle. "I need that coffee." Paula flicked the kettle on.

"Why would he lie?"

"Good question. What else have you found out?"

"Luckily the owner here saw it all. He spotted a dark blue Mercedes, a silver BMW and a maroon Jaguar, with only one person in each. He says he's seen these cars a couple of times before. He couldn't remember the make of the other two cars, only that they were dark colours. He was able to give me some partial registrations."

"A rather observant local…"

"It seems he used to live in a rough part of Glasgow where he ran the neighbourhood watch, it became a habit to make a note of unusual comings and goings. Like everyone else round here he's curious about the new occupants of the house because they've kept so much to themselves."

"Hector Sinclair has a dark maroon Jaguar." Gavin said almost to himself.

"You think he was here, don't you?" Paula said looking quite shocked. "That's why this was so hush-

hush. You were hoping he'd show. You think he's up to something, don't you?"

Gavin was impressed. Paula was smarter than he'd thought. "Maybe, but what makes you think that?"

"Station gossip. I heard that a drug bust had gone pear-shaped and you had blamed Sinclair for messing with the evidence. And that it wasn't the first time you and he had come head to head."

Gavin was surprised that the story was still circulating. His problems with Sinclair happened long before Paula joined up. But Hector Sinclair's recent return and unexpected promotion was bound to resurrect stories of his clashes with former colleagues.

Paula pulled two cups out of the cupboard, "Sorry I've only got instant coffee. Do you take it black or white?"

"White, two sugars, please."

Paula spooned out the coffee, added the sugar, water then milk and slid the cup towards him. "Asking Steven to take over really stuffed things up, didn't it? He's Sinclair's nephew, which might explain his lapse of memory."

"You're probably right, but don't blame yourself, I should have confided in you."

"Is any of the information we collected any use?"

"It could be. Is there anyone left at the house?"

"I took a walk up there earlier. The shutters are all closed. Both Trench and Hill were out searching the grounds for someone, or something. Later they lit a bonfire, and piled a load of clothes, shoes and old suitcases on it. Looked like the contents of someone's wardrobe."

"Men's or women's clothes?"

"Mainly women's, I think." She sipped her coffee. "Hill had a bloody great plaster stuck on his forehead. Judging by the string of abuse Trench was hurling at him the relationship is far from amicable."

"Did anything else happen?"

"Yes. A transit van arrived and the driver unloaded several tea chests and a bundle of cardboard boxes. Everyone went inside, and I came back to wait for you."

"Could you see into the van?"

"Yes, it was empty. It's still up there. I was debating whether to follow it or stay here and see what Trench and Hill did."

"Following that van when it leaves is more important than worrying about that pair. Get ready to go."

Chapter 4

It was dark. It was warm. It was quiet. She knew that much, but no more. Her eyelids were glued together, her limbs leaden and painful.

A soft spoken, non-threatening, voice sometimes broke the silence with tales about an island. A radio programme, she thought, as she lay still, enchanted by the description. How she would love to go there, especially with the owner of the kind voice as a guide.

She loved hearing the details about his childhood, his life as a doctor, his family, and his dog that slipped into the monologue. She was glad he was a dog lover. There were even times when she imagined that he touched her, put his arms around her, lifted her, coaxed her to drink, but she knew it was impossible. A voice on a radio couldn't do that. When the voice stopped she felt herself sink into a dark, bleak place, one she longed to escape from.

She was fighting to pull herself out of the horror when she felt a hand pulling her up. She could hear screaming, and someone calling, "Wake up. Wake up." Her arms shot out flailing about, making contact with something hard, followed by a sensation of hot liquid running down her neck. Her hands instinctively went to her chest. She went rigid and the screaming stopped. She opened her eyes.

All that registered was the colour red.

She raised her hands. They were red. She looked down. A vivid red stain was steadily creeping down her right arm and all over the front of her nightdress. She groped with her left hand touching the warm sticky liquid. Blood. No. She shivered, it couldn't be. But blood was all she could think of. She closed her eyes again hoping to block out the image. The picture in her mind changed. The blood was still there, but it was not hers. Slowly the image came into sharper focus. There was a big, angry looking, balding man coming towards her. Blood blurred his features. It dripped down his face, down his shirt. The huge hands that reached out for her were coated in it. She opened her mouth to scream, but before she managed to make a sound the hypnotic voice started talking again.

"Don't worry, it was an accident." It was the voice from the radio; the same wonderful comforting voice that had kept her company before.

She opened her eyes again. The bloodstained man had vanished. In his place was a young, clean-shaven, fair-haired man.

She became aware of her heart pounding, and of it slowing as she surveyed her non-threatening surroundings. Her trembling hands touched the bowl and spoon resting on her lap. She dipped her finger in the warm sticky liquid. She licked her finger. Soup. Tomato soup.

She turned her attention to the man sitting on the edge of the bed. His smile was friendly.

"Hello, welcome back," he said as he reached out and picked up the empty bowl.

She was confused. His was the voice on the radio.

"It was only an accident, it won't take a minute to clear up," he continued. She reached out, touching his arm. The smudge of soup on his sleeve was proof that he was real. His arm was muscular, and the fresh spicy aftershave he wore drifted towards her, but still she was unsure of where reality began and the dream ended.

Reality was that every inch of her body ached, and moving required more effort than she could muster. Where was she? Who was he? He didn't look as if he intended to hurt her, though she was conscious of his strength as he lifted her onto a chair, washed, dried and dressed her. It wasn't long before he had her tucked up in the freshly-made bed. The intimacy of the whole procedure should have been embarrassing but oddly it wasn't. She felt safe.

She struggled to speak, a whispered, "Thanks," was all she could get out.

Her reward was an even bigger smile, one that lit up his eyes and held warmth that matched his voice. "Everything will be fine. I'm just going to refill this," he said pointing to the empty soup bowl.

He left the room closing the door behind him. The sense of security felt in his presence departed. Her mouth went dry, her hands shook. She had to escape. Throwing back the covers, she swung her feet down and stood up. She managed three steps before her legs buckled under her and she hit the floor. The door flew open. Her guardian returned and scooped her up into his arms.

"What's wrong?" he asked.

"Please don't lock me in," she begged.

"It wasn't locked, I only closed it to keep the room warm, I can leave it open if you like."

"Yes."

"Now you stay put, I must get you something to eat, you haven't had anything for at least four days."

"Four days?" she echoed.

If she hadn't eaten for four days, what had she been doing? Why did everything hurt so much? It required too much effort to concentrate.

She clung to the soft, silky, quilt that covered the enormous double bed. Her inspection for soup stains revealed none. She was relieved. She would have hated to have damaged such a spectacular work of art. The quilt was made up of a series of panels, a mixture of patchwork and appliquéd designs, all embellished with embroidery, lace work and ribbons. The subtle peachy tones were mixed with soft shades of green. The same delicate colours had been used in the paintwork and furnishings, giving the room a distinctly feminine feel. Much too feminine to belong to a man even if he did have a kind voice. Maybe he had a wife.

"It's a beautiful quilt," she said when he returned and handed her a fresh bowl of soup. "Is it very old?"

"It belonged to my grandmother," he answered as he sat down on the edge of the bed.

"Aren't you afraid I'll spoil it?"

"Not now that you've come round."

"Come round?"

"Yes, you've been unconscious."

"I don't understand? What happened?"

"I think your boat capsized, I pulled you out of the sea four days ago, and brought you here.

She looked at the piece of toast in her hand, while trying to picture a boat. She couldn't remember any boat. She nibbled at the toast.

"Is your name Jim Cullen?"

"Yes."

"You're a doctor?"

"Yes."

"And we're on an island, and you can't get help, and you have a dog called Digger?"

"Yes, it's my sister's, but she lets me look after him sometimes."

"You're the voice I heard, I thought it was part of a dream, and I was listening to a radio."

"I talked a lot of rubbish. I can't remember what I said, I thought it might help. Now it's your turn. Tell me your name." he said.

She toyed with the plate, trying to come to terms with the situation, wishing she could just close her eyes, go back to sleep, anything to avoid the truth. She began to shake again.

He reached out, took the plate from her grasp, and enveloped both her hands in his. "Relax, you don't have to tell me if you don't want to," he said.

She shook her head, "You don't understand. I want to tell you. But I can't... I can't because I don't know."

"What do you mean?"

"I can't remember my name. I can't remember anything."

Chapter 5

The only thing that marred Hector Sinclair's promotion to Acting Chief Superintendent was that the posting was in Oban, and Gavin McKay would be working from the same office. Hector remembered Gavin as unforgiving, a trait that was unlikely to have vanished in the years since they last worked together. Detective Inspector or not Gavin McKay would still have to obey his orders, but Hector knew he'd have to be careful not to rub him up the wrong way, or he'd have Gavin sticking his nose into matters that didn't concern him.

Hector had one piece of good luck. His nephew, Steven, was actually working in Gavin's department, in a position to watch what Gavin was doing. What he hadn't realized was just how necessary it would be when he'd briefly primed Steven to let him know what was going on.

He'd only had the job for a couple of weeks when Steven phoned to say he had been working on surveillance on the outskirts of Mallaig. During which he had logged Sinclair's car. He wanted to know if he should mention this in his report. It had been an awkward moment. Sinclair had no knowledge of any activity there that would be of interest to anyone in Oban. A fact that had him more worried than he let on.

Dan Trench or Ron Hill had to be up to something he didn't know about.

"Talk me through all you have so far," he said to gain time to think, "I have been in meetings and missed reading up about it."

Steven obliged without hesitation. "I don't know very much, I was only called in at the last minute. Paula Dawson was out there and had to go to see her sick mother, and I was the only person in the office, so she asked me to take over for her."

"Didn't she have a partner?"

"No, she seemed to be doing it on her own. I thought it was a bit odd, but she was in too much of a rush to get off for me to find out more. All she told me was that there were two men at the house. One of whom, Dan Trench, had one conviction for handling stolen property, while the other, Ron Hill, had several convictions for more serious offences of actual bodily harm, for which he had served terms in prison. She said something about checking out the car registrations of their vehicles, but nothing had shown up. They still don't know who owns the house."

"Did she say why they were interested?"

"No. My instructions were to write down details of any vehicles going up or down the drive. When I saw your car, I thought I should check with you first."

"I'm glad you did. You're still alone?"

"Yes."

"And no one else knows I went to the house?"

"Not yet."

"Good. It's really important that no one else finds out. I shouldn't be telling you this, but I'm currently working on a high security undercover investigation. The last thing I need is Gavin McKay sticking his nose in and messing up all the work I've put in so far.

I trust you not to tell anyone about seeing me there, especially McKay. Do you understand?"

"Yes. What about the other cars?"

"Don't mention them either. If you want to help you'll keep me informed of what McKay's doing. I don't like to ask you to spy on your boss. The truth is, McKay has had a grudge against me since we first joined the force. He's jealous of my promotion and is determined to undermine me so he can have my job."

"I never saw him as the jealous type."

"Believe me, he is. Contact me at home every evening to keep me informed of what he's up to. That is presuming you are prepared to watch out for me."

"Of course I will. What do you need to know?"

"Everything," Hector answered, damage control was all he could hope for at this stage. Then while he had Steven hooked, added "I might need your help keeping my cover safe, someone I can trust, would you be willing?"

"Of course," Steven answered, without a trace of hesitation in his voice.

Maybe something good would come out of the situation after all, Hector thought to himself. But care was needed.

This unscheduled investigation proved McKay was more of a threat than anticipated. He made Steven go over the whole incident, questioning every detail from the first call to go to Mallaig, to what had been said when he left. "Try to find out more from Paula when she gets back? But make it sound like casual curiosity. Do you think you can do that?"

"No problem."

"Steven thanks for calling when you did. I promise you won't regret it." Hector said, happy with Steven's demonstration of loyalty.

Chapter 6

Gavin was late for their regular Wednesday lunch at the Royal Hotel not far from the station. Tom Jackson was settled at his usual table and as Gavin sat down two coffees arrived. Gavin would have preferred a pint, but had to respect the rules about drinking while on duty.

"I hear Paula's moved into your place," Tom said with a disapproving look.

Gavin couldn't resist winding him up.

"God, I'd never have offered if I'd known you fancied her."

"Not funny," Tom answered. "I think you've made a mistake."

"She'll liven the place up." Gavin hoped that Tom's lack of humour was only temporary, but decided not to stretch it. "She needs support. I don't think she's had much in the past. And she has been invaluable to me with the Mallaig surveillance. I am not going to chuck her out for making a bad call."

This seemed to placate Tom slightly, but Gavin sensed something still bothered him.

"How's Neil?"

"I've been round to check on him a few times, taken some food over, but I don't think he bothers to eat it. He's more interested in drinking."

"That's no surprise." Tom pushed his coffee cup away, looked as if he was going to say something, but didn't.

"Go on, spit it out. What have I overlooked?" Tom and he had been close enough to be able to mind read each other.

"I'm worried about Steven Fowler. Everything you do or say will get back to Sinclair."

"That rather depends on what he gets to hear. After what happened in Mallaig, he'll be lucky if Paula ever speaks to him again. And if we get proof he reports things back to his uncle no one else in the office will either." Gavin had liked the lanky red headed graduate who, in spite of the fact he was related to Sinclair, had managed to impress everyone in the department.

"I never understood why you picked him. I warned you about his family connections."

"I know. I had hoped that it wouldn't matter, he's had some great results, and is so damn keen."

"Yeah, but if you can't trust him… what use is he?" Tom said.

"Wait and see, perhaps his family loyalty will work to our advantage." Gavin could tell that Tom didn't believe him. Obviously Sinclair's new appointment must be bugging him. "Do you want to eat?"

"I've ordered. What about you?"

"Sorry, I don't have time. I've been summoned to see Sinclair."

Tom nodded, but didn't comment. Gavin knew Sinclair's promotion and move back to the Oban area was harder on Tom than anyone. Past history was hard to brush aside with a wheelchair as a constant reminder.

"How is Paula?" Tom asked, changing the subject. "Is she going to press charges against the boyfriend?"

"Seems reluctant, wants to avoid the gossip a court appearance would generate. Anyway, that's up to her, I can't interfere. Her face is looking better, but her ribs are still causing pain."

"What are you going to do now about Mallaig, hand it over to internal investigation?"

"Nothing. We don't have any viable proof that would nail Sinclair. And even if I did, I'd not risk him interfering and contaminating evidence again. Who knows what influence he has in other departments?"

"Make sure you don't do anything he can use against you." Tom said, "Remember there's a spy in your camp."

"Yes, but he doesn't know we know. Or that we've found out about the vehicles that were at Mallaig when he was supposedly watching.

"The maroon Jaguar in particular?"

"Yes. I'm pretty sure it was Sinclair's? The partial registration matches his."

"What do you think Sinclair will do?" Tom asked.

"I'm guessing he'll try to shut down the investigation. My best bet is to pretend to lose interest because nothing seemed to be going on. With luck Sinclair will think Steven managed to prevent us knowing he was ever there."

"That won't stop you, will it?"

"No. The Mallaig house is probably not worth watching, we saw Dan Trench and Ron Hill leave. I doubt they'll be back. I'm more interested in what they took out of the house. A self hire removal van took a load of boxes and some quite valuable looking furniture to a storage depot just outside Crieff."

"Hard to figure out what those two have in common," Tom said.

"I'm more interested in what happened to the woman, the one who arrived with Trench. I guess she left when Steven was watching. The photo of her wasn't that great, and we didn't manage to identify her."

"What do you want me to do?"

"Keep working on who owns the house." Gavin put some money on the table for the coffee. "Call me at home with updates. I don't want Sinclair suspicious that we're working together on this."

Gavin made his way to the office to see the Acting Chief Super, after which he would get in touch with his friend, Alistair Duncan from rescue services, who needed help identifying a woman who'd been washed up on one of the islands.

First he had to speak to Paula. He called her mobile.

"Did you find everything you needed at the house?"

"Yes, thanks."

"There's no hurry, you can stay as long as you need to. But I have another job for you. I'll extend your sick leave, say your ribs are causing problems, no one will be suspicious. They all know what happened to you."

"And give them even more reason to pressure me into pressing charges."

"Sorry, I didn't think of that. I'll talk to them, because I need you out of the building."

"Has this got anything to do with the mess I made at Mallaig?"

"In a way, but that was my mistake. I should have told you Sinclair's name was in the frame and that there was a need for secrecy.

"How has he reacted?"

"I am about to find out. What I am hoping is that I can get him to believe I was acting out of turn, and let him think we were fooled by Steven's actions. He has no cause to suspect that I was expecting him to show."

"That's true. If we had, we'd never have asked Steven to take part."

"That's one of the reasons I want you out of the office."

"What do I have to do?"

"First of all tell me again exactly what you told Steven before you handed over to him."

"That some drunk who'd been arrested had been mouthing off about the place, and it had made you curious. It was all you told me. Did I say too much?

"Did you name the informant?"

"No, you never told me." Paula paused for a moment. "When I came back he stuck around for a while quizzing me about why I was there. I didn't think it odd at the time."

"What did you tell him?"

"There were two petty criminals staying at the house and we suspected they were planning something. I didn't know more to tell."

"Good, but from now on, you know nothing. I don't want Steven or anyone other than myself or Tom, to know that Steven hid stuff from you, or that we followed the van taking the stuff from the house."

"Trust me, my lips are sealed."

"I'd like you to go to the store where the crates and furniture from the house were taken, try to find out who is being billed, and how long they expect it to be there."

"That shouldn't be too difficult. One of my brother's best friends works there."

"Great, then I want you to go and talk to the named registered owners of the two Volvo's, find out what they do. You can report to me this evening. I'll sort out the paper work about your pay when you get back on duty"

"Do you think Sinclair will close the investigation down? He is renowned for doing just that."

"Is he?"

"Yes. I've heard several moans in the canteen about him pulling people off cases."

"Well it might be what he's planning, but this time I'll beat him to it, I'm going to tell him we gave up on Monday morning because nothing happened over the weekend. That way, he'll think we believed Steven and never know we saw the van take the crates to the store. And thanks for the tip off about Sinclair shutting down other investigations. I'll get Tom to check up on which cases he's shown an interest in. Now I'd better go and see Sinclair before he gets upset."

"Are you really sure about me staying? Think of the gossip it will generate."

"I suppose they think I'm a dirty old man taking advantage of you."

"Not at all, they'll reckon I've made a good catch."

Gavin laughed as he disconnected.

What a turnabout, three weeks ago Neil Gillespie had worried him by telling him he was turning into a sad case, and now he was at risk of being classed as a good catch. What phrase would Hector Sinclair use to describe him? How two people as different as himself and Sinclair had chosen the same occupation was a mystery. They'd led parallel lives, been brought up in the same town, attended the same schools, shared so many of the same experiences, and to all outward appearances were still running on the same track, doing the same job. Anyone looking closely would soon find the similarities stopped there.

Gavin had never been too bothered by fashion and rather remiss about buying anything new. He still made an effort to make sure his suits were regularly dry cleaned, and he always ironed the fronts of his shirts, and made sure his tie matched his jacket. Today he had been in a hurry, and his shirt only got the fastest flash of an iron, which meant that the front and collar looked barely passable, but it did go with the tie he'd chosen.

Hector Sinclair would be togged out in one of his many designer suits, with a professionally laundered shirt. Gavin remembered the early days when they first joined up. Sinclair never missed an opportunity to wear his full uniform, complete with badges and gleaming buttons, razor sharp creases in his trousers, and shoes he could see his face in. Sometimes he used to volunteer to go to events just to dress up for the occasion. Everyone in the station used to joke about him practising clicking his heels.

As he walked down the corridor he wondered how Hector would act. Would being elevated to rank of Acting Chief Superintendent have really gone to his head? Though Gavin was sure that Oban would not have been Sinclair's chosen posting even though it was technically his home town. For three weeks Gavin had avoided direct contact, afraid his disrespect would show.

"Good afternoon," Gavin said, carefully omitting to add the polite, Sir, he would normally have used to a higher-ranking officer.

"Sit down," Sinclair replied. "Fill me in on what your department is dealing with at the moment."

Gavin sensing that Hector wanted to lull him into a false sense of security, sat down, and launched into a detailed report of all the cases currently in progress, deliberately making no mention of Mallaig."

Sinclair's fingers drummed on the blotting pad in front of him while Gavin spoke. Then he fired the question. "What about the surveillance at Mallaig?"

"Oh that," Gavin said trying to sound as nonchalant as possible, "we gave up."

"Why were you there, it is out of our jurisdiction? What did you expect to find?"

"I had a tip off that something was going on there, and I thought it was a good excuse to keep young Paula busy while she recovered, and she got your nephew to stand in for her at the weekend, perhaps he told you."

"He did, and that's why I queried it. Private investigations are not permitted. You know the rules as well as I do."

"It was nothing personal. I was given some information I felt ought to be followed."

"From some drunk who had been arrested? Neil Gillespie by any chance? I saw he'd been picked up a few weeks ago."

Gavin hesitated for a moment, the fact Sinclair had bothered to make the connection with Gillespie was cause for concern.

"I hear he's very civic minded, when sober," Hector continued. "What exactly did he tell you?"

There was no point in denying Neil's involvement. A denial could complicate matters. "Only the location of a house," Gavin replied, trying to make it sound as if he really wasn't interested. "He'd overheard part of a conversation and seemed to think there was something dodgy going on there. I felt it was my duty to check it out. Nothing was happening so we pulled out."

"So what are you working on now?"

"I believe that Alistair Duncan from Search and Rescue, wants help identifying a body that got washed up on one of the islands. The call came in as I was leaving my office. I haven't had time to get any details."

"Then I'd better not keep you."

Chapter 7

Jim placed a log on the block. His axe came down, splitting it in two, with a satisfying release of tension. He had been chopping logs for over an hour, not because he needed so many, but to get him out of the close confines of the cottage. He'd have to stop or he wouldn't have an excuse next time he needed to escape. He put down the axe, loaded the basket and went inside.

Mer was still sitting at the kitchen table, head down, studying the list of questions he'd created. He stacked the firewood by the fire, opened up the log burner, stirred the glowing embers and threw in some more wood.

The list she was working on had begun when he set about writing up his patient notes. Not knowing her name, he'd written 'Mermaid,' in tiny letters on the top corner of the page. She laughed when she spotted it, and insisted he ditch the maid insisting, Mer, would be sufficient. He left a space for address, age, family, and so on. On a separate page he'd noted her injuries and his impression of her physical condition at the time he found her and the improvements since then. This sheet he kept in the desk drawer. On the other pages he'd jotted down headings, hoping they would trigger memories to her past. The topics were diverse, ranging from favourite foods, animals, subjects at school, television programmes, sports, and countless other trivial things.

"How's it going?" he asked as he put the kettle on.

"Nowhere," she replied pushing the pages away.

It wasn't the answer he wanted, as he was running out of ideas to help her. Nothing he'd tried had prompted her to remember anything.

"I'd love to go for a walk," she said.

Her request surprised him. He hadn't thought outdoor pursuits would appeal to her. "It's a bit late now. But we can go tomorrow, I'll see if I can dig out a pair of my sister's walking boots for you."

"Sit with me for a while," she begged. "You've been so busy all day I've hardly seen you."

He filled his cup and moved to the far end of the table. Her request made him feel awkward because he could hardly tell her he'd been avoiding her. It wasn't her fault. She had done nothing in the four days since she had come round that was even slightly encouraging. But it had not stopped him from dreaming about a relationship with her.

His crazy fantasy could never be fulfilled while she was a patient in his care. Never mind the fact he suspected she was a mother and someone else's wife. These details he had omitted to mention because he had so little to go on. Was he being overprotective, making too much of her vulnerability?

He was just confused by the thoughts her presence provoked, which had nothing to do with what she had been wearing when he found her. Rubber, leather and that sort of thing did nothing for him. He admired her courage, cheerfulness and adaptability. She looked good in an over-sized jumper and baggy leggings.

Up to now she seemed unaware of the effect she had on him she when brushed past him in the kitchen.

He wondered how she would react if she knew all he wanted was to reach out and grab her and... God, he'd better stop thinking about it in case he did something insane. The sooner Ned got his transmitter working and got word to the mainland and someone claimed her, the better.

"When do you think Ned will come over with some news?" she asked.

At times it was as if she could read his thoughts. He was pleased that she seemed excited at the prospect of meeting Ned, and had started talking about him as if he was an old friend.

"Some time mid afternoon. Let's just hope he's managed to get through to the authorities on the mainland."

"Why? Getting desperate to get rid of me?"

No way of giving a truthful answer. Changing tactics he offered her a fresh cup of coffee, and a sandwich. After eating he retreated to his room and lay down on the bed. He must have dozed off, because the next thing he knew Mer had come to wake him.

"Ned's here," she said as she shook his shoulder gently.

"I'll be out in a minute," he muttered, struggling into a sitting position, watching her graceful movement as she turned and left the room.

He looked at his watch. He had slept for two hours, his first decent sleep since rescuing her. Most nights Mer had been tormented by nightmares. They were so terrible, and so frequent, that she would wake screaming and shaking and drenched in perspiration. Because the dreams were so bad, she'd tried to stay awake for the rest of the night to avoid them. And more often than not, he would sit with her, the result being that neither of them got much sleep. She was exhausted too, but there was little he could do to change that.

Jim came out yawning. "Sorry to keep you waiting. I take it you've introduced yourselves."

"Yes, unusual name, Mer!" Ned said as he filled his pipe.

"Best we could come up with." Jim was about to explain but she smiled and shook her head. Jim grabbed a cup of coffee from the pot on the table and sat down.

"Any luck with the transmitter?"

"Yes" Ned said, then quietly began to relay in his typically spartan style the information he had gleaned. "No missing boats reported. So, no search. The storms hit worse further south. Supply ship won't be calling, unless it's a matter of life and death."

A look at her concerned expression prompted Jim to say. "Don't worry, there'll be someone out there looking for you."

"He's right, lass," Ned added. "They arranged for a spare transmitter to be dropped tomorrow, weather and time permitting, but say they won't take you off the island unless hospital treatment is absolutely essential."

Jim nodded. He was happier now with the progress Mer was making with her recovery. While an X-ray might confirm a fractured cheekbone, there was little that hospitalization would achieve. She had physically recovered with amazing speed. Only the memory loss was serious. She wasn't suffering severe headaches, or having any trouble with her vision so there was little to be gained from rushing back to the mainland, especially as there was no miracle cure for amnesia. Peace and patience were the best treatment, and she would certainly get that on the island.

Jim watched with interest as Ned began to relax. It was always the same. He'd be stiff and official until he had dispensed with all the business side of his trip, now he'd indulge in the luxury of a rare social chat. His smile broadened as he animatedly responded to Mer. There was no doubt in Jim's mind that Ned had been totally captivated by her charm. Ned, well into his sixties, had a craggy, weather beaten face, which lit up as he told Mer about his family, his cottage, the joys and hardships he had encountered over his lifetime on the island. The main sorrow of his life was that both of his sons had been forced to leave the island to work from a bigger port in order to earn a decent wage. He described the six other cottages further to the west, most of which were occupied by his relatives. He told her about the fortnightly supply boat that served as their lifeline, socially as well as physically. But he quickly assured her the islanders always kept reserves for emergencies.

He explained that Jim's was the only holiday cottage on the island, and the only building on the eastern side. But it was his detailed description of the rest of the island's inhabitants that finally brought a smile to her face. The pedigrees of the sheep, the cattle and the chickens were of great importance, and he duly lectured Mer on the merits and failures of an assortment of breeds. Jim caught her eye as she pretended intense interest in the subject, and had to stifle a laugh. Then, oblivious of the response of his audience, Ned veered onto his next favourite topic, wildlife.

"You'll have seen the barnacle geese if you've been to these islands before?" he said, "You have been before, haven't you?"

Her smile faded. She shook her head, her eyes filled with tears which she blinked away and whispered, "I don't know."

Ned looked across to Jim, puzzled, but aware he had blundered somehow. There was a deathly hush as they waited for her to add something.

Ned broke the silence. "I think I'd better go." He grabbed his hat and hurried to the door. "I'm sorry I didn't mean to upset her," he muttered to Jim as he left.

"Good thing he got put off his stride," Jim said as they watched Ned walking down the path. He knew he'd be taking a risk getting her talking when she was so on edge, but it was a risk he had to take. She was exerting such effort in stemming the flow of tears she had probably already forgotten what had created the desire. "Once he gets going about wildlife, he can go on for days, with even more passion than he had for the farm breeds."

His comment was rewarded with a faint smile.

"What did he say that upset you?" he asked quietly.

"It wasn't what he said, it was his questions. I just can't cope with them," she answered. "That's why I was so relieved yesterday, when you said his transmitter was broken."

"I knew it would be difficult, but I never expected you to find it so hard. I don't suppose you slept at all last night?"

"No."

"Is it fear of dreaming, or something else?" he asked, aware that he might be opening the floodgates.

"Both," she sobbed, her poise breaking down.

"OK. Let's start with the dreams. Are they always the same?"

"Yes, always the same. A man covered in blood chasing me. When he reaches me I wake up."

"Is it someone you know?" he probed intending to press to her limits. Tears were running freely down her cheeks, all efforts at curbing them abandoned.

"I can't remember his face, only that he's covered in blood. It's everywhere. I feel as if there's something, something so awful, about to happen that I've blacked it out. Jim, what am I going to do?" she stopped to wipe away her tears. "I'm so afraid of what I shall find out. It's so frightening not knowing who you are, or where you come from."

"Perhaps you have blacked something out, it can happen," he said softly, thinking to himself he had taken her far enough for now. She was so vulnerable, he couldn't stop himself taking her into his arms, holding her tight. Her sobbing eased. She barely reached his chin. Her silky hair brushed his face. Raising his hand he touched it, enjoying the feel of it. He wanted to hold her forever, breathing in the fresh scent that he associated with her, but realized just how unrealistic that wish was. Too many factors stood between them.

He felt the rigid tension in her body ease. She gradually began to pull away from him, looking up to thank him for being there. Looking down at her face his reaction was instinctive. There was no premeditation, no thought to the consequences. He simply lowered his head so their lips met.

Her lips were soft, warm and welcoming, and for a few moments Jim lost touch with reality. Seconds later he knew he had overstepped his boundaries. He drew back holding her at arm's length. He felt her try to pull him back as if she didn't want him to let go.

"Sorry, that shouldn't have happened," he said softly. Her expression forced him to add, "It's not that I don't like you, I want to kiss you, but…" The whole situation was getting out of hand, he was out of his depth and the harder he tried to explain his feelings the deeper he floundered, her silence unnerving him. "You have to sort out your past first."

"What difference will knowing make?"

"It's not just your past. I'm a doctor, I'm responsible for you, and that means we can't have a relationship."

"Is that the only reason?"

"No, I wish it was. There are so many other things that need to be sorted. You might have a husband, a child or children." He knew as he said the words that whatever intimacy there had been between them was shattered.

"Why do you say that?" she demanded.

"Oh God, I'm sorry. I should have told you what I suspected before." He knew he had been blinded by his infatuation with her, which was why he hadn't pointed out the clues earlier. "Look at your hand, see you have a pale band round your ring finger. That could be a sign you have been married."

"And children?"

"You have very faint stretch marks," he told her, hating how his clumsy handling of information was hurting her. "I hadn't really connected everything till now."

She stepped away from him and stood motionless letting the information sink in. She moved like a robot, silently attending to menial tasks like picking up dirty cups, taking them to the sink, washing them, drying them, actions that required little or no emotional input.

He respected her need for silence as she absorbed the implications of his deductions.

The longer the silence the wider the gulf between them seemed to grow. Did she think he had kept her in the dark deliberately? Was it the facts that would come between them, or was it that he had failed to inform her sooner? What else had he failed to tell her? Would she be upset to know he suspected she had been a drug user? He had no proof. She wasn't even showing any signs of serious cravings. Could telling her now do more harm than good? It would worry her, and there was no benefit in her knowing now. If he was wrong, and she found out later it could hardly do more damage to their already doomed relationship.

Mer kept her focus on household matters avoiding deep and meaningful conversation by keeping busy. She offered to cook dinner. Jim was happy to agree as it seemed to be what she wanted. He did his best to keep out of her way. The meal she prepared was simple, but her subtle use of herbs made it special. The smells wafting from the kitchen were so delicious Jim decided to complement the meal with a bottle of wine. They began the meal in silence, then as the food and wine relaxed them they began to talk more freely, and by the end of the meal Jim felt confident enough to broach the subject of his lists.

"I know you think it's a waste of time but I'd like to go through the lists again. Perhaps we can add something."

Mer drained her glass of wine before nodding her agreement. Jim sensed that her earlier enthusiasm to fill the gaps was missing, which was odd. He'd expected her to be fired up by the curiosity sparked by his clumsy revelation. He spread his almost blank questionnaire on the table. It covered so many areas but, as they went through it, Jim kept trying to think of new categories to add. They pored over them, Jim adding more questions than answers. The list seemed endless, but still she remembered nothing. Jim hid his disappointment, and undeterred refilled her glass until the wine was finished. He ignored her plea of exhaustion, bringing out the whisky to round off the evening. But several tots of that failed to get new answers on the pages.

"OK. Let's call it a day," said Jim accepting defeat.

"You'll have to help me," she said as she tried to get to her feet. "I've had far too much to drink."

"You can manage."

"No, I can't. The room's moving." she said staggering slightly as the effect of the drink became more apparent.

"OK," he said linking his arm in hers, "One last question. What was your husband's name?"

"Denis."

There was no hesitation. It took a second or two for the sobering impact of that single name to ring home.

"Denis," she repeated, shivering as she said the name.

"Denis, who?" Jim asked, regretting for a moment that he posed the question.

She shook her head. "I can't even picture him. I don't know why I said it. Surely I'd remember being married? But I must have been. Why else would I have come up with the name?"

They knew Denis was a fact of life, one they both had to come to terms with.

Chapter 8

Gavin sat down at his desk and restlessly flicked through the Mallaig file again. Sinclair had looked so pleased when he told him he was giving up on the investigation. The fact that he had bothered to link the drunk with Gillespie was worrying. The sooner Paula found out more about the registered owners of the vehicles the better. There had to be some clue there, without new information he'd have to give up. Instinct alone wasn't enough to keep an investigation going.

Once he was back at his desk he returned the call to Alistair Duncan.

"Hello Alistair. Sorry about the delay in getting back to you," he said. He'd known Alistair since childhood, and still occasionally enjoyed a round of golf with him, when Alistair came back from Stornoway where he was based for work.

"What grim task have you got in store for me today?" Gavin asked, recalling the last gruesome task Alistair's team had presented him with after a fishing boat from Oban had capsized.

"Believe it or not a nice one."

"I'll wait till I've seen it before I comment."

"Honest. This one is still alive."

"What? Alive! Are you sure you are ringing the right department?" Gavin replied. "You've never offered me a live one before."

"Well, we had a call from one of the islands. They say that a woman was found in the water a few days ago. So I thought I'd let you deal with it."

"Thanks. But if she's alive why do you need me?"

"She's lost her memory and has no idea who she is, or where she came from."

"No one reported missing, or boats gone adrift?"

"Nothing we know about. All we do know is that she is in safe hands. She was rescued by a doctor."

"Where is she?"

"Still on the island. There have been problems with their only transmitter which has caused delays. And now with the bad weather, the best we could do is air lift in a replacement set."

"Why didn't they take her off the island?"

"No room on the helicopter, and she didn't require urgent medical attention. Once they have the new transmitter set up you'll be able to talk to them yourself. It should be up and running by late afternoon."

"Fine, I'll do that," said Gavin sighing. This was why he had stayed with the force so long. You never knew what would turn up next. Then it occurred to him. Trying to find the identity of a person, who had lost their memory, would provide perfect cover to check out a few niggling loose ends in connection with the Mallaig file. This mystery lady could be very useful indeed.

Gavin reacted with text-book precision. Even with the limited knowledge he had so far, there were several channels to be checked. Soon he had the team sorting out missing person lists from the surrounding police forces. Once he knew the woman's age and height he would be able to eliminate a lot of names. Then he contacted the coastguard for a list of all missing vessels. Within an hour he had print outs of all the available information making him appreciate the advantages of modern technology.

Alistair Duncan called back later to confirm the radio had been delivered.

"I hope this one isn't going to muck up the weekend," Gavin said jokingly. "Unlike a dead body, it won't wait patiently till Monday."

"No, but I don't think you'll complain when you hear who's involved."

"Come on. Don't keep me in suspense."

"Ellen Cullen's brother. He's the doctor who rescued the girl."

"Ellen's brother… I can't remember her married name," Gavin answered.

"She doesn't use it these days. They got divorced some time back."

"Divorced? How come you didn't tell me?"

"It happened a couple of years ago. I must have told you."

"No. You didn't. But where does she fit in?"

"The young doctor involved in the rescue is her brother, Jim."

"Yes, I remember him, but I never knew he'd become a doctor."

"I wish I could stop and chat, but I'm off to a meeting so I'll be brief," Alistair said. "When they dropped a transmitter off they arranged to make contact at five o'clock. It might be worth talking to Dave Morgan, the Doctor who was on board the helicopter that delivered it. He spoke to her himself. You'll like him. He'll be touching down at Oban airport in the next half hour to pick up supplies. Perhaps you could talk to him then. Good Luck."

Gavin checked his watch. If he left now he would make it in time. It would be good to get out of the office and enjoy the sunshine offered by a brief break in the weather. He drove over to the airport and strolled over to wait near the helicopter landing zone.

Ellen Cullen, the name sparked a million happy memories. It was years since he had seen her, but she was not someone you could easily forget. He recalled that Alistair had been keen on her. Gavin knew that if he had not been so deeply involved with someone else at the time he might have been in the running. It would be interesting to see what her brother was like. Ellen always had family in tow, mainly her younger brother and her sister, sometimes a crowd of their friends too. No one minded. Ellen was such good fun to be with. His only hope was that divorce hadn't knocked the fun out of her. The more he thought about her the more he wanted to see her again. In fact, he was surprised as it was the first time since his own divorce that he felt a thrill at the prospect of an encounter with another woman.

He waited till the helicopter crew were well clear of their machine before approaching them and introducing himself, and told them he was looking for Doctor Morgan.

"Can you tell me anything about the woman who lost her memory?" he asked as they waited for the supplies to be loaded.

"Yes, I was able to examine her briefly. She's made a remarkable recovery physically, but the memory loss is serious. However there are encouraging signs. She has remembered her husband is called Denis, but so far can't put a face to the name."

"It's a start though."

"The main problem with her is that we don't know whether the loss of memory is caused by physical damage to the brain or purely psychological. There is always the possibility she might be deliberately trying to forget something. But she had taken quite a battering, so it could well be physical."

"Which do you think it is?"

"Difficult to answer. The fact that she has remembered something is a healthy sign. But Jim said that was after a hefty quantity of booze. I didn't get a chance to talk to him privately. I was under the impression he was holding back information because she was there. Her face was in a mess, looked as if she had been in one hell of a fight. I tried to discuss it but he veered off the subject."

"Well, by all accounts, she's lucky to be alive. I presume when you say Jim you mean Dr. Cullen. Do you know him well?"

"Fairly well, we were at college together."

"Did he say anything else?"

"Yes. He's trying to let her remember on her own. He's very anxious not to force information on her or press her too hard for answers."

"Would you agree with his method?"

"Oh yes. He did extensive work on psychology as a student, and he must have a good reason for choosing that approach to the problem. He asked me if I remembered a particular case, even suggested that I look it up. It should give a clue as to what he thinks is going on."

"Have you remembered it yet?"

"No. I'll check the details, and call you with the information."

"Can you remember what her voice was like? Did she have a distinctive accent that might give a clue to her background?" Gavin asked.

"She certainly didn't sound like a local. I don't know how to describe it, educated, fairly neutral, definitely no distinct regional accent. She's petite, about five foot two, dark shoulder length hair, very attractive, somewhere in her mid to late twenties.

Gavin thanked him and returned to the office. He was beginning to enjoy this assignment. It certainly beat identifying dead bodies. And the possibility of meeting Ellen again was an added bonus.

The radio call came in on time. Gavin explained who he was and how he would try to locate her family. He got Jim to give a more detailed description, which confirmed the one the doctor had given him earlier without adding to the little information gathered so far.

Jim asked if he'd spoken to Dave Morgan the helicopter doctor. Gavin assured him that he had.

"Get back to him. Ask him to tell you about the Hennessy case, and also ask if he remembers the Turner brothers, I think he'll understand the relevance."

"Is she with you?" asked Gavin, recalling Dave Morgan's comments about Jim being cautious in her presence.

"Yes."

"What sort of clothes was she wearing?"

"What difference does that make?"

"Depends on whether they were designer labels or high street brands."

"She had on some old, over-sized waterproofs, and underneath that a leather outfit."

"What?"

"Shorts and a laced up bodice - not exactly normal sailing gear!"

"Nothing else?"

"No."

"Any jewellery?"

"A necklace, silver I think. I haven't looked closely."

"Sorry if the questions seem endless, but any extra information from you would make our task easier. We'll call again in the morning."

Gavin stared at the notes in front of him. Apart from referring to the Hennessy case and Turner brothers he had added almost nothing to help her cause. Certainly nothing that would help to locate her relatives. The greatest problem as he saw it, was that the information to date was fragmented, each piece insignificant on its own. In one respect, her normality, and lack of distinguishing features put her in a category with millions of other attractive married women in their twenties and made his task harder. The details about her clothing added confusion. Finding a man called Denis who had lost his wife would not be any easier.

He left a message for Doctor Morgan asking him about the two cases Jim Cullen had mentioned. The reply came quickly.

"Glad I caught you. I looked up the Hennessy case Jim mentioned. "It was the most severe case of drug withdrawal that we witnessed during our final year."

"He asked me to ask you if you remembered the Turner brothers."

"Hard to forget them, they were twins who spent their whole time beating hell out of each other."

"He said you'd understand the connection."

"Was she with him when he made the call?"

"Yes."

"Well I'm presuming he was trying to tell us that the bruising on her face was caused in a fight, and he thinks she's a drug addict."

"And at a guess, he hasn't told her?"

"I can't think of any other reason why he would bring up the Hennessy case or the Turners unless that is what he wants us to think. When are you making contact again?"

"Tomorrow at ten. Can you spare the time to be in on the call?"

"I'll try. Perhaps we'll be able to clarify a few points but obviously we must be careful how we put our questions."

"Thanks, that'll be a great help. Goodbye."

Gavin stared at the phone when he had replaced the receiver, thinking that his golf was definitely going to be disrupted. First he must find out more about amnesia, its causes and treatment. Being well informed was a habit of his, and gave him the edge when tackling a problem he had never previously faced. Gavin called an old friend who happily explained in simple jargon the root causes, and the ins and outs of the problem that faced Ellen Cullen's brother. He listened to his friend for nearly half an hour and in that time his estimation of Jim Cullen as a doctor rose sharply. He seemed to be very much in control of this case, and had done everything he could to prevent her from suffering shock from sudden revelations. It was now up to himself to ensure that the same care was shown in all future calls.

Gavin decided that he would not wait to reacquaint himself with Ellen. It had been so long since he had felt the urge to contact someone from his past. He was worried if he didn't act quickly he might end up postponing indefinitely.

Her voice was exactly as he remembered it, and he was glad he had not put off making the call. They exchanged greetings and both acknowledged surprise at the departure of their respective partners.

"Ellen, I was really contacting you to try to discover more about Jim."

"What's he done now?"

"Nothing to be alarmed about. He's rescued someone and I just thought it would be nice to know more about him, and to be honest, I couldn't resist phoning you as I had such a good excuse."

Ellen laughed. It was the same happy sound that he had always associated with her name.

"I'm glad some things don't change. And by the sound of your voice you haven't changed at all. What do you want to know?"

"Well anything you think might be useful."

"He attracts patients like a magnet," she announced. "I have never known him go anywhere without finding someone who needs his help. And finding one on an almost uninhabited island is fairly typical."

Ellen continued talking with pride about Jim. It didn't take Gavin long to realize that she had a very good relationship with all her family and particularly with Jim. She described how Jim had worked with their father until his death two years ago, since when he had worked fiendishly expanding the practice.

"Everything was going well until his partner was injured in a car crash. Jim cancelled his own holiday, and coped reasonably well until the flu epidemic hit. He got a locum in to help, but it wasn't enough. There was still too much to handle. The work load trebled because of the epidemic."

"I can believe that. It's been terrible down here too."

"His phone never stopped ringing. He couldn't get a decent night's sleep. Perhaps the exhaustion made him vulnerable, and he caught the virus and collapsed. I thought he was going to die, but just as he began to pick up he got a secondary infection on his lungs."

"You must have been very worried."

"Yes. Anyway his partner, Andrew McPherson, was by then sufficiently recovered to return to work. And he insisted that Jim take time off to recover, plus his full holiday time. Andrew thinks it could be months before he's completely well again."

"What took him to this island?" asked Gavin.

"He wanted to get away from the practice. He's a terrible patient, and couldn't bear being close to the surgery without being involved. The island seemed like a sensible place to go. We foolishly thought he'd be safe from patients. But, from what you have told me, it sounds as if we were wrong."

While she had been talking Gavin decided he had to meet up with her.

"I take it you still play golf?" he said.

"Occasionally, but what has that to do with Jim?"

"Nothing, I was just looking for an excuse to see you. We could meet at the club after I've spoken to Jim, I could be there by eleven."

"Forget the golf, come to the house. I moved back to the parent's house, you must remember where it is, better still stay for lunch," she added, which was an unexpected bonus."

Chapter 9

Mer leant against the wall, basking in the warmth of the weak winter sunshine, with Digger curled up beside her. He had become a comforting companion in the last few days.

She wondered why Jim had suggested abandoning the lists in favour of exploring the island. Was it because he didn't fancy spending the day cooped up with her in the cottage? Could she blame him? Not really, if the clothes she had been wearing were anything to go by, that outfit was only fit for someone on the game or someone with strange sexual fantasies. Maybe that was the real reason for his aloofness.

True there had been one passionate kiss, but it hadn't lasted long, and then she'd remembered that name which had changed everything. Since then, Jim's hands off approach had seemed icy. His changed demeanour was most noticeable when he appeared with tea after she had woken yet again with one of her nightmares. Gone was the comforting arm around her, gone was the reassuring touching of hands, gone the gentle caress as he wiped away her tears.

Everything would have been more bearable if she could have confirmed the answer to his question about her husband, if she could have remembered even one detail about him, other than his name. But she had failed. Denis remained a mystery. Perhaps if they had some information from the mainland, she would have felt slightly less depressed.

But as she looked around she felt her mood change. It was as if the island had some magical healing effect. She began to understand his love of the place. The air of tranquillity steadily obliterated her depression and frustration. For now, she didn't care if she couldn't remember who Denis was. She wasn't even upset that there had been no identifying debris washed up on the shore of the cove where Jim had found her. It didn't matter. Nothing mattered.

"Are you warm enough?" he asked.

She just nodded, and snuggled deeper into the soft jumper he had lent her, revelling in the lingering scent of his aftershave.

"Have a glass of wine," he said

"No. Not after the other night. You don't want to have to carry me back to the cottage."

"One glass won't hurt," he said, passing her a sandwich and a drink.

"Is this your favourite spot on the island?" she asked, surveying the scenery from their vantage point at the ruined monastery.

"Yes, I used to hide up here with a book when I wanted some quiet. You can always find a spot sheltered from the wind. I don't know whether the atmosphere has anything to do with the fact it was a holy place, but I always feel calm and peaceful here."

"Yes, I feel it too."

"I used to lie in the grass and imagine what it was like when the monks lived here, and dream of finding buried treasure."

"You were never tempted to excavate?"

"Never. I couldn't bear to have other people trampling all over it."

"What about me?"

"That's different," he said quietly and very gently touched her hand.

She held her breath, savouring the moment. Then he took his hand away to point out a flight of geese, whose noisy wing flapping and raucous honking had attracted his attention.

"Look, those are the barnacle geese Ned was about to tell you about. We've been lucky this year not too many have turned up. The last really icy winter we had, the whole island was covered with both barnacle geese and white fronts. They usually stay on the sand flats, but there were so many of them, they moved further inland and devoured most of the grass, stripping the island bare. Ned and his family were badly hit by it. They're still fighting for compensation on the grounds that they can't shoot them because they're protected."

"Where do they come from?"

"Greenland."

"It's hard to believe they come all that distance." she said before settling into contemplative silence, watching as the formation went from a neat arrow head to a ragged line as they changed leader and regrouped.

The next thing she knew was that Jim was shaking her shoulder to wake her.

"Come on, there's another storm brewing. We've been here too long."

"I must have been asleep for hours. Why didn't you wake me up earlier?"

"You needed the sleep," he said as he hastily packed up the lunch things.

Keeping a wary eye on the rapidly approaching storm clouds, she struggled to keep up with Jim on the route back through the woods. There was a brief respite, when he stopped to point out a young deer as they passed a clearing. He strode along at a brisk pace, making her wonder what speed he'd go if he hadn't been convalescing, he must have been very fit beforehand, and obviously enjoyed keeping himself in good shape physically.

She had dropped about fifty yards behind, when the first splattering of rain hit. Within minutes it beat down in freezing torrents, stinging her arms and face.

The thunder rumbled. Jim had disappeared out of sight. She could feel panic rising. The rumble got louder. Closer and closer, then crashed with an ear-deafening blast directly above her head. A simultaneous flash of lightening cracked the sky, bathing the forest in an eerie electric blue light, so intense it left her dazzled and paralysed.

She had no idea how long she was rooted to the spot, before Jim reappeared yelling her name. She was unable to respond. She felt the pressure of his hand on her arm as he grabbed her, pulling her with him just as more thunder and lightning boomed and cracked. Gradually her legs began to function as he guided her to shelter. It was hardly more than a shed, but it had a door, which slammed shut behind them as he pulled her into his arms. It was almost pitch dark in the windowless room. Slowly her eyes adjusted to the change of light. Jim coaxed her towards the ready laid fireplace, disentangling himself to set it alight. Another crash of thunder drove her back into his arms. She was shaking from fear rather than from cold.

"It's alright. I'll look after you. You're quite safe now," he whispered to her.

Enveloped in his arms she felt completely secure, her fear of the storm diminished, but her feelings for him did not. Just being held by him was heaven, and she clung tighter. Soon she was unable to prevent herself stretching up and turning her face towards his and kissing him.

For a fleeting second she felt his muscles tense, as he tried to pull away. She clung on. His initial response to her kiss had told her all she needed to know. If she could hold onto him long enough she had the power to conquer his intention of keeping their relationship platonic.

"It mustn't happen. Stop," he murmured.

Her reaction was to kiss him even more passionately, knowing she almost had him under her control. All the odds were stacked in her favour. She was driven by a desire that had started on the first morning when she had regained consciousness.

Jim was soon returning her kisses with equal fervour. Then, so slowly, so gently, he caressed her, his hands moving cautiously over her body, tenderly touching and exploring. She could tell from the way he held her he was afraid of hurting her and avoiding the worst bruised areas.

The fire crackled into life unheeded along with the storm, the thunder and the lightning. The rain sodden garments were eased off and discarded. Not a single word spoken, touch was enough.

There was a last brief moment of hesitation from Jim, but she fought to prevent his retreat the only way she could, with her lips, her hands and her body, triumphantly overwhelming his caution.

He carried her to the small cot-like bed that took up one side of the hut. The roughness of the blankets and the damp musty smell of the mattress went unnoticed. Joy obliterated everything else. Passion reached heights never experienced or dreamed of before. With a feeling of euphoria she lay in his arms, confident he would not be able to give her up now, no matter what problems lay ahead. She snuggled closer, the glow from the fire giving enough light for her to watch him as he slept.

As dawn approached she stirred, filled with a glorious feeling of contentment as she recalled the sensations of their lovemaking. Then deep disappointment set in as she realized he had gone. Turning, she saw him sitting on a low bench, staring into the fire.

"Jim, come back to me," she called softly. The second his eyes met hers she guessed his reply. Hoping to change the response, she begged, "Please."

She could tell nothing she could do, or say, was going to change his mind.

"We can't Mer. It's no good pretending. Not until we know who you are."

She wanted to scream, yell, beg, to do something to force him to take back those words. Not a sound escaped her lips. A part of her knew he was right. But could she accept life without him?

"The sooner we can get you back to the mainland the better," he added.

Mer sat speechless, deeply hurt by his swift and almost brutal rejection. She held back the threatening tears. She loved him. She watched as he backed out of the hut escaping her gaze. Couldn't he bear to witness her agony?

Shivering from shock and cold, she dressed mechanically, hardly conscious of the fact that her clothes were still wet from the storm. Numbed she sat on the edge of the cot in a trance. She watched him return unable to tear her eyes away as he damped down the fire and restored the hut to the order in which they had found it. His obliteration of all evidence of their ever being together was too much. She fled. But Jim caught her only yards from the entrance, gripping her firmly.

"Please don't hate me," he begged softly. "Try to forgive me."

"I don't hate you, only what you're doing to us," she whispered.

Jim kissed her softly on her forehead.

"I hate it too," he admitted. "Last night should never have happened. I'd do anything to change things back to the way they were, but I can't."

She shivered.

"What am I thinking of? Letting you stand out here in the cold in sopping wet clothes. I didn't save your life to let you get pneumonia through stupidity and neglect. Come on, let's get back to the cottage and get warm and dry."

It didn't take them long. They walked in complete silence. Not even the scenery raised a comment from either of them. Jim having resumed his role of doctor insisted that she had a hot bath and change immediately. Then he presented her with breakfast. She struggled to eat it, feeling choked with emotions. When she'd finished, he plonked the dreaded sheets of questions in front of her.

"These will keep you occupied till the next transmission."

His brusque manner surprised and angered her. If that's how he wanted to behave, maybe it was better to end their relationship now. It was unbearable to be so near to him, yet so totally apart. Defiantly she grabbed up the bundle of papers and made her exit to the other room. She sat and faced the sheets. Angry with herself for thinking he might have seriously cared for her. She went through them again and again, rage and misery dominating her thoughts.

His appearance bearing a fresh cup of coffee created an interruption jolting her back to the present. How long had she been working, trying to answer his silly questions? He didn't even care about her. She had to answer them so she would never be in a position of dependence on him again, and with that in mind she set to work in earnest. Starting at the beginning, she read through all the filled in information. It was some time before she was aware that most of what she was reading was fresh. She had written it, without registering her actions, while her anger was at its peak. With increasing surprise at the details scrawled on the sheets, she read on and on in amazement. Snippets of her life unfolded.

When she read her answer to the question about children she finally cracked.

It was there, written in her own untidy handwriting. Was she going mad?

Twins - Michael and David.

She read the names again and again. Michael and David. Michael and David. Michael and David.

Chapter 10

Since finding the names of the twins written down Mer sat rigidly gripping the sheet of paper. She neither spoke nor moved. Jim was beginning to give up hope of getting through to her. He could no longer treat her objectively. He bitterly regretted the complication their love affair created. All his effort to keep her at arm's length had been for nothing.

"Let me give you something to calm you down," he offered in desperation.

The violence of her reaction surprised him. The papers flew from her hands, littering the table and floor, as she jumped up and ran to the kitchen.

"What is it?" he yelled, chasing after her.

"Don't touch me. Don't come near me."

An internal alarm stopped him at the first sight of glinting metal. She stood with her back to the sink, silhouetted against the window, menacingly brandishing a knife.

"Leave me alone," she screamed.

Jim stepped back one pace, then slowly back another. He must stay calm, and give her room to manoeuvre. Her posture reminded him of a cornered animal. Was she capable of using the knife? Had he hurt her so much she would want to use it on him?

"I'm not going to hurt you," he said quietly, watching as her grip tightened, her stance defiantly indicating that to invade her territory would provoke trouble. "Can we talk?"

"Don't come any closer." she shouted.

"Can I go and sit over there?" he asked, pointing to a chair in the furthest corner of the room. "Then you can sit here by the door," he added, knowing that he had to leave her an exit. He needed to restore her trust in him.

She didn't answer. He had to test her. He moved half a pace. No reaction. He moved another, then another, gradually working his way across the room till he eased himself into the chair he had pointed to earlier.

The only sound in the cottage was the clock ticking, as the hands moved slowly round.

She began to tremble. He held his breath, waiting for her to attack.

"Why don't you sit down?" he suggested bravely.

Her expression changed from terror to bewilderment as she stared down at the knife in her hand. Then without warning, she spun round, flinging the knife into the sink, the noise shattering the silence.

Slowly her knees buckled, and she sank to the floor like a limp rag doll; her head pressed against the cupboard door and then she let out an anguished cry.

"Oh God. What's happening to me?"

Jim warily approached her.

"What sort of person am I? Why did I do it? Please help me. I didn't mean to hurt you." she sobbed.

The rage had gone. Tenderly he helped her to her feet, and drew her into his arms, feeling an overwhelming desire to protect her.

The clock chimed. Jim groaned. He had lost track of the time. He was due to make a transmission. He had missed the previous scheduled call because of the storm. If he failed to make this one everyone would assume there was trouble.

"Trust me," he whispered, and led her into the lounge and across to the settee. "Just sit quietly and try to think why you got so frightened. I have to call the mainland now."

The connection was so prompt he was taken by surprise. But when Gavin McKay complained about the missed call, Jim cut him short.

"I'm sorry about yesterday. Got caught by a storm, I can't talk now. I'm in the middle of a therapy session."

"How much time do you need?"

"Three hours minimum. Have you come up with anything?"

"Nothing. Are you sure you're OK?"

"Yes, but the sooner you can get us off the island the better. I'll talk to you later."

"We'll expect another call at five. Don't miss it."

"I won't. Thanks."

She looked up at him after he had switched off.

"Therapy, is that what you call it?"

"Can you think of a better description?"

"No."

"Right, I want to go over everything you've said and done today." He knew exactly what had upset her, but wanted to check if she was conscious of it herself.

"I'm afraid. What happens if I suddenly decide to attack you with a knife again?"

"Don't worry, I won't let you."

"I can't."

"You have to. If you don't find out why you threatened me, it'll drive you crazy."

As she poured out her troubles, he became aware how clumsy and brutal his efforts to reinstate a professional but impersonal relationship had been. He had never intended to hurt her, but he had. From the minute she had woken, her day had been hell. His rejection as a lover had started the agony. Finding the names of twins on the lists hadn't helped. But neither of these problems explained the terror she had exhibited.

There was no avoiding it. He would have to tell her.

"You were fine until I offered something to calm you down."

Before he had finished speaking he knew he had pinpointed the problem.

Her colour drained from her face, her body went rigid, her fists clenched.

"That's what scared you?"

She nodded.

"Do you know why?" he asked.

She shook her head. He could no longer keep his earlier fears, about her drug withdrawal symptoms from her; nor could he suppress his speculations about the extensive bruising.

The clock chimed again and again, but Jim chose to ignore it. They talked about everything except the storm and their affair. Silence on that topic being the only defence mechanism available.

"I can't take any more," she announced, ending the session.

It was a statement, he had to accept.

"Sorry, I didn't mean to push you so hard," he said knowing how tired she must be. "How about having something to eat?"

"No. I'm too tired."

"Go and lie down for an hour or two."

Jim read and reread every question and answer written on the sheets, adding a few of his own comments. He also carefully double checked and completed her medical notes. He wanted to be able to hand over her case at the earliest moment and with the minimum of fuss. He would have to explain to his partner Andrew McPherson the full story. Then one obstacle would be eliminated, that of the doctor - patient relationship.

When the clock struck five, he was ready to make his call to the mainland.

"How did your therapy session go?" asked Gavin McKay.

"Not too well. There are still too many incomplete answers, and very little that would help you. Have you had any better luck?"

"Not about her. But I have been trying to arrange for Jamie McNeil to pick you up tomorrow. He should be there at eleven to catch the high tide on his way back from one of the other islands. But I'll have to confirm it in the morning."

Jim sank into the chair beside the fire, and closed his eyes.

"Jim. Are you alright?" she asked, waking him from his doze.

"Yes, just tired."

"I'll get you something to eat, then I think you should go to bed and try to get a good long sleep." she said. "I shall be alright."

When he finally gave in and climbed into bed sleep was elusive. He lay still listening to her moving restlessly about the cottage. Should he go to her? No. That would be asking for trouble. He must keep his distance.

He heard his door open. He held his breath, and prayed she would go, but at the same time willing her to stay.

"Jim," she whispered. "I can't sleep."

He grunted, afraid to speak. What could he say?

"Will you hold me?" she said as she eased herself into the bed beside him, snuggling down, her body fitting neatly alongside his, her head resting on his shoulder. Then she very quietly mumbled, "Thanks."

He pretended to be asleep, though every nerve in his body had come tingling back to life at the thought of her lying there beside him. He must not move, he told himself. It wasn't long before he sensed she had fallen asleep. He felt good, she trusted him, needed him. He'd look after her, no matter what transpired. He listened to her quiet even breathing, savouring the delicate scent from her hair, longing to run his fingers through it.

Finally he slept. Ned's knocking at the door woke him. He gently placed a kiss on her forehead as he eased himself out of the bed, grabbed his clothes, dressed and left her sleeping.

Jim signalled to Ned to keep quiet.

"She's asleep. I don't want to disturb her. What's up?"

"We need a doctor. My niece has gone into labour, she's six weeks early."

"Of course I'll go. Can you stay here until nine? I'm expecting a transmission, to confirm Jamie McNeil will get in at eleven, and could you see Mer onto the boat."

"Yes, I can do that."

"I'll go and tell her what's happening."

It was such a shame to disturb her when she was so peaceful. But time was running out.

"What time is it?" she murmured, yawning.

"Sorry I had to wake you. But I have to go, there's an emergency, a premature delivery. Ned's going to stay with you and see you onto the boat at eleven."

"I can't go without you."

"You must. I promise I'll come as soon as I can. But I'm sure that Inspector McKay will take good care of you." He bent down, and kissed her tenderly on her forehead. "Take care."

Grabbing the cottage first aid kit, he made a quick exit. He had a long walk ahead and couldn't waste time while lives were at stake.

Chapter 11

Dan Trench knew nothing would cure the unbearable itch on his rash covered hands except finding Jenny and extricating himself from all dealings with Hector Sinclair and his psychopathic henchman Ron Hill.

He paced round the bland two-room holiday flat he'd rented on a short lease on the outskirts of Oban. He had decided staying on at Mallaig with the police taking an interest in the place was not a good idea. The bare magnolia walls, the beige carpet, curtains and furnishing were beginning to drive him crazy. He flopped into a chair, flicked on the television, but couldn't block out the fear of what Ron might do.

Ron had gone back to his flat in Sterling. At six foot four, all of it well muscled, he was scary, but it was his volcanic temperament that scared Dan most. Dan knew Ron wasn't fussy who he lashed out at when his temper kicked in. Age, size, or sex made no difference.

Taking the woman to Mallaig had been a mistake. Not just because he'd made a foolish assumption she was ready for a more intimate relationship. She had made him forget the danger. Worse still he'd forgotten Ron Hill might turn up.

He was ashamed at his cowardice. He should never have trusted Ron to keep an eye on her, and worse still had been too petrified to intervene when he realized what Ron was up to. His fear had even prevented him from making the final blow that could have solved the problem of Ron for good.

His relationship with Sinclair was different. Sinclair's cold, calculating hold was more sinister than a physical threat. For years he had been trying to get free of Sinclair. The harder he tried the more pressure Sinclair managed to apply, including financing part of Sinclair's latest deal. Shit he didn't want to get involved with drugs. Antiques were his strength and his weakness. Right now he was in danger of losing everything.

He wasn't sure if he could trust Sinclair's story about a surveillance team watching the house at Mallaig. The cunning bastard, using his position as Acting Chief Superintendent, had probably set it up himself to scare him into deeper commitment. If not, then it was either Hill or Sinclair himself who was under investigation. Dan was confident he'd done nothing lately that would have anyone after him. Not that it mattered, neither option was good.

He went to the alcove that served as a kitchen and peered out the window. There was nobody in sight. He grabbed a can of beer off the pseudo marble counter and angrily yanked the ring pull. He hated the paranoia that came with the job. He needed some sort of plan to protect himself. If only he could find a weak spot in Sinclair's armour, to make him defensive and less dangerous.

He was just finishing his third can of beer when the phone rang. He didn't dare answer it. If he was under surveillance his phone might have been tapped, and he was determined to take every precaution possible to protect himself. As only two people knew the phone number of the flat, it had to be one or other of them. He would return their call using a public phone. He put on his coat, picked up the car keys, then, remembering he'd already consumed a couple of cans of beer, put them down. Getting breathalysed would be the last straw. He let himself out, and made his way down the street to the nearby pub. He nervously surveyed the other patrons, ordered a pint and asked for change to make a phone call. There was a newspaper lying on the bar, he flipped through it. There was nothing about the girl. Nothing at all. He could feel himself go into a cold sweat. The call had to be about the girl. He had tried to contact her at home without success. Where the hell had she gone? He downed his pint and made for the phone and called Ron Hill.

"Ron. Did you just phone me?"

"No. But Sinclair's trying to get hold of you."

"Did he say why?" Dan asked.

"No. He's worried about some drunk called Gillespie, who's supposed to have tipped them off about Mallaig. Any idea who he's talking about?"

Dan shivered. He remembered Gillespie. Gillespie was the drop-out who had been sheltering in empty crates in the warehouse on the night they'd arranged the deal. A bad fit of coughing had alerted them to his presence. He'd sworn he hadn't heard a thing, but that didn't stop Ron from punching and kicking the poor fellow until he was unconscious, Ron would have killed him if he hadn't intervened.

"I remember him. And so should you. He's the tramp you beat up in the warehouse the night we collected the crates."

"That old fool… You should've let me finish him off."

Dan shivered, unable to think of a reply. He had to make a break from these people before they dragged him down to their level.

"I wonder what Sinclair wants us to do."

"Nothing for the moment," answered Dan quickly. "Leave it with me to find out, meanwhile just stay out of trouble."

"OK."

"Are you sure you didn't say anything to him about the girl?"

"You must be joking. He was in a bad enough mood without that. He'll go mad if he finds out."

"He's not going to. I don't intend to tell him. And neither are you."

"Of course I won't. But what do I say if anyone asks what we were doing in Mallaig?"

"Say you've been helping a friend to pack up the contents of a house to go into storage. You don't know who owned the stuff. It was a cash in hand job. Is that clear?"

"What about the car?"

"They won't delve too deeply, the number plates match the colour and make, so there's no reason to suspect it's stolen."

"Where can I contact you?"

"At the flat, but I'd rather you didn't unless it's important. If anything comes up I'll keep you informed."

Dan noticed as he put the receiver back on the hook his knuckles had turned white. He had never wanted Ron Hill on the job. But Sinclair had insisted. Maybe Ron's violence would be the key to solving some of his problems. If Sinclair gave orders to silence the unfortunate drunk, and he could get proof, he'd have the protection from Sinclair that he craved. All he had to do was ensure he had a totally watertight alibi.

Instinct led him back to the bar, where he ordered another pint. He had to make some plans before he spoke to Sinclair. He wanted a normal life. He had been living a lie for so long he had forgotten what normal was. He stared at his pint. What a mess. The six month prison sentence he'd served at the age of twenty, for possession of stolen goods had spiralled his life into a cat and mouse game, the stakes growing all the time. His dreams of quitting came close to reality when he inherited the house at Mallaig from a distant uncle. He at last had a place to house what he referred to as his retirement collection. The frustration of not being able to brag about his haul had led to carelessness, and now he was further from retirement than ever.

Sinclair had worked it out, and used the knowledge to pressurize him into jobs he didn't want to do. Worse still, he had to work with others, which didn't suit him at all. Sinclair was always in too much of a hurry, and greedy beyond belief.

Meticulous planning had been Dan's forte. Working alone, or with an expert if the job required specialist knowledge was his preferred mode. He smiled, the ideas were coming together to get himself out of trouble and out of Sinclair's clutches. It wouldn't be easy but if he could pull this off, his retirement plans could be salvaged.

Chapter 12

"She's going to hurt him." Ellen said as she put the tray down. "It's a pity she didn't get off the island the first day you got the boat arranged."

Gavin understood the sisterly concern, Jim was getting emotionally involved with Mer, but he didn't want to interfere because it gave him an excuse to see Ellen. Since their first meeting, they'd had dinner together and even gone on a five mile run.

"Jim's well able to look after himself," he said, as he looked round taking in the details of Ellen's comfortable living room. He loved the way she blended the pick of her parents' antiques with modern furniture and art.

"I hope so. Knowing she's married and has children worries me. How much longer will it take to find out who she is?"

"Depends on if we get lucky or not."

"You seem worried."

"Not about Mer, I'm sure we'll come up with something soon. Sorry I've been a bit preoccupied because of another case I'm working on."

"Want to talk about it?"

Gavin smiled at her, "Sorry, I can't." He really wished he could share more with her. The fact that she knew Hector Sinclair from their days at school made him wary. It was a risk he couldn't afford to take.

"Would you like to stay?" she asked.

"No," he answered without thinking. An invitation to stay had been the last thing he'd anticipated when she invited him in after dinner.

Having given his answer he realised that he was a total moron to have turned her down so sharply. "I'd love to really, but I have an early start in the morning," he said trying to make his reaction seem less brusque, and to hide his confusion as to whether the offer was simply to sleep in her spare room or something infinitely more preferable.

"Before you go," she said, with no hint of disappointment, "please recount exactly what happened earlier when I was out of the room. She seemed perfectly happy all afternoon."

"It's hard to describe. She was fine right up till the time we came into this room. Jim and I both noticed right from the start she was restless. She made a comment about it being a beautiful room, and then started pacing round, examining all the ornaments, one after another. There was something odd about the way she moved. Jim spotted it too. She'd been studying the vases on the mantle-piece, when she looked up at the painting she freaked out."

"Who is it by?" he asked, making a closer inspection of the incredible misty landscape.

"Henry Hillingford-Parker," she answered

"Well known?"

"Not a big name as such, but fast becoming very collectable, the way he captures the sun of the hills and the water is magical."

"Yes, even I can see that."

"Anyway, she went from relaxed and happy to being so tense you could actually see her muscles stand out. Her whole body shook as she tried to speak, but the words wouldn't come out. I don't think I've witnessed that much terror in all my life."

"That's hard to believe."

"Well it's true. Perhaps the closest I've ever seen were a group who had been held hostage for five days by a complete madman. When we rescued them they wouldn't allow themselves to accept they were being released, they were quite convinced that we were going to harm them."

"What did she do?"

"Jim reached out to her and started to say something, but she ran out. He couldn't stop her."

"Poor thing, you wonder what's going on in her head. Jim told me he was surprised that she had locked her door, said she'd been upset at the cottage once when he closed a door. Why should she react to a painting?" Ellen asked.

"No idea, especially over such a beautiful work of art. I'm envious. Hard to believe it could evoke terror. I only hope we can discover the reason." Gavin answered, putting his empty cup back on the tray. "I'd best be on my way. I've a long drive ahead and hectic day tomorrow."

"Next time, bring a toothbrush." Ellen said.

"Now there's an invitation I won't refuse. Dare I suggest another run followed by dinner next week, even if all this has been sorted out"?

"Another run? That's brave of you. I thought I was too slow for you." Ellen answered, smiling.

"No, perfect pacing. I'll be in touch tomorrow," he said quietly and gently kissed her forehead. "Thank you for a beautiful evening." There was no doubt about it. He would be back. The extra delay in Jim returning from the island had given him a good opportunity to renew his friendship with Ellen, one he wished to maintain.

When he reached home exhausted, all lights were blazing. He still hadn't got used to having company and had quickly learned Paula never switched things off. He hoped she was in bed already as he wasn't in the mood for conversation. His luck was out. As he opened the door she called out. "Thank god you're home. I've been trying to get hold of you for the last half hour."

"What for?"

"There's an urgent message on the answer-phone. I probably shouldn't have touched it, but I've been waiting for a call from my mother, so I checked for messages when I came in."

Gavin had never seen Paula looking so flustered. Not even on the night he found her after her boyfriend had beaten her up. "So what was it?"

"You'd better listen yourself," she answered.

Gavin stabbed the play button, and tapped the edge of the table as the machine clicked and beeped into action. He yawned, he needed sleep. Eventually the message machine ceased winding and clicking and a slurred voice started speaking. At first he had trouble making out the words. He concentrated so hard the impact of the message was lost. Suddenly he was fully alert, the tone of Neil's voice jarred. He pressed the replay button, this time every word and nuance grabbed his attention.

"McKay." said the drunken slur. "Sinclair's the bastard you want. He's the one. He's out to get me. You've got to get him first."

The line went dead.

He played it again. No doubt about it being Neil Gillespie. Why leave a message like that? He wished he could put it down to drunken ramblings, but instinct told him it was genuine. The man was terrified. What had Sinclair done? Neil had to be desperate, because if Sinclair was the cause of his fear, he was taking quite a risk to trust anyone, let alone another member of the police force.

"Any idea when he phoned?"

"Sometime between seven and nine when I was out," she answered. "I saw the light flashing when I came back, then I didn't know what to do. I presume it's the same man who put you onto the Mallaig house?"

"Yes."

"There's a second message from Tom. He said he had some interesting information for you, and to call him when you got back regardless of the time."

"Must be important," Gavin muttered to himself. Tom was well known for not taking calls at home. Not that he was a nine to five copper. His routine rarely changed but in an emergency he had been known to stick at his screen for as long as forty-eight hours if he thought he could get a result. To be asked to call his home was rare.

He looked at Paula, thinking she could do with a good sleep. "Thanks, anything else I need to know?"

"No I don't think so. Do you need help looking for him?"

"I'm not sure," he picked up the phone and dialled Tom's number, "it depends on what Tom has to tell me." The ringing tone went on and on, until at last a sleepy voice answered.

"Hello."

"Sorry to wake you Tom. But I got your message, you said it was urgent."

"Yes. I think it is. I have a problem. Sinclair's nephew spent the day in my department. I can't do a thing with him there."

"I'll try to get him moved. But did you find out anything before he arrived?" Gavin said.

"Yes. Sinclair gave the final order in every case that has been closed down recently. And young Steven has been accessing all those case files."

"Any idea what he's been doing?"

"Who? Hector or Steven?"

"Either…. both…. come on blast me with your theories."

"Well I didn't want Steven to feel we were nosing into what he was doing, so am on the whole ignoring the fact he's there. But have set up a system to monitor his machine from afar. He has no idea we know what he's up to."

"Good."

"Hector's definitely covering tracks. From what I've seen so far, he is methodically erasing some of the evidence from the files of the cases Sinclair closed. I have a snapshot of the before and after files showing all the information they tampered with."

"Good. Is there a pattern? Similarity in type of case? Something we can concentrate on?"

"No. At least I can't see one. I have the files here if you want to go through them yourself. I have made a few notes of the things I know were left out."

"Have you any ideas where to go next?"

"No. I started checking out the last posting Hector was at, to see if he worked the same way there. No results so far."

"Fine. Would you mind if I sent Paula over for those files now?"

"Why not, I'm awake."

"She'll be there in about ten minutes. Thanks."

"Looks like you've been volunteered for the late shift," he said to Paula. "Can you pick up the files and see if you can make any sense of them. I'll go and see if I can find Gillespie.

Chapter 13

"Be rational Jim. You're letting her become too dependent on you." Andrew McPherson said. "I thought you got Ellen to put her up, because you didn't want to get too involved. I see now, I was wrong."

"It's what I want."

"Be careful, she has history, with huge complications."

"That's not true. I love her. She has immense courage. She must have to have coped so well. And she's beautiful." Jim replied.

"Is it enough? Remember, she's been a drug user."

"Even more reason for needing my help."

"She's married, has children, you could be destroying a family."

"Not much of a family unit if they don't bother to report her missing. Why should I turn my back on her?"

"You should ease off."

"Oh hell, life's so messy. I've never felt like this before. Not since Felicity."

"Well you and she never had much in common, and you have even less with this girl."

"You're wrong."

"I think the doctor patient relationship has blinded you."

"I don't."

"Fair enough, but you must be prepared to let go once she's found her family."

"Yes." Jim answered thoughtfully. "Are you sure you can cope without me for a while?"

"Yes, we weren't expecting you back for at least another couple of weeks."

Jim was relieved. He wanted to use the time to help Mer. What bothered him most was that since they had left the island she had become more withdrawn. He no longer knew what she thought, or how she felt. On the surface she was maintaining an amazing air of control, but refusing to discuss her fears. Bottling everything up was creating severe tension. Ellen had heard her crying during the night and when he'd asked about the dreams she always clammed up.

"I have to go and fetch her from the hospital now. They finish the last tests today."

"Keep me informed, and do be careful," Andrew answered.

Jim kept a close watch on the hospital entrance, expecting her to emerge exhausted. So far there had been no physical cause found for her loss of memory, confirming his fears, psychological issues were to blame. The challenge now was to uncover the cause without creating further trauma.

"Sorry I was so long." she said, as she slumped into the seat of the car, showing obvious signs of relief at escaping.

"Do you want to go back to Ellen's place?" he asked.

She shook her head, leaving him wondering if she was reluctant to face the flat, or actually wanted to be alone with him. He hoped for the latter.

Jim drove off, telling her about his day.

"I'm a free agent, totally at your disposal for the next few weeks."

"I shall never be able to repay you for being so kind."

"I'll think of a way." he answered. "Shall we go and visit one of the most beautiful houses in the area? I hear they lay on a sumptuous tea."

He turned off up a tree-lined avenue, which led to a wide gravel car park in front of a magnificent house. Before she had time to protest he got out and waited for her to follow. Did he detect a feeling of reluctance? What was holding her back? He began walking up the main steps. He rambled on about the history of the house, all the time feeling he didn't have her full attention. He turned to ask her a question to find her running down the steps towards the car.

Jim was caught out by her taking off like that. No explanation. What had he been saying? He hadn't said anything to offend. Baffled, he raced after her.

"Please take me away from here." she pleaded.

Jim opened the car, and set off. When they were a few miles away, he pulled into a lay by. She was still shaking and had tears close to spilling. He reached over, took her hand in his. She did not shy away, so he put his arm around and drew her towards him and quietly questioned her.

"Did you feel the same the other night, when you ran out of the lounge?"

She nodded.

"How did you feel physically?"

"Funny, my stomach was churning. I felt hot and cold at the same time. I knew I couldn't go in. I can't describe it, sort of sinister."

"Calm down, no one is going to force you."

"There must be a reason for being so scared, not knowing terrifies me."

"You locked me out of your room the other night. Do you remember?"

"Yes, I'm sorry."

"I thought it very odd that you locked the door. At the cottage you freaked out when I shut a door."

"It has to do with the difference between being locked in and locking oneself in."

"You can't explain any better?"

"No. Sorry."

"OK. Let's go back to Ellen's. You can have a rest before we go out for dinner. Gavin is coming. I have a sneaking suspicion he's coming to see Ellen, not you."

Mer smiled. "I think you could be right."

It was good that something had made her smile.

By the time they arrived back at the flat Mer was calm and Ellen had no reason to guess there had been a problem. Jim thought about going to sit in the lounge and go through the list of questions, but Ellen suggested it first. Immediately Mer's nervousness reappeared.

"It would be easier in the kitchen, there's more room to spread them out." Mer quickly responded.

Jim now knew it was not the lists bothering her. She was simply making an excuse to keep out of the lounge. He agreed. No point in pushing her into doing something that felt wrong.

While they were going through the lists the phone rang. Ellen had her hands full and asked Jim to answer it.

"Jim, good news!" announced Gavin. "We've located the shop where her necklace came from. It's a little shop in Comrie. It might be worth going there to jolt her memory."

"I'm not sure. She had another fright today." Jim filled him in on the details.

"How odd, but you can't be too overprotective. How is she otherwise?"

"Subdued. But they've finished all the tests at the hospital, nothing physical showed up."

"Well, in my opinion I vote for trying Comrie. I have a friend who owns a comfortable little hotel in the centre of town, and I think you should consider going because it's the only lead we have." said Gavin.

"You're right, we have nothing to lose."

"Good. I can't make dinner tonight. So let's make it lunch tomorrow in Comrie. Ask Ellen to join us, and we can have a round of golf then dinner and stay the night. I'll fix the hotel booking."

Jim quickly checked with Ellen that she was free to join them, confirmed details and hung up.

He could tell Ellen liked the plan just as he knew Mer didn't.

"Something wrong?" he asked.

"No." she snapped at him.

"Tell me why you're so angry then."

"OK. I'm fed up. All you seem to be interested in is your game of golf. You don't care that this is the only clue to my past. Or that it might be the only chance of finding my identity."

The pent up frustrations poured out. Jim listened without saying a word until she stopped.

"I love you when you lose your temper," he said. "You're just mad because you don't want to be a golf widow."

She looked shocked then began to laugh.

"You're crazy, and probably right. Am I forgiven?"

"Only if you keep laughing. I don't suppose you remember if you've ever played golf?"

"No. But I'll have a go, to see your face if I beat you."

She was transformed back into the girl he had fallen in love with on the island. Jim wondered how he could help her avoid building up tensions that worked like barriers between them.

Chapter 14

Since receiving Gillespie's message Gavin and Paula had hardly slept. The time was spent studying the files Tom Jackson had supplied, or scouring the back streets day and nights searching for Gillespie. Gavin was so concerned he even considered asking others in the department for help. But fear of alerting Sinclair prevented him from doing so.

He had managed to give Tom Jackson a bit of respite to dig into Sinclair's activities, by dispatching Steven Fowler to locate the sales outlet for Mer's leather outfit, and her unusual hand crafted necklace.

Fowler had surprised them all with the speed with which he had fulfilled his mission. The leather goods were from an online marketing setup with some retail outlets spread all round the country. Thousands had been sold making it almost impossible to get a list of purchasers. But the necklace was much more individual and came from a small shop located in Comrie. Gavin was delighted. Comrie was small, which could work in their favour. The chances of her being recognized were good. And he had friends running a comfortable hotel in the town, who could be helpful.

It was nearly lunch-time when Jim, Mer and Ellen arrived at the hotel. Gavin came out to greet them, anxious to be present if Mer responded to being in a place she might have visited before.

"Let's have lunch while we decide our next move."

"I thought we came to play golf," said Mer. "Jim's worried I might be able to beat him."

"I didn't know you played."

"I don't either!" she replied laughing. "But I'll have a go."

"No need to rush into things, but I do think we ought to check out the jewellery shop first." he added puzzled by her lack of concern." That is what we're here for, isn't it?"

"You're right. I gave Jim hell yesterday for not being concerned enough. I know you're all doing your best, but I've decided to enjoy myself instead of getting all het up about things out of my control."

"Great news. I vote we have lunch, then go and check the shop, after which we can relax and enjoy ourselves," said Gavin. His suggestion met with unanimous approval.

The shop owner was very sympathetic. The design of Mer's necklace was very distinctive, she remembered it but didn't remember selling it. And it had not been included in the stocktaking done over six months ago. There was a possibility that her part time assistant might have sold it, but she wouldn't be in until the morning.

Gavin watched Mer's reaction to the information as they agreed to return the following day. There was none.

Jim chased them out of the shop, eager to test her skill on the golf course. It didn't take long to decide she had played before. More interesting to Gavin was the fact she seemed to know her way round the course. An observation he chose to keep to himself.

After their game they returned to the hotel and settled down by the fire for tea and Gavin announced his plan.

"Graham McDonald, who owns the hotel has invited us to a party this evening. I've told him a little about Mer's dilemma, and he's offered us help."

"How?" Mer asked.

"The party we've been invited to is one of the biggest local functions in the area. Everyone will be there, and he can easily spread the word that we're anxious to find anyone who recognizes you. There will be lots of Scottish dancing and music, they like to keep the old traditions going."

"Sounds too good to be true, and should speed up the process of finding out if anyone knows me. Trouble is, I'm not sure I can cope," she said nervously.

"Of course you can. We'll be there for support," Jim replied.

"Graham will be leaving the hotel just after seven thirty, so if we meet here at seven, we can have a drink before we go."

"Looks like I had better go and prepare myself for this evening." said Mer, getting up to leave. "I feel like Cinderella going to the ball. Are you going to come and help me find my slippers Jim?"

Gavin was glad to see them go. He hadn't had a moment of privacy with Ellen all afternoon. He had a sneaking feeling both Jim and Mer were aware of his feelings for Ellen, which was why they tactfully disappeared.

"She's in much better form than the other day," he said.

"I think a lot of it was tension, the tests and coming to terms with her situation," answered Ellen. "You aren't worried about tonight are you?"

"No. I'm sorry I couldn't come last night. That other case is causing problems, forgive me if I'm a bit preoccupied."

"I'll forgive you if you promise to make it up to me another day."

"You're on," he said smiling. She was more attractive than he had remembered. She had kept her figure in great shape, and her casual elegance made him slightly self-conscious of his own rather untidy appearance.

Graham and his wife were perfect hosts who within minutes of meeting Mer had put her at ease. She looked happier now she'd met them, and knew they understood her difficulties.

What a crowd, all ages were present from the smallest children to aged grandparents. Mer looked radiant. The music started and the evening got into full swing. Gavin, when he wasn't partnering Ellen, joined Graham and Jim taking turns dancing with Mer guiding her through the steps until she picked them up as if she had danced all her life.

Midway through the evening there was a supper break. Their party grouped in an informal circle. Suddenly a little red headed girl rushed up, skidding to a halt beside Mer and tugged her skirt. Gavin wondered what the child wanted. Then he heard her question.

"Where are the twins? I can't find them?"

Gavin watched helplessly. Mer's flushed glow from dancing faded to deathly white, she opened her mouth to answer while her knees slowly buckled. He was so absorbed by her reaction he failed to act.

Fortunately Jim responded instantly, sweeping her up into his arms before she hit the floor.

The little girl looked puzzled. She stepped out of the way shrugged her shoulders, and having decided she wasn't going to get a reply, darted back to her friends, with no idea her innocent question had caused Mer's reaction.

It was not quite what Gavin had hoped for, but at least the exercise had resulted in positive recognition.

"She's in a state of shock," Jim said.

"Take her back to the hotel," instructed Gavin. "I'll find the little girl and get some more information."

Chapter 15

The sensation was strange. She could feel everything, hear everything, see everything, but she couldn't get her body to co-operate. Not even to communicate verbally. Her legs felt too heavy to move, her arms, even her fingers felt as if they were being sucked towards the floor. Why couldn't she move?

Jim and Ellen were struggling to undress her, and she was unable to make the task easier. Deep lethargy made every movement feel laboured but soon they had her tucked up in bed.

"Do you want me to sit with her?" Ellen asked.

"No. You go and wait for Gavin, I'll stay here."

Ellen left and he sat on the side of the bed holding her hand.

"Please Mer, don't shut me out. Trust me," he whispered, brushing her forehead with his lips. "I love you. Let me help."

A tear rolled down her cheek. He wiped it away with his thumb.

"Can you hear?" he asked looking directly into her eyes. She tried to answer but nothing came out.

"I love you. Talk to me," he said again. She wanted to tell him about the little girl, the one who'd asked about the twins. Then he kissed her. The kiss started so softly, she could barely feel his lips on hers.

The intensity and tenderness was bitter-sweet, stirring up memories of the night of the storm. Memories she had been forced to suppress. The pleasure diminished by the certainty it would not last. He drew away. She wanted to scream for him to carry on, but couldn't. He smiled and lowered his head and kissed her again, this time more passionately. Her body responded. Her arms reached out and clung to him as he pulled her into his.

His lips left hers and he whispered in her ear, "Welcome back."

Welcome back, what a strange thing to say. Maybe in a way she had gone. Gone where? Why? Then the memory came back.

"Fiona," she muttered. "The little girl is called Fiona."

"Go on," he said.

"That's all."

"It doesn't matter," he reassured her. "At last we have positive proof you've been here. We'll find out your name and the rest of the picture will start to fall into place like a jigsaw puzzle."

"I'm so afraid it won't," she said, hugging him tightly.

"Do you think you can sleep now?" he asked. "Or shall I get you something to help?"

"No!" she snapped.

"Sorry. I shouldn't have offered."

"It's OK. I'll sleep alright, but only if you kiss me again."

Jim smiled and lowered his lips to hers.

"I'll go and find out what Gavin has discovered," he said as he eased himself from her grasp. "I'll be back as soon as I can."

In the silence that followed his departure she relived the moment he told her he loved her. It was the one statement that she had longed for. Now she could be happy.

A dazzling ray of sunlight hit the pillow. Mer lay still, watching the dust motes dancing in the beam of light streaming through the chink in the curtains. She snuggled deeper into her cosy cocoon of bedclothes. Then she remembered Jim was going to find out something for her. She stumbled out of bed. Where was he? Why hadn't he come back? She groped for her dressing gown in the semi-darkness.

"Mer are you alright?"

She jumped at the sound of his voice, coming from the chair by the window.

"Oh. You gave me such a fright. I didn't know you were here. What happened? What did you find out?"

"Very little. Gavin talked to the little girl Fiona who recognized you. You, your husband and the twins sometimes stayed at their house. She couldn't remember your name. Her parents, Ken and Maureen Campbell are away, and she's staying with her aunt till they get back later today."

"Ken and Maureen Campbell," she said pensively, "the name doesn't mean a thing."

"How do you feel about meeting them?" he asked.

"I'm not sure," she answered. "Do I have a choice?"

"Not really. If it worries you I could delay it."

"Let me think about it?"

"Of course."

"I'm starving."

"I'm not surprised," Jim replied. "You missed supper last night. Get dressed and meet me downstairs for breakfast."

It was a delicious breakfast. Having gulped down her eggs and bacon she pushed her empty plate to one side and reached for the coffee pot to pour another cup.

"I feel better now. I do hope Gavin and Ellen will forgive us for not waiting for them." She glanced up when the dining room door opened expecting it to be them. But it wasn't. Ignoring the newcomers she turned back to Jim.

"Coffee?"

A woman interrupted, "Hello Jenny, it's so lovely to see you. Why didn't you tell us you were coming? "

Mer looked up. The person standing by their table seemed to be targeting her question directly at her. Odd she thought, there isn't anyone else in here, then horror struck.

The question had been addressed to her.

All eyes were on her, waiting for a reaction. She fought to maintain some composure, and to overcome the desire to run. Jim removed the coffee pot from her shaking hand as she took a deep breath.

"Are you alright Jenny?" queried the woman.

"Sorry," she stammered, struggling to stay composed. "Jim, I'm not ready for this. Please do something," she begged. He took her hand in his and squeezed it.

"I'll handle it. Promise you'll stay here till I get back," he said quietly.

She nodded. Then she heard him address the couple. "You must be Ken and Maureen Campbell." They nodded. "Come with me." He firmly ushered them away from the table. "There are one or two things I'd like to discuss with you."

Gavin and Ellen appeared at that moment, and he quickly explained the situation. "Can you stay with her for a while," he said to Ellen, as he, Gavin and the others moved out of the room."

"I wish I hadn't reacted like that," Mer said to Ellen a few moments later. "I feel such a fool. But the shock of discovering my name after all this time, especially when it doesn't even sound familiar made me so scared."

"It's fine."

"I hope they don't think too badly of me."

"I know they won't, in fact they probably feel more embarrassed than you do. At least now you know your name's Jenny. I hope you won't mind if I call you Mer by mistake."

"I'm not sure whether I'll even respond to Jenny. Could they have made a mistake?"

"Have your coffee before it gets cold," Ellen said, cunningly avoiding the question.

Jim returned at that moment, looking very pleased.

"Go gently, she's having trouble accepting the name Jenny," Ellen said.

"Don't you remember them at all?" he queried.

She shook her head, watching as he sat down next to her.

"OK. Let me fill you in. Your name is Jenny Marshall. And your husband, Denis is a solicitor."

"What about the twins?" she interrupted. "How old are they?"

"The same age as Fiona, about six."

Six. The word kept echoing in her mind. She found it hard to concentrate on what Jim was saying about where she lived. It was somewhere in Devon, near Exeter, and the Campbells had visited their house. They even had photos of her husband and the children.

"I've arranged to drive over to their farm later, I hope by then you might feel easier about talking to them. Think you can handle it?"

Mer hesitated, nodded assent, relieved not to have to face them immediately.

"I'd like to go for a walk," she said.

"I'll come with you," answered Jim. "Want to join us?" he added looking towards Ellen.

"No. You two go on your own. I'll stay and have breakfast with Gavin.

They set out along the river in silence, stopping by the waterfall, taking the path up to the monument that overlooked the town. The view from the top was breathtaking. The air so clear even the most distant hills were clearly visible.

"You've been here before, haven't you?"

"I think so. But I can't remember when, or with whom," she answered, attempting to puzzle out what it was about a particular direction that attracted her attention.

"See something?" he asked.

"No."

"Come on, it's time to go," he said, taking her hand and leading her down, not relinquishing his grip till they reached the hotel.

"You go and order some coffee and I'll see what the others are doing, I'll meet you in the lounge," Jim instructed her.

Mer came down to find him busy filling in the latest discoveries onto his original question list.

"Come and help, perhaps it will bring something into focus," he suggested.

She still couldn't picture her family.

"We ought to go now they'll be expecting us soon," Jim said as he packed up the sheets of paper, and helped her to her feet.

"Where are Gavin and Ellen?" she asked.

"Gavin left a message, something has happened and they need him back at the office. Ellen went with him. She thought we'd probably want to head down to Devon."

"But I still have some of Ellen's things."

"It doesn't matter, I'm sure she meant you to keep them. And anyway it will give you an excuse to come back and see her."

Suddenly she knew she could not face the Campbells. And she knew her feelings for Jim were the reason. The information they would provide would mean ending their relationship.

"I can't go to the Campbells."

"What?"

"I can't do it."

"Why?"

"I'm afraid."

"Of Denis, the children."

"No. You'd never understand."

"Try me."

"I'm afraid of losing you."

"I don't suppose it occurred to you that I have as much to lose," he answered angrily. "You have to face up to your past until you do you can't make the decision about me or them. Without that you'd be living a lie."

"But I can't cope."

"You can. And you will. Come on let's go."

They drove in silence. It was the first time Jim had pressured her to do something and been angry with her. She was dreading the meeting.

Jim stopped the car at the top of the drive, took her in his arms and kissed her. Was it meant to give her courage? Or was it the kiss she feared most, the farewell kiss?

He had warned her all along that the past would come between them. And now that prediction was coming true, there was proof of a marriage and a family. It wouldn't hurt so much if she could remember her husband and children. But she felt trapped, doomed to accept an unknown person to whom she was legally bound, but who obviously didn't care about her or even bothered to search for her?

Jim held her firmly by the shoulders and said, "I'm only making you do this, because I love you. Do you understand?"

What choice did she have? None. His determination to make her face up to her past was unshakeable. She allowed herself to be led into the house, gripping Jim's hand as she entered. The Campbells smiled nervously, waiting for her or Jim to start the conversation, and she surprised herself, by thanking them for coming over. Then she thanked Fiona for recognizing her.

Her bravado was short lived. She was beginning to panic when Jim stepped in, suggesting that it had been a difficult day for her, and that if they had sorted out some photos it would be easier for her if they could take them away, to give her a chance to study them on her own. Her relief at his suggestion was even greater when she saw the size of the heap of photos they had gathered together. She sifted through a few of the pictures on the top of the pile, without any joy.

"Those two are the best ones." Maureen said selecting one of two boys sitting side by side, and one of what she presumed was her family, herself, a man and the same two children. What was wrong with her? Didn't she have any maternal instincts?

"Thank you," she said tugging at Jim's arm. She had to get out. Get away from here.

"Take these," Jim said, pushing a pile into her arms, and guiding her to the door. "Wait for me in the car."

She didn't need any further coaxing, and eagerly rushed from the house, clutching the bundle of pictures.

Jim followed several minutes later. He told her he had taken down details of her address, telephone number and as much information about her home and friends as they could remember. The Campbells had tried to phone the cottage in Devon but got no reply. She was very relieved she needed more time to take in all the fresh information.

"I feel so guilty. I can't find even one photo in this huge pile that brings back even the faintest of recollections. I've had more fun looking at a mail order catalogue. I can't believe they're related to me."

Chapter 16

Gavin was angry. He had been daydreaming instead of concentrating on solving the mystery about the Mallaig house. Ellen was responsible for a lot of changes in him, from his appearance onwards. During the last four years he hadn't met anyone he'd consider an intimate relationship with and wasn't sure how she would react to the idea. Perhaps it was good he was too busy to rush things.

He heard a car pull up outside. It was frustrating not being able to talk freely in the office and having to resort to meeting after hours. Apart from the inconvenience, the situation was making them edgy, but until his suspicions about Sinclair were allayed they had to put up with it.

"Good to see you Tom," he said opening the door. "Come in, you look as if you could do with a drink. Coffee or something stronger?"

"Thanks." answered Tom, as he manipulated his wheelchair into the space Gavin had cleared for him. Then he gave his thick-lensed glasses a ritual polish. "Coffee. Please."

"Here," Gavin said, proffering a mug. He heard a key in the door. "Good, that will be Paula." Soon they were all settled.

"I've enlisted Ewan Murray. I think we need his specialized help," answered Tom. "He's a hundred percent reliable, and an absolute genius at extracting data most people would never know was on a computer."

"Fine. What are you hoping to find?"

"For a start we've pinpointed every terminal used when files were tampered with. Now he can probably restore all the information previously deleted so we can analyse it. Best part is that he doesn't work in our building so there's no danger of Sinclair, or his nephew finding out what we're doing."

"Good. What else are you working on?"

"I'm checking out stolen cars. Paula told me about the two vehicles you followed from Mallaig. They appear initially to have bona fide numbers. When she called on the registered owners, both claimed neither of their cars had been near Mallaig, then or at any other time, and could prove it. Therefore we must assume there are two similar cars bearing forged plates matching the colour and make of the registered ones. Quite cunning, except Paula found out from one owner this wasn't the first time inquiries had been made about his vehicle. When it had happened before the police had apologized for bothering them, saying someone must have made a mistake when taking down the information. Which got me thinking, so I ran the makes and numbers through the computer and found similar vehicles have been reported at several different incidents. I haven't found the common denominator yet, though there must be one."

"Paula, tell us what you've been up to," Gavin said.

"I didn't get very far in my search for Gillespie. No one seems to have seen him. Or perhaps I should rephrase. No one is admitting to having seen him but I got the distinct impression I wasn't the only person searching."

"That's what I was afraid of."

"I think it's time you told me your history with Sinclair?" Paula said.

Tom pointed to Gavin. "Go ahead."

"Well, we all joined up on the same day. We'd been to school together and never seen eye to eye. Of course we ended up in the same unit, which proved to be a disaster."

"Yes," Tom agreed.

"The main differences between us all, is that where Tom and I always try to find the good in people, Sinclair concentrates on the bad. His mode of work was to find a weak spot and exploit it. He'd brag about the number of informants he was collecting, though they never came up with useful information."

"Hardly a reason for hating someone," Tom piped in.

"No. The trouble started when a close friend of ours was badly assaulted. He was so badly injured he was forced to quit. Naturally there were a few of us who were determined to get the man responsible. Sinclair surpassed himself and actually made an arrest. The good impression didn't last long. He made a complete cock-up in procedure that even the most incompetent solicitor would have found it impossible not to get the man off, even though the evidence of guilt was strong. When the guy walked out of the dock he laughed. We all knew he was guilty, but there was absolutely nothing we could do about it. Initially we made allowances for Sinclair's inexperience, swearing we'd never make the same mistake ourselves. It was a hard lesson, particularly because the victim was a friend and a conviction would have satisfied our need for revenge. I could have forgiven Sinclair, except one week afterwards I saw him buying the man he'd arrested a drink. To all appearances they were great buddies, no hard feelings and all."

"What else?" Paula queried.

"After that several other similar incidents occurred. Tom here got caught up in the cross fire on one of Sinclair's stake outs. We all know that the people involved were expecting a raid. Situations where people had warnings of arrest giving them enough time to fabricate alibis. We could never pin anything on Sinclair, but we were certain all the leaks had come from him. To my relief, he was moved to another section, and I was spared from working with him, though rumours filtered back down the line."

"Surely if it happened as often as you imply, his incompetence would have shown up on his records."

"Oh no. The slippery bastard never looked bad on paper. He wasn't careless, and nothing ever happened when he made an arrest. He made sure if he did make the arrest he always got a conviction. He was always generous at giving his partners information, cunningly engineering them into making the mistakes. He'd get the glory for coming up with a name, and someone else would take the flak for fouling up, by either not double checking the alibi, or failing to read the man his rights or something similar. We all knew the men arrested were guilty for the crime they were accused of, but getting the case to stick was another matter."

"So you think that in addition to telling them that they were about to be arrested, he actually planned how they could cover themselves."

"That's about it. Then he'd meet them for a friendly drink about a week later."

"Why did he do it?"

"That's what I never managed to find out. I personally think he craved power, perhaps money. It was difficult to tell, especially after he married Stella Bairstow, the bookmaker's daughter, and his life style changed dramatically. There's no way of proving where the money comes from, Stella was very wealthy in her own right, and was never coy about flashing cash."

"What you're saying is that you think he wanted power more than money?"

"Yes."

"I wonder how he uses the power?" Paula poured herself some tea from the pot. "Weren't the Bairstow family mixed up in a recent fraud investigation?"

"Yes. Stella's brothers. It isn't the first time they've been in trouble. And guess what? They got off once more because of a technicality. What a coincidence!" Gavin answered. "It makes me wonder if there's more to his promotion than meets the eye. I don't trust him. If he is using his position to squash investigations we need to find his motive."

"You think he's after personal gain?" said Paula.

"If it is, he's covering his tracks very well," said Tom. "There's no financial benefit showing in his bank accounts."

"You'd better be careful about breaking the rules yourself," replied Gavin smiling.

"In exceptional circumstances, one has to bend the rules" Tom answered.

"So what's his link with Mallaig, and Gillespie?" Paula asked.

"The fact he wanted us out of Mallaig was enough to get me curious, then the message from Gillespie, who was the person who gave me the tip about

Mallaig naming Sinclair really got me worried. If Sinclair is involved I want him nailed."

"You've checked out just about everything" Paula said

"Everything, except the contents of those crates. I wish we knew what was in them. I can't get a search warrant without alerting Sinclair. But, I'm more worried about Gillespie."

"By all accounts he doesn't wander far," said Paula.

"That's why I sense he's in real danger."

"From Sinclair?" said Tom.

"Yes."

The shrill ring of the phone interrupted the conversation. As Gavin reached out to take the call, the file on the arm of the chair fell off.

The call was from the Devon police who had been trying to find out more about Jenny Marshall's address.

"Are you certain?" he queried, not able to believe what he'd heard, scribbling notes as they talked.

"You dealt with it yourself? There is no doubt about it being her family. OK. I'll pass the information on, I hate to think how she'll react. Thanks I'll keep you up to date. Goodbye."

"Bad news?" asked Paula.

"Yes. The worst, another chance to be the bearer of bad tidings," Gavin answered. "Excuse me, I have another call to make, why don't you glance through that pile of papers, you might spot something I've missed. Tom, pour yourself another cup of coffee."

Jim's initial response to the phone call made it hard for Gavin to get a word in edgeways.

"It's fantastic," Jim said, "she's beginning to remember details about the children. She even remembers how to tell them apart, and if you'd seen the photos you would understand how difficult that is. I was worried she'd be swamped under with all the information we got from the Campbells, she's coping well. What did you discover?"

"You're not going to like it," Gavin answered.

"It can't be that bad."

"Believe me it is. We contacted the local police station in Cullompton. They knew the address and the reason we didn't get a reply. Prepare yourself. Denis Marshall and both his children were killed in a car crash about six months ago."

"No. There must be a mistake."

"Sorry, it's true. They even checked out her photo with the neighbour who's keeping an eye on her cottage. She thought Jenny was staying with friends in Scotland, which is why no one reported her as missing. There's no doubt."

"How the hell am I going to tell her, she's just getting used to the idea of having a family?"

"Jim, could she have been attempting suicide?"

"Never."

"Nervous breakdown?"

"Well I suppose something like that would make one keen to block out the past, hence the memory loss."

"I wish I could be there to give you moral support, but you're probably the best person to break it to her."

"I'll manage somehow."

"Let me know how she takes the news."

Gavin replaced the receiver and buried his face in his hands for a moment. He stretched out to pick up the file that dropped on the floor earlier to add this last dreadful piece of information. Paula had rescued it and put it on the table leaving a photo of Jenny sitting on top.

Paula put her hand out pointing at the picture, "Why didn't you tell me you had a picture of her?" she demanded.

"What? Who?"

"The girl from the house at Mallaig, I didn't think my description was that good." Paula added, waving a photo of Mer at Gavin. "Why didn't you say anything? Don't you trust me?"

"Paula I'm tired. What the hell are you going on about?"

"This girl," she said, as she slapped the photo of the newly identified, Jenny Marshall on the table, "this is the woman who was at the Mallaig house. You remember, the woman who vanished. The woman we never saw leave the house. You could have told me you'd found her."

Gavin sat bolt upright in his chair, all earlier tiredness forgotten. Ideas began racing through his mind. Was it possible for her to have drifted from Mallaig to the Island? If so why? What was her connection to Sinclair?

They went over and over every detail they knew about her, from Paula's first glimpse at Mallaig, to the latest information Gavin had moments earlier conveyed to Jim.

"Do you think she really has lost her memory?" asked Paula.

"I had no reason to doubt it. At least we'll be able to maintain contact until we find out what she was doing in Mallaig."

"How?" asked Paula.

Gavin explained about Jim and Ellen, and how through their friendship he was sure he would be able to keep in close touch.

"You need some sleep. I'll carry on searching for Gillespie for another hour or two," Paula said as she got up to leave.

"I'll come," said Tom and Gavin together.

"Forget it. I'll be less conspicuous on my own. You both need to save your strength for tomorrow, I promise I'll call if I find him."

Chapter 17

Jim caught a glimpse through the glass door. Her eyes were focused on the photo her face devoid of expression. The photo was of the family which had prior claim to her affection, which had earlier roused intense jealousy on his part. He had found himself admiring her children, thinking how happy and carefree they looked, while hating the good looking, fair haired husband who exuded irresistible charm.

"It's the only picture I feel any connection to," she'd said. "The house is more familiar than the people."

When Jim questioned her about telling the twins apart she answered without hesitation.

"That's easy. David has a scar over his eye, it happened when he fell onto a toy train when he was two." At which point she had faltered and went silent. So he didn't know what else she had remembered.

Then he'd been called to the phone to speak to Gavin, and hear his devastating news about Mer's family. He wished he could delay imparting the information he had received. Maybe a stiff drink might help to numb the pain. He stopped at the bar and ordered two large whiskeys before returning to his seat. He felt like an executioner about to destroy her.

The family might have died six months ago, but only minutes ago she'd begun to accept they even existed. The task of informing families about the death of their loved ones was hard enough without the complication of personal attachment.

She paid no heed to his return, her gaze riveted to the picture. A tear trickled down her cheek unchecked. Her stillness disturbed him. She had remembered something, but how much. And would she talk about it?

Jim put down the drinks and moved the photo.

She looked up and their eyes locked. She whispered, "They're all dead. Aren't they?"

He wished he could deny it. How could he?

His nod of assent confirming her statement triggered a change. Subtle, but Jim spotted it immediately.

Withdrawal coupled with an air of independence distanced him. One wrong move could drive a permanent wedge between them.

"Why didn't you tell me?" she demanded.

"I didn't know. That was Gavin on the phone. He found out from the police in Devon."

"I don't believe you," she snapped.

"Why would I lie to you? What good would it do?" he replied, as he gently took her hand in his. "Tell me about them."

"I made such a mess. Now it's too late to do anything about it," Jenny started hesitantly.

"You can't blame yourself for what happened," Jim replied.

Slowly her story unfolded. She started with her childhood. He wanted to move to more recent times, but had to be patient and let her take her time.

She'd been happy as a child though a little unsettled because her parents worked abroad, rarely spending more than a year in any post. Boarding school provided stability of a kind, but every holiday was spent in some remote exotic location. None of which ever felt like a true home and making friends was difficult as the other children she met went to different schools and moved to other countries.

The constant upheavals made her long for a feeling of permanence. This urge influenced her decision to marry young and pushed her into decisions she regretted, her marriage being the biggest regret.

During her last year at College she met Denis who was studying for his finals in Law. He was everything a girl could ask for, good looking, self assured and would have a steady, well paid, job in his father's law practice. Jenny refused to accept her parent's advice not to rush into marriage. Their lack of enthusiasm spurred her on to get married on her twentieth birthday. She found her dream home, an idyllic thatched cottage about five miles from the town where Denis had been born.

"His parents resented me from the start," she said. "I tried hard to please them. I even gave up my plan to complete my art degree to concentrate on becoming the perfect homemaker. It took a while to understand their attitude. Then I met his ex-girlfriend who was their partner's daughter and realized what I was competing against. She would have suited them perfectly. I set about trying to win them over. I tried to cook elaborate meals for them and his clients. That backfired, as it gave them the impression I was incapable of intelligent conversation about anything other than domestic matters. Denis was oblivious to my efforts, and there wasn't one person among all the guests we entertained that I could relate to. I was lonely and in desperation decided a family would fill the void." She paused, a slight smile on her face.

"I was blissfully happy while pregnant. Identical twins came as a surprise. They were adorable, and it took me weeks to learn to tell them apart. I lavished all my time and attention on them. Their arrival was a perfect excuse to stop giving dinner parties. Denis spent less and less time at home. When he wasn't working late, he'd go out without me, because I refused to get babysitters in to avoid spending an evening with his business associates.

"I made new friends, people with children who seldom had contact with Denis. My happiness lasted until the twins reached nursery school age, when I saw the flaws in my marriage. It was hardly a marriage at all. Denis used the cottage as a place to sleep, change his clothes, and eat. We never sat and talked to each other and he hardly ever spent time with the children. On the few occasions when we spoke he wore me down with critical remarks about the children's discipline, their manners, even the clothes they wore. And on those rare days when he went out with us he'd ruin their enjoyment by constantly correcting them."

"One day he went too far. I let loose every complaint I had. His response was infuriating. He based all his arguments on financial and material matters, and there was no suggestion that he might alter his life to accommodate us. I nearly packed my bags, but I couldn't bring myself to disrupt the children's stability." She stopped, looked at Jim and added, "Sorry, I shouldn't be boring you with all this."

"You need to tell it," he answered, sensing her nervousness. She nodded and started again.

"Then I made the silly mistake. I decided to try for reconciliation. Denis was away at a conference in Birmingham, and I thought the neutral location would help. I got details of his hotel reservation and conference time-table. I left the twins with Anne, my neighbour, and set off to surprise him. I got more than I bargained for. When I knocked on his hotel door, I found myself facing his charming ex-girlfriend, clad in a bath towel, water dripping everywhere. I apologized for disturbing her, when Denis stepped out from behind her, also dripping and wrapped in a towel."

I managed to stammer that I'd see him in the lobby and ran.

By the time he appeared my embarrassment had turned to anger and the anger to joy.

Now I could leave him, take the boys and get on with my life after eight years of marriage.

Jim decided to resist the temptation to point out how late it was. He knew she had not finished, so sat back prepared for a further instalment.

"All my great ideas and plans for the future came to nothing." She wiped her eyes, and took a sip of the whiskey that had been waiting untouched in front of her.

"I got home to find that Denis had packed up his things, and collected the children. He told Anne we were getting divorced and that he intended taking them away for a few days.

I was so angry with myself for not anticipating his move, but there was nothing I could do, I was certain once he discovered that children needed clean clothes, and regular meals, he'd regret his impulsive decision and bring them back." She took another sip of her drink.

"When the door bell rang at ten o'clock, I was surprised he was bringing the boys home so soon. But, it wasn't him. It was a rather sombre looking policeman standing on the doorstep with Anne at his side. It took me a minute to register he must have bad news, and tried to convinced myself he was at the wrong house. Then he told me about the accident. Denis's vehicle had spun off the road and hit a pylon. He and the twins and one other person had been killed instantly."

She reached out to pick up the photo, tears streaming down her face.

"I don't remember much more, Anne stayed with me, and there are vague memories of a funeral. I do remember feeling guilty, terribly guilty, because everyone thought I was heart-broken about Denis, but it was the twins that I mourned. Poor Anne. I know she sometimes felt she was partly responsible, because she had let him take the children. But she was the only one who understood what I was going through. No one else knew about the pending divorce or the events that led up to that day."

"Do you still feel guilty?" he asked.

"I'm not sure," she answered sadly. There was something different about her tone of voice and the expression on her face. Jim couldn't pinpoint it. But from then on she was silent, as if encased in a shell. No words were needed but Jim knew she would not welcome even the slightest gesture of help.

Suddenly it was clear. Jenny was here. Not Mer. And he wondered if he and Jenny would ever recapture the magic of the night in the hut?

Chapter 18

Hector Sinclair sat in his wood panelled study, trying to convince himself his instinct, that Gavin McKay was still nosing around areas he shouldn't, was wrong. He was certain there was no evidence to connect him with the house in Mallaig. Covering tracks was something he had done successfully for so many years, so why was he nervous now.

Steven was part of the problem. He'd trusted him, but since asking him to alter some files, Steven had started asking awkward questions. Getting him to report on McKay's activities was risky, but he had no choice.

Steven was his nephew, his sister had married an honest law abiding accountant, who had never committed as much as a traffic offence. So it was hardly surprising, Steven turned out the way he had.

Had Steven been a member of his wife's family, there would have been no hesitation. None of the Bairstow bunch were renowned for upholding the law. A fact he discovered early in his own career, when he frequently had to keep them out of trouble. He had mistakenly thought when he married Stella that the family would not be able to influence him. It didn't take long to discover he had been wrong. They had used him to such an extent that now there was no way he could get out, not even to leave her. They had promised if he did, they would ruin him, and he knew they were serious.

There was a knock at the door. Hector groaned. Stella was having another of her damn parties and no doubt had sent someone to fetch him. "Come in," he called. The door opened and Dan Trench strode in.

"What the hell are you doing here?" Sinclair snarled, angered by the smug look on Dan's face. He actually looked pleased at the discomfort he was causing.

"Stella invited me, and I thought it would be rude to turn down her kind invitation."

"I want you to get out. Now."

"No. If you make a fuss I'll make sure everyone leaves with me. And you don't want that, do you?" Dan snapped back

"Why not?"

"I understand Hill's dealing with a small problem tonight, and if they go, so does your alibi. And you need one as much as I do. You can't really improve on twenty people to give you one. And I like the touch of having the Acting Chief Superintendent of Police standing up for me!"

"You'll regret this," Hector answered, straining not to raise his voice.

"No. Remember I have a very large stake in that shipment."

"Yes, but what do you need an alibi for? I'll find out sooner or later, so you might as well tell me."

"Gillespie. He's the reason. I know you've organized that he won't be a problem much longer. Haven't you?"

Hector gritted his teeth. Trench had never been pushy before. There was something threatening about his behaviour. The provocation was deliberate. No way was he going to give Trench the satisfaction of knowing he was worried.

"Don't know what you're talking about?" he answered, trying to sound casual. Dan looked put out by his response.

"That's a lie, I'm telling you now, I want out when this deal is over. I've had enough."

"Well Dan I can understand how you feel, but have you thought this out carefully. Surely the success of this last deal depends on discretion. Something you are showing a distinct lack of by barging into my house. OK, I have no idea why you think either of us needs an alibi. But you can get it just as easily by having a riotous party somewhere else. I'll pay." Hector opened his wallet and took out some notes. "Here take this. And get out before anyone sees us together."

"As long as you understand this is my last deal."

"I know. I saw the inventory. It's all the stuff you'd collected for yourself. I was surprised I thought you swore you'd never part with it. What made you change your mind?"

"Hill. I can't work with him. And I need the cash."

"Fair enough, but don't mess things up. Have your party tonight then lie low. Try to leave here without making a scene," added Hector, showing him to the door.

Hector found he was sweating when Trench had gone. What a nerve. Didn't he realize his visit could jeopardise the whole plan. He poured himself a large gin and tonic and contemplated postponing the shipment until he was sure of what McKay was up to.

There was another knock on the door. This time Steven entered.

"Stella asked me to come and find you," he said.

"How many are here?" Hector asked. He daren't ask if Steven had seen Dan Trench. Not after he'd made the connection to the name when Trench had carelessly given his name earlier in the week when he'd phoned the house. Hector denied knowing him then, but if Steven saw him in the flesh he would recognize him as the man McKay was interested in at Mallaig.

"About twenty I think. People are still arriving, sounds like they had a good day at the races."

"Have you been here long?"

"No, I just arrived."

"Well I suppose I must put in an appearance. By the way, what was McKay up to today?"

"I didn't see him today. I gathered he had gone off to play golf."

Hector nodded, deciding silence was the best policy. He must assume Trench had left the house swiftly, and hope Steven hadn't seen him.

Chapter 19

Gavin fumbled to find the phone beside his bed. It was still dark.

"Who is it?" he mumbled sleepily.

"Paula. They've just fished Gillespie out of the harbour."

"What!" said Gavin suddenly fully alert, "Where are you?"

Paula briefed him.

"I'm on my way. Wait there for me," instructed Gavin as he reached for his clothes. "I'll be there in about ten minutes."

Was he losing control? Suddenly the whole investigation was getting out of hand. He'd known Gillespie was in danger. What could he have done to prevent his death? What bothered him most was the feeling he had been the one who put Gillespie in jeopardy in the first place.

Would Sinclair try to interfere? If he did, it would confirm Gavin's suspicions beyond doubt.

Gavin arrived at the harbour, and checked for himself that the man hauled out of the water was actually Gillespie, before the doctor arrived. Paula drew him to one side.

"Listen, someone else has been looking for Gillespie, I've been double checking, and I am certain from the description it was Hill, the big guy seen at Mallaig."

"Will they testify?"

"I'm not certain. I need his photo to get confirmation. Have you got the file?"

"No, it is with the others, on the table in the lounge, where we left them last night. Go now and try to verify his indentity. I'll stay and talk to the Doctor. I'll tell him I think he's dealing with murder. Tell him we knew Gillespie was being intimidated, but I won't give details of the phone message he left for me."

"Did you keep it?"

"Of course I did. I even took the precaution of locking it up."

Gavin couldn't rid himself of the notion he was to blame. He was the one who had given Gillespie's name to Sinclair. A slip that could have cost Gillespie's his life. The need for secrecy within his own department distressed Gavin more than anything. There had been so little to go on, but Gillespie's death had effectively curtailed their major lead. Gavin decided to recheck everything, even if he had to do it personally. If the pathologist confirmed Gillespie had been murdered he would have to be very careful who found out the girl had been at the Mallaig house. He must make certain nobody else found out about her connection, or more importantly, that he was aware of one.

As soon as he got to the office he called Tom Jackson to break the news about Gillespie.

"Tom, we need help. Could your contact in Devon check out the girl for us? I don't want anyone in this office to know I think there's a connection. And I can't spare Paula to go down and check her out."

"Don't worry. I'll get back to you as soon as I can."

Gavin decided he would send Paula to Mallaig, to scour the grounds in the hope that there was something previously overlooked. He wished he could go too, but wanted to stay at the office to see how Sinclair would react to Gillespie's death.

It was mid morning before he tried to contact Jim at the hotel. He waited patiently while the receptionist tried both rooms without success. He presumed Jim would call him if there were problems with Mer accepting the terrible news about her family, and resigned himself to the fact they must be coping with the information given the previous evening. He left a message stating clearly that he didn't expect to be at the office but they could call him on his home number, or he would phone them later. He hoped it would deter them from calling back. Until he had ascertained if there was a tie up between Sinclair, Mallaig, and Gillespie, he would like them kept well out of the way.

Paula reappeared looking pleased.

"It was Ron Hill who was looking for Gillespie. I found several witnesses who say they would testify if the need arose."

"Presumably no one saw them together."

"No. But at least we have established his interest. Do you think we should go and pick him up for questioning?"

"No. Not yet. I want to hear what the coroner comes up with. What I'd really like you to do is go back to Mallaig. Search the outhouses, especially the places where you saw them go, perhaps you should check out that bonfire, maybe we can discover what they were burning. Bring anything you find back, then we can decide if it's worth sending to the lab. I don't want to rush into anything before seeing how Sinclair behaves."

"Anything else?" Paula queried.

"Yes, just in case anyone wants to know what you're up to, spread the word you've got a toothache, and are going to the dentist."

"Especially if Fowler is around?"

"Most definitely."

Chapter 20

There was a message from Jim to say he was taking Mer home, they were going to travel slowly while she reconnected with her identity. He confirmed that she remembered the family, but nothing since they died. He wasn't sure when they would arrive in Devon as he didn't want to rush her. Gavin noted that Jim referred to her as Mer still.

Gavin knew that he had to find out more about her connection with Mallaig. He didn't want to make a move until he had established exactly what role Jenny Marshall played. So far all he knew was that Paula had seen her arrive, and had since then found debris on the bonfire which confirmed her name. Paula had retrieved an assortment of half burnt items, a handbag which contained a melted lipstick, a partially charred bank card, and remnants of a cheque book, both of which had sufficient detail remaining to identify them as belonging to her. There had also been a discarded syringe and a bunch of keys, which they had yet to link to her. A study of the weather and tide patterns during the days preceding her discovery confirmed the possibility of a boat being swept from Mallaig to the island. But nothing explained her connection with the men at the house.

Gavin looked up when his office door opened. Steven walked in, closing the door behind him.

"What can I do for you Steven?"

"Sorry to interrupt."

"Sit down." Gavin pointed to the chair opposite his desk. There was a prolonged silence, as the young man nervously settled himself. "How can I help? Do you need time off?"

"No. Nothing like that, I need some advice."

Gavin noticed the bundle of files Steven had on his lap clutched with his visibly shaking hands. He was obviously having difficulties deciding what to say. Gavin felt sorry for him, and decided to make the task easier so prompted him, "Is it something personal?"

"Not exactly..."

"All right, let's talk about a hypothetical situation," Gavin said. This produced a noticeable relaxation to the expression on the young man's face.

"Yes. A hypothetical situation."

"Good, let's get on."

"Well, if you knew someone had been tampering with information, what would you do?"

"Report him."

"But if he did it without fully understanding what he was doing?"

"You mean somebody asked him to do the dirty work, without giving a reason?"

"Yes."

"Well, I think my curiosity would probably make me determined to find out why," Gavin answered thoughtfully, "then I'd report it to someone in authority."

The young man looked down at the pile of files he had on his lap. Gavin studied his face, trying to read his troubled expression. Until his display of distrust regarding Mallaig, Gavin had thought of him as a youngster with promise, now he didn't know what to think.

"Steven, have you done something wrong?"

"I'm not sure."

"Someone ask you to do it?"

"Yes."

"Have you asked them why?"

"No."

Gavin was concerned by the direction the conversation was taking. It occurred to him that maybe Sinclair had set the whole scenario up to find if he was still delving into his shady activities. He must be ultra cautious about letting on he already guessed where Steven's revelations were heading.

"Why not?"

"Fear."

Gavin couldn't help thinking that was exactly the emotion that Steven was showing right now. "Is it someone in my department?"

"No."

"Why don't you talk to your Uncle? He's senior enough to handle most problems," he suggested in the hope that Steven's reactions would betray him. What he hadn't expected was an outright honest answer.

"Because he's the person I'm afraid of."

Gavin was stunned. It had to be a set up. They knew he was onto them, and wanted to find out how much he knew.

"What the hell has he asked you to do?"

"Tamper with evidence," Steven answered quietly.

"Sorry, tampering with evidence, how?" he asked, seeking clarification.

"Yes," Steven whispered "by removing information from some files."

"Current cases?

"No. It was mainly old ones, which is why I wasn't bothered at first."

"What do you expect me to do about it?"

"I don't know? Help me work out what he is hiding?"

"You should have gone to internal affairs? Why pick me?"

"Because I trust you, and I want to keep my job."

"I should be flattered, but I won't make any rash promises to you. If you want my help, you'll have to tell me everything. I'll need proof too. I can't do anything without proof."

Steven stood up. He was smiling and looking very relieved. "I thought you'd say that, here," he placed the files he had been clutching on the desk. "These will give you all the proof you require, they are the files I have altered, I've made notes of all the changes I was asked to make."

Gavin looked straight at him. There was one question left to ask.

"What about family loyalty?"

"I got myself into this mess in the first place because of it. Please read the files. Then I'll explain."

"Fine, take a seat," Gavin instructed, wary of being left alone with the potentially incriminating files. He read silently, it took him almost a full half-hour to get to the last one. They were the same files that Tom Jackson had produced earlier in the week. His initial thought was that Sinclair must have discovered that he was aware of the discrepancies in the information and had sent Fowler to make some plausible excuse.

"OK. I've read them. What was I supposed to find? They appear to be a perfectly ordinary set of files."

"Yes. But all the highlighted stuff is what I deleted. I was worried about it, which is why I kept a copy of the files for myself."

"And you don't know why he wanted this done?"

"He said it was important, and not to ask too many questions."

"So what made you come to me? What do you expect me to do? Did something happen to make you think twice about obeying his orders?"

"No."

"I need to know why you don't wish to discuss this with your Uncle Hector."

"He's lied to me."

"What if I were to call him in here to explain why he asked you to do the alterations."

"No." Steven begged, leaping to his feet. "Please don't do that. He'll kill me."

"That's a bit over dramatic. Why should he want to kill you?"

"I know too much."

"If you want my help, start talking. First tell me what he's lied about, if you don't want to do that, then get out and stop wasting my time."

The young man stood rigid by the desk, his fists clenched so tight his hands turned an unnatural shade of white. He looked directly at Gavin, and started, "I don't know what grudge you have against my uncle, but I am aware that you and he don't see eye to eye. That's the reason I feel I can trust you. You have to believe me." He paused for a moment, seeming to wait for a reaction, then reached into his jacket pocket and took out an envelope and placed it on the desk. "Here. Look at this."

Gavin picked it up, turned it over, before quietly saying. "Perhaps you should sit down again." He proceeded to open it and study the content.

It contained a single photo. A photo showing Dan Trench getting into a blue Volvo. Gavin looked at it carefully and asked, "Well, who is he?"

"Dan Trench, he was the man being watched at Mallaig."

"And?"

"Well the other day, while I was at my uncle's house, I answered his phone, it was Dan Trench. I asked my uncle, if it was the man who'd been at Mallaig, he flatly denied it."

"OK, so he made a mistake. There's no law against receiving telephone calls, not even from ex-convicts. I get several every year."

"Yes. But you don't understand."

"That's because so far there has been nothing to understand. I'll need more than that," Gavin answered impatiently wondering if Steven would come up with anything useful or better still admit his part in covering up the presence of those vehicles at Mallaig.

"I was there a few days later and I overheard another telephone conversation. I thought I'd made a mistake. I couldn't believe what I heard, until Gillespie's body turned up."

"Well come on. What did you hear?" Gavin snapped.

"I heard him give orders for Gillespie to be dealt with."

"He could have meant, pay off a debt, or something quite innocent with that remark. How do you know it was the same Gillespie? And what would he have to gain from it?"

"I don't know. I only know it all ties in with the Mallaig house."

"What makes you so certain?"

"I took that photo of Dan Trench at my Uncle's house two nights ago. I saw him arrive, and followed him in. He went into the study and they were in there alone for about ten minutes. I deliberately listened in on part of their conversation. Trench talked about needing an alibi, and that my uncle would need one too. I didn't understand it at the time. But that was the night Gillespie was fished out of the harbour, I knew that was what he was referring to."

"Did they talk about anything else?"

"Yes. My uncle wanted to know why he suddenly wanted to take part in the deal. Trench said it was because of Gillespie, and Hill, and that he wanted the money and to quit."

Gavin stretched his arms over his head, leaned forward over his desk. "What will you do if I refuse to believe you?"

"I don't know. I don't even know what I expect you to do. I can see there is not enough evidence to do anything with. But I had to talk to someone. Someone I could trust."

"Why do you go to your uncle's house so often if you don't get on with him?"

"I have to. He asked me to report to him all that goes on in our department on a daily basis."

"Did he give a reason?"

"He told me you were gunning for his job."

"And you believed him?"

"Yes."

"Well, I'll have a hard time proving anything at all. It's going to take a lot of hard work and you're going to have to help. And that means being stuck in the middle. Do you think you can handle that?"

Steven nodded. "Where do I begin?"

"Motive. Without it we haven't a case."

"And if I find one?"

"I'll back you all the way, and that's a promise." Gavin then added, "About the files. I'll be honest with you. I already knew that information was being removed. But like you, I still don't know why. Any suggestions?"

"No. I was obeying orders."

"Fine. He's bound to know you've been to see me. Tell him I called you in here to ask about one of the files you altered." Gavin rummaged through the pile, extracting one. "Here this one will do. Convince him you fobbed me off with an excuse that you had been rushing to finish your work and had left loads out. Say I threatened to get you fired if you ever took another short cut."

"What if he doesn't believe me?"

"He has to. I can't do anything without evidence, and a motive." His tone softened. "Don't think I don't care, because I do. I hate to see the system abused."

"Thanks."

"Don't thank me yet. There's a lot to do. And I suggest we start with a rundown of his or perhaps I should say your aunt's family."

Chapter 21

Jim liked Anne from the first moment when she rushed over and flung her arms around Jenny to welcome her home. Jenny looked a little flustered by the warmth of the greeting, and seemed glad to have a reason to break away in order to introduce Jim to her neighbour.

"Come on in, I've got the kettle on," Anne said, pushing open the gate, "I'll bet you could both do with a cup of tea before you go home." Jenny followed quietly casting the occasional glance towards the house on the other side of the hedge. Her jaw was clenched tight but she still managed to keep a semblance of a smile for her neighbour. Jim wondered how long she could keep her poise. He felt the best way to help was to keep talking to Anne, which would take the spotlight off Jenny.

His task was easy. Anne bustled around the kitchen, tossing toys into a basket in the corner, as she cleared a space on the table to put down the tea things. "Children, god they don't half mess up the place," she said, then turned pink, clapped her hand over her mouth in horror.

Jim checked for Jenny's reaction to the comment. To his relief Jenny was gazing out the window, deep in her own thoughts and oblivious to Anne's tactless remark. He changed the subject by asking, "Is it possible for me to have coffee instead of tea?"

"Me too," Jenny piped in.

"Of course," Anne answered, she looked relieved and happy to be doing what she obviously enjoyed doing, entertaining guests.

Anne flitted about her spotless, highly organized kitchen, while the water boiled. A couple of times she looked as if she was about to speak up, but didn't. Jim wanted her to act normally, Jenny needed that more than anything, but explaining that in Jenny's presence was impossible. Jenny had described Anne as a bubbly, warm-hearted, whirlwind of a friend, just what Jenny needed to make her return home less traumatic.

"How do you take your coffee?" she asked, pointing to the milk and sugar. Jim took his black and once he had his cup in his hand, Anne said to Jenny, "I've a load of messages for you."

"I'll deal with them later. I've changed my mind about having something. I want to go next door," Jenny announced, adding quietly to Jim, "on my own."

He knew he shouldn't agree to it, but what choice did he have. She had made her decision and made it clear he wasn't welcome. He caught sight of Anne watching them both, shrugged his shoulders and casually nodded his agreement. If he let her go without an argument, he could talk freely to Anne.

"Fine, I'll come over in a while." He turned toward Anne. "This coffee is good, are you having some?"

"Of course." She handed Jenny the keys, and as soon as Jenny had gone she turned back to face Jim. "You didn't want her to go on her own, did you?"

"No. But I didn't think it was worth arguing about."

"Well, I'm quite glad, it gives me an opportunity to find out what happened," Anne said as she filled her mug. "I was quite worried when the police called about her. They didn't say much beyond that she'd lost her memory and they needed more information about her. Has she remembered everything?"

"Not quite," Jim explained the problems they'd had finding out who Jenny was.

"They wanted to look round the cottage. I wasn't sure whether I should let them or not, but the inspector who came is a friend of my husband's so I felt it would be all right. I went with them, and made sure they didn't disturb anything."

"You did the right thing," Jim said reassuringly. "But can you give me some idea how she spent the last six months. That's the biggest blank. She says she can't remember anything after the funeral."

"Well to start with she did nothing. She was in such a state of shock it was an effort even to persuade her to go to the shops let alone be sociable. She surprised us all by doing a course on "The History of Art" at the local college. That seemed to help. She became very friendly with the person who ran the course, and used to go off exploring junk shops, museums, galleries and historic houses. Jenny began to write about her trips, her whole attitude altered, she seemed happy and several of her articles were published. It gave her quite a thrill. I know she had plans to develop her writing career, she already had a commission from the local paper to do a regular feature."

"Funny about that, she got the shakes over a painting and refused to go into an old house near where I live that's full of antiques, which is open to the public. I wonder what went wrong." Jim put his cup down and wandered to the window. "She hasn't mentioned an interest in either art or writing."

Jim felt comfortable enough to confide to Anne the complication of their mutual attraction and growing emotional ties.

"I'll admit I did wonder about your relationship, you seem very close."

"We have been, but I'm worried, something she's remembered has destroyed what we had. I'm being shut out again and I don't know how to fight it. In the month since I found her we've become very close, but I still have so much to learn about her."

"Well something has changed. Jenny would never have missed the chance of a cup of coffee in the past. I was surprised when she rushed off like that."

"Her moods vary. She can swing from tears to laughter in a matter of seconds, without any warning," he said.

"The police wanted to know when she left here, I wasn't sure of the date, but I've just remembered it was the day I took my daughter to the dentist. I had to drop Jenny off at the station early so I wouldn't miss the appointment, so it must be written down in my diary," Anne said as she rummaged in her bag.

Jim tried to collect his thoughts into some semblance of order. He must phone Gavin. He hadn't spoken to him since the call with the news from Devon. Every time he had intended to call, Jenny had found some excuse to delay. All he'd managed was a string of texts.

"I've found the date, and I'm positive I dropped her off at the station before eleven. It's all I can offer. Perhaps the ticket office can help. She might have paid by cheque. Do you think the police could find out?"

"Anne you're brilliant, can I use your phone?"

Luckily Gavin McKay was in his office, but his reaction to the call was not what Jim had expected.

"Where the hell are you?" Gavin demanded. "Why didn't you call me before?"

"I'm sorry, but Jenny needed to get away, she didn't want me to call."

"Why?" Gavin snapped.

"I don't know. She said she wanted time to think."

"Well has it done any good?"

"What do you mean?" Jim asked somewhat puzzled by the rather unsympathetic responses he was receiving.

"Has she told you how she landed up on the island?"

"No. I don't think she's remembered anything like that."

"Are you absolutely sure?"

"As far as I know, the children's funeral is her last recollection. The last six months are still totally blank."

"Are you certain?"

"Yes, I'm pretty sure. But I get the impression you know something I don't. What have you found out?"

"Nothing. But remember you thought she might have been taking drugs and had been beaten. We still don't know who was responsible. There's always the possibility she might have remembered and be afraid to speak up. Or worse still be protecting someone."

"That's crazy," Jim answered.

"No Jim. Because you're so personally involved, you're not as objective as I am. Bear it in mind, and let me know if she does anything odd."

Jim relayed the information Anne had given him about the date of departure and ended the call.

"What was all that about?" Anne asked.

"Well I don't suppose it will hurt to tell you the condition Jenny was in when I found her. You might even have an explanation."

After he described the situation Anne shook her head. "Sorry, I can't help. Drugs thankfully are almost unheard of in the village, and I can't think of anyone with a reputation for violence."

Chapter 22

Collecting her spare keys from Anne had started her speculating what else had disappeared; credit cards, cheque book and drivers licence were among the most likely items. Where were they? Would she ever find them? Those thoughts vanished as she approached the front door. She fumbled with the keys. The back door key was familiar to her. She remembered they rarely used the front entrance so wasn't surprised she couldn't pick out the correct key instantly. Perhaps she should use the back door after all. No. The occasion demanded the use of the front door. The heady scent of mahonia wafted towards her. The big bush by the door was covered with yellow blooms. The rest of the garden looked untidy with lots of dead leaves lying on the uncut lawn. A few clumps of snowdrops shone like bright jewels at the base of the thick beech hedge. She inserted the key in the lock, and turned it.

Her stomach churned at the prospect of entering. Perhaps she had been a fool to insist on coming alone.

Her hand tightened on the doorknob. She needed to sit down, she felt sick and dizzy. She could picture the carved oak chair just inside the door. Her instincts of self-preservation took her over the threshold, propelling her forward to collapse onto the chair. She dropped her head between her knees, forcing herself to take deep breaths until her nausea and dizziness subsided.

The worst was over. She had made it. Gradually she allowed herself to study the hall. Nothing had changed, except there was a lovely bowl of deep blue hyacinths in full flower on the hexagonal table, filling the room with heady perfume. Anne had been expecting her, and had probably left a freshly baked cake in the kitchen too. Anne was an expert at providing those wonderful little touches to take the edge off difficult situations. Anne's help before, during and after the funeral had been the only thing that had enabled her to get through the ordeal. Jenny felt guilty, certain she had never thanked Anne properly for all her support.

She looked round again. There were two pairs of very small boots on the hall-stand. She shuddered. Had she deliberately left them there? Had she been hoping the boys would wear them again? With a sinking feeling in her heart she faced the fact she had never accepted their deaths. Slowly moving round the downstairs rooms, she picked up one object after another, examining each one before replacing it. She shuffled through the papers on her desk. What did she hope to find? She moved on, aware that there was one particular pile of papers she'd left untouched. Like a magnet it drew her back, but every time she went to open the top file a tingling sensation at the back of her neck made her stop. A subconscious voice screamed at her not to look.

She fled upstairs. She knew instinctively, before opening the door that the children's room would be exactly as it had been before their deaths. Steeling herself, she peeped in. Her premonition was correct. Nothing had changed. How on earth had she lived here for six months without clearing their things? Had she spent hours sitting in their room waiting for them to return? It didn't bear thinking about. Hastily she closed the door and moved on.

Her own room had only one reminder. A large photo dominated the dressing table. It was of herself and the boys on the beach at Exmouth. She sat on the stool in front of it, remembering the day with absolute clarity. She looked up, caught sight of her reflection in the mirror. She had changed. Not just physically, the lost weight, and longer hair were obvious differences, the carefree mother had disappeared forever. The reflection she was studying was one of a stranger; someone she knew virtually nothing about. And she wasn't certain she wanted to find out. Carefully she examined the fading scar on her temple. As Jim had promised there was almost no trace of his handiwork. Her skin might have healed but one thing she was pretty sure of was her mental scars were still intact, even if they were obscured by the loss of memory. She doubted she would be able to explain her feelings to anyone, making it hard to get help unravelling the mess.

One thing became painfully obvious to her as she sat looking at her reflection. Coming back with Jim had been a mistake. Their newfound relationship would not survive the return to her marital home. Here her insecurities would flourish, destroying the possibility of recapturing the closeness they had experienced on the island, in Comrie, and during the last few days on the journey down. But she could not leave here yet. Tears filled her eyes. She mustn't break down. She had too much to do, too much to find out.

Frantically she rummaged through her overfilled wardrobe. Could she possibly have worn those clothes? Somehow she couldn't imagine herself wearing any of them. Had she changed so much?

A thought struck her. There was absolutely nothing left in the room to remind her of Denis. Had she deliberately removed all trace of his existence? She stopped in her tracks. Why? Had it been easy to erase his memory? Had she been so bitter about his affair? Jealous maybe? No. The answer was more basic. She blamed him for the death of the boys. He had been driving. He had been trying to take them from her. She could see now how she simplified the situation, heaping all the blame on Denis, ignoring her own failure to keep her marriage going. Now she had to face up to the fact she was at fault. She should never have pressed Denis into marrying her, and certainly knowing their relationship was flagging she should never have allowed herself to become pregnant. Too late to worry about that now, the boys had been real. She had loved them more than anything in the world. Now they were gone. Gone forever. The time had come for her to accept the fact and remember the happy times. Forget the bitterness and anger.

She went back downstairs and once again the papers on the desk made her shiver. She could not keep avoiding them. With determination she drew up a chair and pulled the offending pile in front of her, and gingerly prised open the first file, which contained detailed notes on paintings. The more she read the more tense she became, experiencing the same reaction she felt in the lounge at Ellen's flat and at the historic house Jim had tried to take her to. The temptation to push the papers away, or hide them in a drawer was great, she fought it. She had to define the reason for her terror. There must be a common factor and this might be the one. What she didn't know was how she'd deal with it. Jim couldn't help her, his presence would inhibit her. She'd have to persuade him to leave. He'd not go willingly. A great deal of tact and skill would be needed to convince him to go.

There was a knock at the door. She heard it open.

"Can I come in?" Jim called out. "Are you all right?"

Before she had time to answer, he was there in the room. She was angry she hadn't had time to hide the papers. She didn't want him to see them. It worried her that she felt so strongly about it. But that didn't stop her from pushing the papers back into the desk and slamming the lid shut, locking it and stuffing the key into her pocket.

"Sorry I didn't mean to interrupt," he said.

"No, you didn't," she lied. "I was just looking through some papers. Did you enjoy your coffee with Anne?" she added trying to change the subject.

"Yes, she's not a bit as I had imagined her. You're very lucky to have such a good friend," he said. "I found out quite a lot about you."

"Gossip," she muttered, leading the way to the kitchen.

"Maybe. But she told me lots about the last six months."

He outlined briefly what Anne had told him about her attending a course studying art history, and the progression to writing articles that had been published, even that the local newspaper had offered her a regular column.

"That explains some of the papers on my desk," she said. "There are lots of notes and things about paintings and antiques. I don't remember doing a course. I suppose if Anne said I did, then I must have." She noticed the puzzled look on his face. "Oh, don't get me wrong, I didn't mean to sound as if I don't believe her. It's hard being told what you've done in the past when you can't remember for yourself."

"I'm sure it is. Would going through them with you help?"

"No," she snapped. Then to avoid further discussion on the subject she added, "Is Anne coming over?"

Jim looked as if he was about to lecture her, instead simply said, "Yes."

"Could you put her off? I know I should apologize for rushing off earlier, I can't face her today."

"I'm sure she won't mind, I'll go in a minute and tell her. But I have a serious problem."

Jenny sighed to herself. How could he expect her to help him with his problems, she had enough of her own.

"Anne told me she'd stocked up your fridge, and I'm starving."

Jenny grinned with relief.

"Is that all?" They were on safe ground at last. "No problem, so am I. I'll fix us something to eat."

Cooking provided a neutral occupation, a chance to draw breath and adjust to his presence in the surroundings she was not yet at ease with. She quickly prepared a salad, and beat up some eggs to make a tasty omelette. Jim insisted on opening a bottle of wine. "Do you good to relax.

"If you say that to all your patients, you'll have to open your own drying out clinic," she joked.

Jenny had to admit to herself she felt more relaxed now than she had since her arrival at the cottage, but she still had to talk to Jim about their relationship. If she didn't sort things out soon he might misread the situation.

"Jim."

"Yes."

"I don't know how to say this."

"Let me guess," he answered. "You're having problems adjusting and don't think you're ready for a full blown love affair."

Jenny couldn't believe she had heard him correctly. "Yes. I mean no. I don't know what I want."

"You need time. You can't absorb the details about your family, losing them, and finding out about the missing weeks at the same time as starting a new life."

"How did you know?" she whispered.

"I was afraid it would happen, that's why I let you talk me into travelling down so slowly, I wanted to make what we had last for as long as possible. I'd hoped it would become so strong nothing could part us."

"I'm sorry."

"I understand. You will let me stay for a while, as a friend, won't you? I promise I won't try to be more. I'll give you as much space as you need. I'm sure Anne will give me coffee if you want to be alone."

Jenny was caught, she had intended using privacy as a lever to evict him, and he had so neatly taken care of the problem. Well maybe it wouldn't be so bad having him around.

"OK, you can stay."

For the rest of the day Jim seemed to be making every effort to keep out of her way. He went out shopping, swept up some leaves, checked out the log shed, and spent an hour splitting logs then once it got dark he came in and sat quietly in the lounge reading a book. It wasn't until after dinner that he pulled out his list of questions.

"Any chance of going through these again?" he asked.

Postponing the inevitable was not going to help, so Jenny reluctantly agreed, rushing through them and handing them back.

"Enough for today. I think I'll go to bed. You can use the spare room at the end of the passage. Good night."

That day set the pattern for the next week. She was feeling so tired, and had lost her appetite, added to which she felt rather antisocial, avoiding meeting anyone except Jim. He did all the shopping, and helped in the garden and the house and doing anything she suggested. They went for long silent walks, and at the end of each day scanned the lists again.

Jim suggested they invite Anne over to go through the lists with them.

"I don't want to be pushy. But there might be some small clue we've overlooked," he said, with a pleading look that made her give in to his gentle pressure.

He had already put in everything Anne had reported of her activities after the funeral, including details of the Art course, her writing and her departure by train, none of which Jenny could confirm or dispute. It was almost a relief when Jim got to the end of the lists, and put them aside.

Jenny sat in her usual spot on the rug by the fire, absentmindedly prodding the glowing logs with the poker. She was half-aware of Jim refilling her glass of wine but she paid scant attention to the conversation Jim and Anne were having about the village. When the conversation turned to Scotland, she was drawn back into it and found herself extolling the virtues of the place, the hills, the heather, the lochs, and then rather dreamily about the island.

There was no warning, her peace was about to be shattered. One simple question from Anne was the catalyst.

"Did you go anywhere near Mallaig?"

Jenny shivered, an icy feeling washed over her.

"You remember Dan Trench was always boasting it was the best part of Scotland, he used to tell us about having a house up there, which none of us believed."

The poker slipped out of her hand. She wanted to escape. From what? Where to? Her whole body seemed to have become detached, out of control, floating. She could feel the blood drain from her head, as if someone had pulled the plug and she was being emptied like a bath, sucked to the bottom. What was happening? The room was spinning round her. Voices. Hands. Then nothing.

Chapter 23

Meetings at Gavin's house were becoming a regular affair. Tom in his usual spot and Paula sprawled in one of the old sagging armchairs. Gavin couldn't help wondering what Ellen would think of his house. He hadn't yet plucked up enough courage to ask her over. Would she realize it was exactly as his ex wife had left it? Except now everything was rather faded and worn. It wasn't a deliberate decision not to change anything, but laziness and lack of time put decorating at the bottom of his priority list.

"It looks as if Sinclair is about to wind down the Gillespie case," Tom said.

"I know. And there's no way to keep it open, unless I produce the taped telephone message he left me," Gavin answered.

"Have you talked to the pathologist?" Paula asked.

"Yes. He says Gillespie died from a blow to the head before he hit the water. There's no reason to suggest it wasn't an accident, especially since the alcohol level in his blood was so high he wouldn't have been able to see straight. The logical conclusion is that he slipped and hit his head on the edge as he fell into the water."

"What are you going to do about Hill?" Paula asked.

"Unfortunately," Gavin said, "there's absolutely nothing we can do. We have no proof he was responsible. And, if we pulled him in for questioning it would alert Sinclair to the fact we haven't given up on Mallaig."

"What about Fowler's information? I thought you said he'd heard Sinclair give orders to have Gillespie dealt with," Paula said.

"Yes. But that's hearsay, and even with the taped message he left me, there is insufficient evidence to do anything. It wouldn't even get us into court. We still don't have any idea what it was about Mallaig that scared Gillespie so much. He never explained his fears, so we can't prove it had anything to do with his death. It could be pure coincidence that ties Gillespie or Sinclair with every lead we get concerning Mallaig."

"Do you think Steven Fowler can be trusted?" Tom asked.

"I think so. But, to be on the safe side I haven't told him about Hill. I don't think he needs to know everything we're working on. He and I came to an agreement about what should be passed on to Sinclair, I can't be absolutely sure that he will keep his side of the bargain. But having said that, I do believe everything he tells me. Today he came in with some very interesting information. Sinclair is a compulsive gambler. That was news to me. I thought I knew a lot about him but I never found that out. He gets his thrills playing cards on a regular basis, for phenomenal stakes, and is up to his neck in debt."

"Of course," Tom said, "we should have guessed, after all, his wife comes from a gambling background. It must have been how they met. She's a bit keen on the horses herself. And both her brothers are still heavily involved in the family bookmaking business."

"It seems so obvious, I can't believe I overlooked it," Gavin said.

"Any idea who he regularly plays with?" Tom asked.

"Not yet, I think some of the dropped cases might make sense when we do. He could be using his position to clear his debts," Gavin answered.

"Dropping cases is one thing, having someone killed is somewhat drastic," Paula said.

"I agree. Maybe he's involved in something even bigger. Fowler has agreed to try to get in on the act. He is bending over backwards to make Sinclair believe he is ready to do anything, honest or dishonest, without question."

"Do you think it will work?" Tom asked.

"I hope so. I told him both of you could be trusted, and if he got into difficulties he could depend on you."

"Well let's hope it doesn't come to that," Paula said. "By the way, have you had anything back from the lab on the syringe I found on the bonfire at Mallaig?"

"Yes. It's an interesting drug, not commonly available here. They were going to check further into its origins. So far all they can confirm is it's a sedative and highly addictive."

"Do you think it belonged to the girl?"

"She never struck me as the type to use drugs, but the tragic death of her children might have driven her to it. The cheque book and bank card were definitely hers, there was enough salvaged to get the account number. I haven't done anything about the keys yet, I have been thinking I might take a couple of weeks off and go down to Devon and check it out," Gavin said.

"Have you told her we know she was at Mallaig?" Paula asked.

"Not yet. I spoke to Jim Cullen two days ago. Seems she's having trouble settling back home so didn't think it was a good time to broach the subject, and was hoping she would come out with it herself. It would help if we knew what we were dealing with."

"What does Ellen think?" Tom asked.

"I haven't told her about the Mallaig connection."

"Will she go with you to Devon?" Paula asked.

"Why do you ask?"

"I wondered how it would affect the gossip. The rumours circulating round the station have, you and I, as the inseparable couple. Everyone thinks I'm responsible for the change of image, you know, new shirt, jacket, etc."

"You didn't put them right on the subject?"

"Umm... no not exactly, well truth is I led them on a bit, told them about a few changes I'd made round the house," she answered, grinning.

Gavin glanced round. What changes? Flowers, nice, he should have noticed them before. His plants were looking healthier, been fed and watered. Other than that he couldn't see anything very different. He raised his eyebrows to query her comment.

"I made it all up. Sorry."

"I don't mind, as long as you're happy? It won't ruin your reputation, going for an older man, and all that, will it?"

"Has to be better than going out with a woman beater, so no it won't do me any harm. But it'll be fun to see the reaction when they find out how wrong they are. It can't be long before someone catches on Ellen is the one you're trying to impress. I was hoping she'd be here tonight I'm looking forward to meeting her, if only to see if she fits the description I've been given."

Gavin smiled. He'd enjoy watching their faces too, when the truth came out. Having Paula to stay was showing him a side of her he'd never noticed before. It was good to see her looking happy and relaxed and lightening the mood around him. He'd better explain the situation to Ellen before she started to get the wrong idea too.

"Go on, tell us what she's like," Paula said. Gavin had to think hard for a minute, and work out how to describe Ellen. She was tall, only an inch or two shorter than he was. She was about the same weight as she had been at college, curves in all the right places. Her clothes were more casual, suited to her love of outdoor activity. But it was her eyes that really had him hooked. She smiled most of the time, at him, and everyone else, but he wasn't fooled. The smile was on the surface, but it hid a deeper sorrow. Something had left her hurting, and he was waiting for the right moment to discover what it was. Whatever it was it had not managed to destroy the quiet aura of peace and tranquillity that had enchanted him all those years ago.

Gavin nodded. "Perhaps I should ask her to come to Devon with me. Jenny gets on well with her, and her presence would certainly make my trip appear more social and less official."

After a few minutes pensive silence, Tom spoke. "While you're gadding about in Devon, what do you want us to do?"

"You can carry on searching for information on the owners of the Mallaig house, and anything else Sinclair has any connection to. There must be something we've missed that will tie him in. Paula, I need you to keep a very close watch on the crates that went into store. They could be the key to the whole thing," Gavin replied. "It will take a couple of days to arrange to get away, I'll let you know my plans and where you can contact me."

Tom edged his wheelchair round. "Well, I think I ought to get going or my wife will begin to wonder what I'm up to."

"Do tell her I'm sorry for keeping you out for so long." Gavin said.

Paula picked up the dirty glasses, and opened the door for Tom. "Good night."

Gavin watched them leave the room, and in the following silence realized he was jealous of Tom. It hadn't bothered him for the last four years that he didn't have someone waiting for him, but since meeting Ellen again living a solitary life held no joy. The house felt empty, even with Paula living there. He wanted someone to share things with. Ellen was the perfect candidate. He'd have to be patient and wait until he was sure of a favourable response.

His happy contemplation of a future with Ellen was rudely interrupted by the telephone. He automatically checked his watch. It was too late for the caller to be Ellen.

The tone of Jim's voice left Gavin in little doubt all was not well.

"Jim, calm down. I can't understand a word you're saying."

"I don't know what to do."

"Well, explain to me again what happened."

"Last time we spoke, you told me not to forget she had been beaten up and on drugs, and to be on the look-out for anything odd. Well she's been rather depressed and withdrawn. Nothing more than one would expect for someone with her problems. Today she began to relax a tiny bit, and invited her neighbour, Anne, over for a drink. We chatted for a couple of hours and everything was fine, until Anne mentioned a particular name. It really affected her. She reacted the same way she did at the dance in Comrie. She went completely white and then passed out."

"And the name?" Gavin queried, grabbing a pen and paper.

"Dan Trench."

"Anything else?" Gavin asked, hardly able to believe that at last the link was beginning to take shape.

"I got Anne to tell me everything she knew about him, but it's not much. He comes from Scotland."

"Mallaig," Gavin muttered under his breath.

"Yes Mallaig," Jim replied, "how did you know?"

"Never mind. What else do you know about him?"

"Anne says she met him at the golf club, and at several dinner parties in the area where he was often invited as the extra man. He never talked much about himself. Once he let slip he came from the Mallaig area. Usually he changed the subject if people asked more about his home. Everyone presumed it was because of a fairly messy divorce or something similar in the past, but she never got the details. His job involved his travelling about most of the time and he rented a small flat in the village."

Gavin went over everything again, delving into details of her behaviour since returning to the cottage. And it didn't require much intuition to sense from Jim's comments the love affair had been under stress long before Dan Trench had been mentioned.

"I've decided to come down to Devon," Gavin informed him. "Try to find out what you can for me. Jim, please be careful, and keep a close watch on her until I arrive."

"I'm glad you're coming," Jim answered.

His answer made Gavin very happy. "I thought I'd ask Ellen to come with me."

"Great idea. This Dan Trench, who is he? What do you know about him?"

"Very little. I can only tell you his name appeared in a file I'm working on."

"In what connection?"

"I wish I knew," Gavin answered. "I promise you'll be the first to know when I come up with an answer. Probably better if you don't tell her I'm coming, or that I've ever heard of Dan Trench."

"Don't worry I have no intention of bringing up his name. I'm not risking triggering that reaction from her again."

Gavin wasn't ready to tell him that her reaction was what he wanted to see most. And when he got there he'd waste no time bringing up Dan Trench's name, and telling her they knew she had been at Mallaig with him. He needed to see her expression for himself.

Chapter 24

He woke to the sound of her scream. Jim pushed back the bedclothes and swung his feet out onto the floor. Then he froze. It was pointless going to her. He knew all he would get would be a yell to leave her alone. The nightmares, which had stopped at Comrie after she remembered about the death of the children, had begun again. The words Mallaig and Dan Trench had been enough to trigger the change in her, making her refuse all offers of comfort. She had withdrawn into a near silent world of her own, limiting conversation to basics like food and weather. And Jim's instincts made him very cautious. Any attempt to delve into her personal problems would only serve to put him in danger. Danger of eviction.

He hated Dan Trench. What power did the man have over her? Why should the mere mention of his name have such a devastating effect? There had to be more to the relationship, perhaps they were lovers, though Anne had assured him it was unlikely. And what did Gavin know?

The worst of it was being hampered by his rash promise not to push her. Thankfully, Gavin was arriving today, and he was under no such obligation. Would he press for answers? And if so, could she take the pressure? Jim wasn't sure it wouldn't tip the balance and destroy what little peace of mind she had managed to salvage?

He was so wide-awake now, it seemed pointless trying to go back to sleep. What he needed was a coffee. He groped in the half-light and found some clothes, then made his way down to the kitchen. The coffee jug was full, its welcoming smell filling the kitchen. Jenny was sitting in her usual place, her hands tightly clasped around her cup. She gazed into the steaming liquid with the sort of intensity reserved for a crystal ball.

"Morning," he said, as he bent to kiss her. She ducked to avoid him, making it obvious she didn't wish any familiar gestures.

"I'm going for a walk," she announced.

"Can I join you?" he asked, noting her pale skin.

She shook her head. He wasn't surprised. She seldom wanted his company now, and he was sure her solitary walks were an excuse to get away from him. He'd be lucky if she returned by lunch-time. If only he could tell her Gavin was coming, but Gavin had specifically asked him not to. Even Gavin didn't sound the same. Perhaps I'm paranoid he thought. Perhaps I should leave and let her get on with her life. But, he knew that option wasn't open. He had to stay until the end for his own peace of mind. Win or lose.

Gavin arrived with Ellen about an hour after Jenny had gone. He poured their coffee and filled them in on the latest changes in her behaviour.

"Mind if I look round?" Gavin asked.

"No."

"You mentioned something about her being disturbed by some papers?" Gavin said.

"Yes. That pile over there on her desk, always seem to make her very edgy. She tends to keep them locked away, she forgot today."

Jim watched as Gavin began to sift through them.

"Gavin, those are her private papers, you shouldn't be snooping without her permission," Ellen stated firmly.

Gavin ignored her remark.

"I want to take these and examine them in more detail," he said to Jim.

Jim was in a dilemma. He agreed with Ellen, they were Jenny's personal files and no one should be reading them. He had already betrayed her trust by giving Gavin access, what harm could come from letting him take a closer look at them. Gavin was only trying to help solve the mystery of her past, too.

"Can't you read them here?" he asked.

"No."

Jim judged from Gavin's tone of voice, arguing would be a waste of time.

"What do you hope to find?"

"Some connection between her and Dan Trench."

Gavin was obviously not going to elaborate on the subject, and seemed desperate to depart with the files. Jim saw them out, listening to Ellen unsuccessfully trying to persuade Gavin to wait and ask Jenny's permission. When their car finally disappeared he sighed with relief, it was too late to change his mind. The papers were gone, and all he had to decide was how to tell Jenny what he'd done.

First he chopped some logs then he read the paper. He couldn't settle at anything, so finally he set about preparing some lunch, hoping Jenny would eat. He was quite concerned as she seemed to have lost her appetite, and he was sure she was losing weight, which was something she could ill afford to do.

"Enjoy your walk?" he asked, as she shed her coat and boots. The fresh air had done her good, her colour had improved considerably.

"Yes, but the path was quite muddy, I'll just go and change. I'd love a cup of coffee."

Jim refilled the coffee machine. He was pleased she seemed more cheerful than she had been earlier. As he reached into the cupboard for a cup, she rushed back into the kitchen shouting, "Where are my files?"

Jim had never seen her look so distressed and angry. He knew his answer was not going to please, still he owed her the truth.

"Gavin has them."

"What the hell does he want with my papers? Who the hell gave you permission to give my belongings to him?"

"He came this morning, I happened to mention the files seemed to bother you, and he asked if he could look at them. I didn't think you'd mind."

Her rigid posture said it all. He had done the wrong thing. Ellen's words echoed in his head. If only he had listened and insisted that Gavin wait. He had blundered. There was little hope of forgiveness for this mistake. A new barrier had come between them. Invisible maybe, but certainly more impregnable than anything he had encountered previously.

She swallowed, took a deep breath then quietly and firmly, like a judge addressing a jury, pronounced her verdict and sentence.

"I want you to leave," then she added the final blow. "Now."

So final. So definite. Did she really mean it? Jim desperately tried to convince himself he had misheard her. Bit by bit it sank in. She was bitter, she was hurt, but surely she did not want him to go. He couldn't accept it.

"No. I'm not going. I love you. I can't go," he countered.

"I mean it. I want you to go," she said with an icy edge to her voice, avoiding looking directly at him.

"Please tell me what was in the files. Is there something in them you don't want Gavin to find?" He was determined to get her answer and prepared to goad her to respond.

"You've remembered something and you're afraid to tell us."

"Stop it!" she screamed, her voice rising in pitch, her steely composure beginning to crack. The first tear was edging its way down her cheek. Jim's instinct told him if he could hold her it would help put things right between them. He moved towards her and reached out to touch her. She pushed him away violently.

"Don't touch me. Don't touch me."

Jim had no choice but to retreat and watch her from a distance as the tears streaked down her face. Then ever so softly she begged, "Please go. If you love me, go. I have to be alone."

Devastated, he accepted defeat. It was the one plea that destroyed all his arguments.

"I'll go and get my things together," he said quietly, hoping to calm the atmosphere, even though he was reluctant to leave the room. It only took a few minutes to gather his possessions together, after which he sat feeling despondent trying to think of what he could do, or say, to change her mind. He returned to the kitchen determined to make one last attempt.

"Can the condemned man eat before he goes?" Jim asked, using the only excuse he could think of to prolong his departure. She answered with a shrug of indifference. He fiddled with the food, soon there was nothing he could add to the meal so he placed her plate in front of her and sat down to eat his own. The silence was broken only by the echoing sound of cutlery touching the plate. His food tasted like sawdust, he wasn't even slightly hungry, but it provided a means of lingering. Her plate remained untouched. He finished. Washed up, stalling for time, he offered her a fresh cup of coffee, which she refused with a shake of her head. What could he do or say to break the silence? Eventually he resigned himself to the fact there was no way to drag out his departure any longer. He deliberately bent over and planted a kiss on her cheek, which got no reaction.

"Jenny, tell me about Dan Trench," he pleaded, knowing he had already been condemned to exile.

"Get out," she screamed at him. "Get out."

He said, one last time, "I love you. Remember that, and I'll come back the moment you want me."

He waited, knowing no amount of prayers would alter her decision. Then feeling as if an automaton had control of his limbs he marched slowly and steadily towards the door. He didn't want to leave, but continued acting like a robot. His hand came up and turned the door catch and pulled. He stepped out, the door closed behind him. The latch clicking shut snapped him back to reality.

What was he doing? He was a fool. He should have stood his ground. He turned and hammered on the door. Silence. He called her name. There was no response. Nothing.

Chapter 25

His patience finally ran out. It was a risk he had to take. Nervously Dan phoned his ex-landlady. She was always chatty, and if he asked the right questions he might be lucky and find out everything he needed to know without having to give much in return.

"Mrs. Miller, Dan Trench speaking. How are you?" he asked, knowing it would take her ages to answer that particular question. She was bound to regale him with all her aches and pains, and those of her family.

"Oh, that's good," he said on hearing about her latest grandchild's achievements, adding quickly, "and what else has happened in the village?" She rattled off all the gossip she had heard, but said nothing about the person he wanted news of. "What about the people who live down Pond Lane?" he inquired.

"Oh, Anne and her husband are fine, lovely children, saw them only the other day. And you remember Mrs. Marshall, well, she was away for a while and I've heard she's been ill, lost her memory or something. Don't see much of her these days, though they say she's much better. But I know she never will be, I mean, you never really get over losing children, do you?"

Dan asked after a few more people, to keep the conversation general. Then she surprised him.

"I'm so glad you called. There was a man round here only this morning asking about you."

Dan tried not to let his panic show, "Was there? I don't suppose you remember his name?" he asked trying to sound casual.

"It was Gavin someone, hold on I wrote it down." He heard the receiver being put down and could picture her shuffling into the kitchen where she kept every scrap of paper available for scribbling down names like the one he wanted. "Gavin McKay," she announced proudly on her return, "I told him you hadn't left a forwarding address. You promised to send me one as soon as you were settled. Are you fixed up yet?"

"No. But I'll call again as soon as I am. It's been nice talking to you. Goodbye."

He had almost slammed the handset back onto the phone. His hands were shaking. Gavin McKay was the detective investigating the house at Mallaig. The coincidence was too great.

He had to have an answer. He stabbed at the buttons on the phone and waited.

"I told you not to phone me at the office," Sinclair snapped at him.

Dan wasn't bothered by his anger; all he wanted was answers. "I know. This is important. I need an answer now. Have you stopped Gavin McKay from snooping into your affairs?"

"Yes. Why? I told you to lie low. The shipment isn't due for another fortnight."

"I know. Are you sure he's given up?"

"Of course I am. I had him busy trying to find out about some woman who'd lost her memory before getting herself washed up on some island. And now he's gone off on a golfing holiday in Devon," Sinclair said impatiently.

Dan shuddered. If Sinclair knew about the girl, why hadn't he said anything? Of course, if she had lost her memory then no one would know where she'd come from. So, why was Gavin McKay making enquiries about him in Devon?

"What makes you think he's still interested? You haven't done anything careless have you?"

"Oh, no, I thought someone was following me, I must have been mistaken. And as I hadn't heard from you I wanted to check that everything was going to plan," Dan muttered hastily. It didn't make sense that Sinclair didn't appear to know McKay had connected him with the girl, but he'd rather like it if Sinclair remained ignorant a little longer. "I'm sorry about calling at the office. I won't do it again."

Dan put down the phone, and rubbed his itching hands together. His rash was red and raw looking, and there was nothing he could do to ease it. He yanked open a can of beer. He had some serious thinking to do.

He didn't trust Sinclair. He couldn't believe he didn't know what McKay was up to. Was he being set up? The more he considered the matter the more convinced he became Sinclair was about to double cross him. Time to change the odds he must beat Sinclair at his own game. If Sinclair planned to make him the fall guy, Sinclair would go down with him.

Slowly his plan began to formulate, one that would take care of everything. He had to protect his own interests. First there was the girl, he had never wanted to harm her, but there was no room for sentiment at this stage. He would use Hill for that task, and perhaps deal with Hill at the same time. But not before he had made sure the finger pointed at Sinclair. Then with luck Gavin McKay would bring the whole thing to a climax, while he would quietly vanish.

Chapter 26

Ellen's wrath was one consequence Gavin had failed to anticipate. What made it worse was that he knew he deserved it. If he had listened to her advice Jim might still be at the cottage keeping watch on Jenny, and Ellen would still be talking to him.

"I'm sorry. The last thing I wanted or expected was for you to be thrown out," Gavin said to Jim. His apology and concern was genuine, he was a fool to have thought Jenny would not mind him barging into her house and taking her things without asking her permission.

"What was in those files? It had to be important for her to react so badly," Jim said.

"That's the problem, I'm not sure. When I first went through them I didn't spot anything, so I handed them over to Roland Hughes, the local police inspector, hoping he'd spot something I've missed. If he does, I promise I'll let you know."

"You're holding something back, aren't you?"

"No. What makes you think that?"

"The fact you are desperate enough to get other people involved."

"Well, the truth is we're suffering from lack of information ourselves. There are too many little things, and none of them tie up. Meet me at six at the hotel and I'll explain it all to you and Ellen. Believe me I never intended getting you pushed out."

"I believe you, but you're going to have a hard time convincing Ellen, she's pretty angry right now," Jim answered, "You keep me informed and I'll try to placate her for you."

"Thanks, I'd appreciate your help."

Gavin put back the receiver and looked round the room Inspector Hughes had put at his disposal. It was starkly furnished, a table, two chairs, and a telephone, but it was all he required. His initial scanning of the files had told him nothing. They were like sale-room catalogues, with items described in detail and an estimated value pencilled in after each one. Some of the estimates had been crossed out and another amount inserted. Who had altered the figures? Not Jenny, she had a different style of handwriting. Her tutor perhaps? Roland Hughes had someone checking that out.

Less than half an hour later Roland Hughes reported back that they had failed with their search. What should have been a simple straightforward task had turned into a more complex investigation. Jenny's tutor had vanished without trace. No forwarding address could be found, and when they checked her previous address and her references they found everything had been forged. All they had was a description of a woman who had called herself Zandra Snow, aged approximately 30 of medium build, with light brown hair.

Gavin began to wonder if he was going crazy. Every single lead he followed became as elusive as a puff of smoke.

First there had been Mallaig, which started because of a comment made by Gillespie. Now

Gillespie was dead, and Sinclair had been instrumental in closing down both the investigation at Mallaig, and the investigation into the cause of Gillespie's death. Then learning Sinclair was responsible for Steven altering records, and the frustration at not finding a motive for the alterations.

The string of coincidences kept growing. Ron Hill had been at Mallaig. He'd also been looking for Gillespie before he died. And Hill and Dan Trench, the other man from Mallaig, were both driving cars with false number plates. Trench had been photographed at Sinclair's house, and he had been seen with Jenny when they arrived together at Mallaig. He had also given up the lease of his flat in Devon two weeks after Jenny had left, without leaving a forwarding address. Nothing added up. Who had beaten Jenny? Why was she taking drugs? Why had she ended up half drowned? Was her memory loss genuine? And now there was the mysterious college lecturer Zandra Snow, who had vanished without trace.

The door burst open. Roland Hughes rushed in full of excitement. "We've found it!" he announced.

"What?"

"The connection you were looking for," Roland Hughes answered, looking pleased about his news. "Three of those files contained inventories of houses burgled in the last six months. The items stolen were the ones with the altered valuations."

"You think the list was their shopping list?"

"That's what it looks like."

"What a relief. I was beginning to wonder if we would ever find anything linked to a crime. Did you make any arrests or have any decent leads to follow."

"No nothing. They were very professional, the only clues we had were the vehicles we think they used. Turns out they were stolen and found abandoned. None of the property has ever turned up anywhere."

"It could be in the crates."

"What crates?"

Gavin settled down to tell Roland everything, starting with the interview with Gillespie, and everything he had so far collected about Mallaig, Sinclair, Gillespie, Hill, Trench and Jenny Marshall.

"No wonder Tom Jackson was so cagey when he asked me to look into the girl's past. He never let on you suspected your Chief Superintendent of being involved."

"Acting Chief Super, please!"

"Sorry."

"Well, he's the reason I haven't been able to get anywhere. I want to keep going until I can be certain he's involved. I don't want the messengers. I want the man at the top."

"Fine. I'll back you up. We'll double-check those files. There might be more in them if we dig deep enough. By the way how many people know what you've told me?"

"Only yourself, Paula Dawson and Tom so far. I shall have to tell Jim and Ellen Cullen too, but I don't want them to know Sinclair might be involved."

"Why both of them?"

"To be honest, I value Jim's professional advice regarding Jenny. Her memory loss may be genuine. If it is we can't charge in, making accusations. I think Jim's sister, Ellen, could be more helpful if she knows the truth, and I want her on my side for personal reasons."

"Sounds to me as if you think Jenny might be bluffing?"

"Yes. But Jim doesn't."

"How much will you tell them?" Roland asked.

"Only that we know Dan Trench took her to Mallaig, and about the stuff mentioned in the files being stolen. They don't need to know more."

"Well, let's see what else turns up now we have a starting point."

Gavin reached the hotel at ten past six. Jim and Ellen were waiting for him, both looking angry. Not that he blamed them? More important, would they be forgiving?

"I'm sorry I didn't tell you everything I knew beforehand. In my job, like yours Jim, confidentiality is vital. I've known since the night in Comrie, when I told you about her husband and children, that Jenny had been to a house in Mallaig. Dan Trench took her there. The coastguard confirmed the wind and currents could have swept her from there to the Island. But we could find no reason for her being there, and none for her leaving."

"Surely you could have trusted me," Jim queried.

"I wanted to. What made it hard was your conviction she had lost her memory, and had told you all she remembered. I didn't want you to doubt her. I did warn you to watch for odd behaviour. Also I wasn't prepared to confront her with that information. I was heeding a warning given about tackling patients with memory problems. And because I wanted to see her reaction for myself when I told her what I knew, assuming you agreed to her being told."

"And if I'd said no?" Jim queried.

"I would have taken your advice. But as she had reacted pretty badly to the mention of Trench, and

Mallaig already, I was prepared to try without waiting for your permission. I called round this evening to see if she would talk to me. I got a fairly frosty response to most questions, and when I asked about Dan Trench she reverted to saying she could remember nothing. It's struck me that she's lying, but was still visibly shaken at the mention of his name."

Jim and Ellen made no comment so he continued with the information about the syringe, cheque book, cards and keys. When he'd finished he sensed Jim had accepted he'd acted with Jenny's best interests at heart. Ellen seemed less forgiving.

"I tried to phone her today. She hung up the minute she realized who I was," Ellen said angrily. "She needs friends and you've effectively cut her off from them."

"I've asked Anne to keep a watch over her," Jim said. "I'll phone Anne now and ask her to check if Jenny has calmed down since your visit."

"Give her time," Gavin said. "She'll come round."

"I wish I was so sure," Ellen said.

Jim came to Gavin's rescue. "Jenny probably has begun to remember. Her throwing me out wasn't all Gavin's fault. Our relationship was suffering already. Forgive him, please."

Gavin watched anxiously to see if her expression softened. He hated being out of favour.

"I know I was wrong, please don't let it stop us helping Jenny. I shall have to stay down here for a while, to see what transpires," Gavin said. "I'd like you to stay too. I can't explain my reasons, beyond internal office politics. I have to keep up the pretence I'm here on a golfing holiday. If you agree to stay we'll be near enough if she needs us, and won't be pestering her."

"Sounds good to me," Jim said. "What about you?" he added directing his question at his sister.

"Yes. But I'll send her a note to tell her I had no knowledge of your intention to violate her privacy. And if I had, I would never have agreed to let you."

Gavin nodded acceptance of her terms. If the letter would make her happy, then he had no wish to interfere.

Chapter 27

Dan was in a morose mood. For the first time in twenty years he felt vulnerable. Meticulous planning was his forte. He hated to leave anything to chance. The viability of his latest scheme worried him. It was complex, and involved more people than he liked to work with, all of which increased the risk of failure.

He ordered a pint and some sandwiches when Zandra walked in, added her drink to the order and moved to a corner table. Zandra and he had a strange friendship that had survived since their teens. A brief passionate affair had altered their attitude towards each other, but still occasionally they worked together. Zandra's valuable contacts were the reason he kept in touch and had arranged to meet. She looked fantastic. He had never seen her hair cut so short, or so blonde, but the style suited her.

"Why the new image?" he inquired.

"No particular reason, I wanted a change. Don't you like it?"

"It's brilliant," he said, and he meant it. "Did you get the stuff I wanted?"

"Yes." She gingerly pushed a carrier bag towards him. "Be careful! Are you sure you know what you're doing?"

"Of course I do."

"I wish you'd tell me what you're up to Dan? I hate it when you won't tell me what's going on."

"Nothing you need to concern yourself about. I don't suppose you're free tomorrow evening?"

"I could be, depends on what you want."

"Good, I'll take you to dinner."

"Dinner? Is that all?"

"Meet me here at seven. Better still, invite a couple of friends, we'll have a party."

"Are you sure you're not in trouble? It's not like you to want a crowd."

"Just do it!" he replied sharply.

"Sorry, I was hoping we'd have some time together, alone for a change," she said.

"There'll be plenty of time for that tomorrow."

They finished their drinks and sandwiches then Dan got up to go, carefully picking up the bag she had brought. "Meet you tomorrow evening, and don't forget to invite some friends."

Once he was back at his flat he worked carefully. The task took longer than he had expected but by breakfast time the following morning he was ready. He stared at the sheet of paper on the table. Perfect. He folded it and put it into a plain manila envelope. Then he fetched a thick, black felt-tip pen and wrote on the envelope and slipped both into a black bin liner. He swept up all the paper cuttings, glue, a reel of tape, and a few spare envelopes into the same bag. He rummaged in the kitchen cupboard and found a supermarket carrier bag into which he placed a jiffy bag parcel, and a neat black box that had been sitting on the coffee table. He put the bags down by the door and removed his gloves.

He was satisfied with his achievements, and felt he deserved a drink. He had a quick look out of the kitchen window to satisfy himself he was not being watched, and made the call.

"Hello, Ron. Dan here. I'm having trouble with my car, any chance of using yours for an hour this afternoon?"

"Sure, shall I pick you up?"

"No. I'll get over to you."

"What time?"

"About three."

"That's OK, I'll be here."

"Sinclair has a job for you to do tonight. I'll give you the details when I see you. Goodbye."

Dan put the receiver down, closed his eyes and went through the whole plan again. All he had to do was make the hotel reservation. He dialled the number of the motorway hotel he had chosen, and made the booking for Ron. He checked he had enough cash, and everything else was ready. He put on his gloves again, and carried the bags down to his car, laying them on sheets of old newspapers, which were lying in the boot. He slipped the gloves off, wedging them in the corner, before shutting the lid.

He got into the car, drove to a pub he liked two miles outside Sterling, and ordered himself lunch. Afterwards he checked his map, and drove towards Ron Hill's flat. He drove round until he found a suitable parking space on the edge of a busy supermarket car park, about half a mile from Ron Hill's flat. He walked the rest of the way.

A few minutes after three he got there, perfect timing. The television was on and a football match in progress. Ron, eager to get back to watch the television, handed over his keys without a word. It was obvious Ron resented the interruption to his afternoon's entertainment. Dan was delighted.

"Go easy on the beer," he said, "You've got a long drive tonight. I'll be back in about an hour."

Ron grunted.

Dan drove straight back to the supermarket car park, to fetch the smaller carrier bag from his car. As he drove out of town he spotted a key cutting shop. He pulled up, took the spare keys off Ron's key ring, took them in and asked for duplicates. Then he found a quiet spot to park. He put on his gloves before he opened the bonnet and set to work. No one disturbed him and within fifteen minutes he was finished. All he had left to do was to give Ron his instructions and wait.

Chapter 28

It was nearly a week since she had evicted him and Jim had so far, resisted the temptation to charge back. Gavin had actively discouraged him, and his fear of her rejection becoming irrevocable had made taking Gavin's advice seem like the only sensible choice.

That was, until he had spoken to Andrew McPherson on the phone. Andrew let slip there had been a request for a copy of Jenny's file to be sent to her doctor. Jim knew something was wrong, and was desperate to find out. He mentally scanned her notes trying to remember every detail he had written on them, wondering what her doctor would expect to find in the files. Or more important, what did he need to know?

"It's no use," thought Jim, as he threw back the rumpled sheets, where he had tossed and turned sleeplessly all night. "I'll have to go and find out for myself." The decision made, meant there was no point in delaying. He dressed quickly, and left the hotel without waking the others. All he had to do was get her to let him in.

The stillness of the early morning struck Jim as he parked. He stepped off the gravel path and walked along the edge of the lawn. The crunch of the frosted blades of grass being crushed by his weight was almost deafening, but Jim paid little heed. His goal was near. He wanted to be on the back step with the milk so when she opened the door he could surprise her. He prayed she'd be up soon. The air was bitterly cold, and he found himself taking short gasps as the freezing air seared his lungs and created clouds of condensation with every breath he exhaled. He shivered. She usually rose early, he hoped today she wouldn't oversleep or alter her habit of fetching the milk and the newspaper before doing anything else. The sky lightened, and eventually the first glimpse of sun emerged with a glorious golden glow and the frosted garden sparkled.

A light went on upstairs. He heard the sound of footsteps entering the kitchen. Alerted he shifted his position, ready to make his move. As predicted she came to the back door, opened it and reached out, sleepily groping for the milk bottle. It wasn't there. Jim stepped forward, bottle in hand, and using surprise to his advantage crossed the threshold before she could protest.

"We have to talk," he said. She closed the door and nodded.

Taking the initiative, Jim asked, "Shall I make some coffee?" She shook her head.

"Tea?"

She nodded but made no effort to throw him out. He watched her every move as she sat herself down in her favourite chair at the kitchen table. He filled the kettle, and stood by the Aga warming himself while he waited for it to boil. Jenny seemed to have forgotten he was there. She fiddled with a pile of unopened letters in front of her. He presumed she must have picked them up from the front door mat before coming for the milk. It struck him as odd that she seemed more bothered by the post than by his presence. Quietly he poured the boiling water into the teapot, and waited a while before taking it to the table. She sifted through the envelopes a dozen times before picking one to open, there was no doubt the contents disturbed her, what little colour she had in her cheeks drained away as she read the letter. She was so engrossed he got the impression she had forgotten he was there. He carefully put the pot down, noting how flustered she became when she saw he was looking at the letter in her hand. A fleeting look of panic crossed her face as she stuffed the sheet of paper back into its envelope, and hastily shoved it back into the depth of the pile of unopened and discarded letters.

Jim pretended he hadn't noticed her actions and turned away to fetch the cups, as he put them down, he asked, "Are you sure you're all right?"

"I will be very soon," she answered abruptly.

Her reply puzzled him, but he let it go. He felt so out of touch. They drank the tea in silence. Neither of them wanted confrontation and silence was safe. He tried to behave as he had before he'd been thrown out, he opened the bread bin, and asked, "Fancy some toast?" Her reaction was unexpected. She shot from the table into the cloakroom off the hall. He could hear her retching violently.

He was angry with himself. How could he have missed such obvious symptoms? Her loss of appetite, slight dizzy spells, her refusal of coffee in favour of tea, all added up to one logical conclusion. Morning sickness.

How long had she known? Did she know? If she did, why keep it a secret? He knocked on the cloakroom door and asked if there was anything he could do for her. All he got in reply was a very firm response, "leave me alone." Frustrated, he returned to the kitchen to wait for her.

He was hurt and worried by the fact that she had failed to inform him of her condition, feeling he had a right to know, as it was his child too. The request for her notes from Andrew made more sense now, but he couldn't shake off the feeling there was more to it? Jim puzzled over her behaviour, something didn't fit. Then he remembered the letter. What was in it that had made her panic when she had seen him watching her? He rummaged in the pile until he found it, studied the envelope for a moment, it was plain white, high quality paper, with a typed address and a local postmark. He was about to give in to his desire to find out what it contained when she returned to the kitchen. Jim slowly replaced the unread letter on the table, assuming that it had been confirmation of her pregnancy. A glimmer of hope came to him. She been waiting for confirmation before breaking the news to him?

"Why didn't you let me know about the baby?" he asked. There was a long silence. He broke it, by saying quietly, "As its father, I have a right to know."

"You have no rights as far as I'm concerned," she replied sharply.

"Jenny I love you. I want to help you and the baby."

"I don't need any help. Anyway you wouldn't be able to help me," she murmured.

Jim took a deep breath, he was going to have to go along with her or he would lose her altogether.

"Let's not argue Jenny. I am here to help, in any way you want."

"I can't believe you really mean that," she answered quietly. Jim was about to repeat his offer but a telephone call interrupted their discussion.

"Wonder who that is," Jenny muttered as she rose to answer it, "seven thirty is a bit early to be ringing." She left the room, and closed the door behind her.

How could he restore communication with her? Perhaps he was making some progress, he was still here, but he wasn't feeling very secure. It would only take one mistake to be thrown out again, and he'd never get another chance to get her to accept the support she needed.

As Jenny re-entered the kitchen, he inquired, "Who was it?"

She didn't answer. She looked frightened and rather shaky.

"Jim, I need... I have to...," then she hesitated seemingly lost for words, then suddenly managed, "I must go and get dressed." With which she shot out of the room, so fast he never got a chance to speak.

He heard her moving about in the room above him. Her footsteps sounded hurried, different to her usual pace in the mornings. He didn't even manage to refill his cup, before she was back in the kitchen, still buttoning up her blouse.

"Can you go and get Gavin. I need to talk to him."

"I'll phone him."

"No," she snapped.

"We have to talk. About us. If I phone then it will give us time," he argued.

Jim, please. I have to speak to him first and I need a few minutes alone."

"If I go, will you promise you'll talk later?"

"Yes. But please go."

Jim was torn between the desire to stay, and the desire not to upset her. Trust, that's what was needed between them. He wanted to believe she would talk to him if he went and fetched Gavin. But couldn't understand her sudden urgency to speak to him? Was it the phone call? It could hardly be that he'd found out she was pregnant. He reluctantly accepted her ultimatum and went to his car knowing she was watching his departure from the window.

Chapter 29

She had gone. He had been a fool to leave her. He should have stood his ground and insisted on phoning Gavin. He had driven as fast as he dared back to the hotel. Gavin had already left. Jim decided then not to waste any more time in pursuit, and had left Ellen with the task of locating Gavin and had returned to the cottage. Too late. She had already vanished.

She hadn't even bothered to lock the back door. He wandered round the cottage. It had changed. She had moved things about. What? Why? The more carefully he looked and thought about the changes, the more obvious they became. She had removed everything personal. The photos had gone off the mantelpiece in the lounge, so had her collection of ornaments. In their place were dried flowers, shells, and some very simple candlesticks, all very neat, the effect impersonal, the sort of glossy magazine look totally lacking the homely atmosphere that impressed him the first time he entered the cottage.

Curiosity led him upstairs to her room. Again there were changes. The dressing table had been cleared, and he found her wardrobes were almost empty. All that remained were a few very basic items of clothing. What had she done with the rest? He knew the cupboards had been bulging with clothes when he had brought her back. He had a quick look in the room he had used. That was unchanged. He reached the door to the children's room. The patches of missing paint on the door where a pair of name plaques had once had pride of place, should have prepared him. He was astounded by the change, the room had been stripped right down to the carpet, and the freshly painted walls were stark, clinical white.

Obliterating the past was one thing. This was rather drastic. True he had thought it unhealthy to keep the room as a shrine to their memory, but what had driven her to this extreme.

He heard a car engine running and thought it must be Gavin arriving. He looked out of the window and caught a quick glimpse of a man climbing into the driver's seat of a blue Volvo, the car moved off before the driver had even closed the door properly. He was too concerned about Jenny's disappearance to give the matter any further thought.

He heard another car. This time it was Gavin. Jim went downstairs to open the front door. There was a parcel wedged in the letter basket. He went to pull it out, but it was too big and firmly wedged in place by the draught flap. He opened the door, waved to Gavin, who was pulling into the driveway. He turned back to try to dislodge the parcel from the outside. He tugged. Nothing happened. It was well and truly stuck. He tugged again. He heard the sound of paper tearing, but as there was no other way of getting it out, he gave another tug.

The blast threw him ten feet clear of the doorstep. The solid oak door was blown out complete with its frame, landing heavily across his legs, pinning him to the ground. Windows on either side of the door and on the landing above shattered, spraying glass in every direction, becoming embedded in the lawn and flowerbeds, jagged edges exposed, ready to inflict further damage to the unwary. The smaller debris resembled a sprinkling of sugar adding to the sparkle of the early morning frost.

Jim lay there, not quite sure what had hit him. He opened his eyes to find Gavin hovering over him.

"Jim, can you hear me?"

"Yes," he groaned.

"Thank God for that. Lie still. There's an ambulance on the way. I've got to get Jenny out."

"She's not there. Get this off me."

"I can't it's better to wait for help. Are you sure she's not in there?"

"Yes."

"Where is she, then?"

"I don't know. She disappeared when I came to find you."

Jim watched as Gavin moved off, giving orders to the arriving ambulance crew, and firemen. He could see the thatch above the porch was burning, the acrid smoke billowing overhead, blocking out the sunshine. All he wanted was for someone to come and shift the weight off his legs. He thought he could do it himself, and that's when the pain kicked in, and he registered how badly his hands had been caught by the blast. Carefully he raised one hand, tested each finger in turn, then the other hand. All his fingers were intact, though the skin was starting to blister and swell out of proportion. He knew it would take weeks before he would be able to do much with either of his hands. He moved his head, but couldn't move his body, because he needed his hands to lever himself up, and they were useless. The heavy oak door was pinning him to the lawn. The solidity of it had no doubt saved his life, even though it now lay with its inner surface splintered, ripped apart by the explosion. But his greatest fear was the lack of pain in the lower half of his body.

People were surrounding him. The pain in his hands was becoming unbearable. His head was ringing from the noise of the blast. His greatest anxiety continued until the door was lifted off his legs. When it was, he felt an excruciating pain in one leg. To Jim it was a marvellous sign, an indication he was not paralysed.

Chapter 30

"I know it's difficult, but it must be hushed up," Gavin argued. He had been battling for what seemed like hours, to get them to get Roland Hughes to agree to hold back information from the press. "We know it was a bomb, but can you tell the press it was a gas cylinder explosion."

"Why?"

"To give us time and have a better chance of finding the person responsible."

Roland Hughes was reluctant to agree. "They're not fools. Think of the panic it could cause."

"It might cause some alarm, but even if you only hold out until we find Jenny and give her the protection she obviously needs it would help. Then you can tell them anything you like, except of course that she's somehow connected with the house at Mallaig," Gavin answered.

"You think she must know something to have become a target? I don't suppose she'd have kept all those notes in her house if they were likely to incriminate her."

"Talk to her neighbour. She might have some ideas."

"You do that, while I try to match up her lists with the lists of stolen goods I'll see what pressure I can exert to get more men on the investigation. Then we can try to connect your theories concerning a connection between Mallaig and the explosion. Don't worry once we've located her, she'll be given our protection," Inspector Hughes said.

There was a knock on the door. A message was handed to Gavin. There was a call from Ellen.

"Looks as if the job is being made easy for us, Jenny's been found. Here's the address," Gavin said as he handed over the slip of paper to Roland Hughes, before reaching for the phone. "Get someone over there fast."

Gavin was eventually connected to Ellen who had been hanging on patiently. "How did you find her?" he asked.

"It was Jim. He made me take him to the cottage. He kept on about a letter she had been looking at. He didn't give me a choice."

"I thought he was supposed to stay in the hospital overnight."

"He was, but he discharged himself, and said if I didn't take him he'd walk."

"How did he get in?"

"He got the spare key from Anne. Anyway he found the letter. She's gone to have an abortion."

"His child?"

"He didn't say, but I think so,"Ellen answered her voice breaking as she spoke. "I left him talking to the doctor. He's going to try to stop the procedure. If he fails I think it'll break him. I've never seen him in such a desperate state before."

Gavin wished he could console her. All he could do was try to be reassuring. "Don't worry. He'll be all right."

"Jim said he remembered seeing a man get into a blue estate car moments before he found the parcel."

"Are you sure?"

"Yes. Does it help?"

"Possibly, one of the cars at Mallaig was blue. We'll check it out. I'll get onto Paula Dawson, straight away. After that I'll come over to the clinic to see how you're getting on."

"Thanks."

"Perhaps we can arrange for Jim to stay there as a patient. He really shouldn't be charging about in his condition."

"I would be grateful if you could, but I won't bear any grudges if you fail, he can be very stubborn," she answered in a challenging tone.

It was clear from her comment she expected Jim would be reluctant to be admitted to any hospital, but Gavin was determined to rise to the challenge. It was an opportunity to restore her faith in his ability to be caring, which had been so badly damaged when Jim had been thrown out of Jenny's cottage.

"I'll try."

As soon as he reached the clinic, he was ushered in to see Dr. Matthews.

"Tell me more about Dr. Cullen. What exactly is his relationship with Jenny Marshall?" the doctor asked.

"What do you mean?" Gavin asked, surprised at the line of questioning and the tone.

"Is he the father of her child?"

"What difference would it make?" he asked boldly.

"His career is on the line. He told me a long story about Mrs. Marshall losing her memory, and how she'd not fully recovered. He said you could confirm that fact."

"Well I can, I've been working with him since we found her and have been having a tough time trying to find out what happened to her and what caused her loss of memory. So far we've had little success. As for the matter of whether it is his child or not, I can assure you he's too professional to let that affect his medical opinion."

"Good, I'm glad you said that, and were able to back up his story. I was concerned that I might have to take disciplinary action."

"Never mind disciplinary action, what he needs at the moment is hospitalisation. He discharged himself this morning, because he was so concerned about Mrs. Marshall, and he's in no fit state to be out and about."

"Don't worry, he's already been admitted." The phone on his desk started ringing. Dr. Matthews picked it up, and said sharply, "I'm with someone. Oh. Yes he's here. I'll put him on." He held the receiver out. "This call is for you. Paula Dawson, I think she said. Will you excuse me? I have something to attend to. I'll be back shortly."

"A bomb explosion on the motorway. No I hadn't heard. But what's the connection?" Gavin asked.

"It was a blue estate car. I think it could be the one from Mallaig."

"Are you sure?"

"No, I haven't done anything about checking it. The person you need to talk to is Inspector Waverly at the Birmingham Station. He's keen to rearrange your round of golf."

"What?"

"Sorry, it seems Angus got his wires crossed and double booked. He'll explain everything if you call him."

"Is someone in the office with you?" Gavin asked, puzzled by Paula's message.

"Yes. Are you ready to take down his number?"

"Yes, go ahead."

Gavin frantically scribbled the number down and queried, "Does anyone there know you've made a connection?"

"No, I don't think so," Paula answered.

"Good. What I want you to do is forget you know anything about it. Since the bomb blast at Jenny's cottage I've got plenty of support here, and we can check out his address without Sinclair knowing. I need you to keep an extra close watch on those crates."

"Fine, I hope you have a good game."

"OK. I'll let you know what we find out. And thanks Paula, great work spotting the connection."

Gavin put down the phone, and wondered what else could happen. No sooner had he sorted out one problem, a whole lot more appeared. He made his way back to the reception area where Ellen was patiently waiting. He put his arm around her and gave her a hasty kiss on the cheek. "Sorry, I have to desert you again. Can you cope here with both Jim and Jenny? Jim can stay and Roland Hughes is arranging for police protection for Jenny, so you won't be on your own. Something's come up which may lead us to the bomber."

Chapter 31

Dan Trench reached across the bed and peered at Zandra. His head ached from lack of sleep, and his mouth was dry, even though he had been careful not to drink too much the night before. He'd wanted to keep a clear head for the two vital calls he had to make at dawn. He slipped out of the bed and out of the room closing the door quietly behind him. Then he made the first call. He had to ring the number in Devon to make sure Jenny was there, after which he'd spoken to Ron Hill at the motorway hotel, and instructed him to deliver the parcel within the next half hour. Having done that, he climbed back into bed with Zandra.

Zandra had organised a memorable party. It was like old times, too much booze and not enough food, and very loud music. He hadn't intended bringing her back to his flat to sleep. Now he was glad he had. It was good having company again, he spent too much time on his own, and he could use her today. She was just what he needed to get the job done right.

She groaned. "Go away, leave me alone."

"Sorry," he said, as he ran his hand over her naked shoulder. "We've got things to do."

"What. Are you mad?" she muttered as she focused on her watch. "It's too early to get up," she said as she burrowed deeper under the bedclothes.

Dan remembered how difficult she could be in the morning. He propelled himself out of bed, threw on some clothes and went to get her a cup of coffee. Perhaps then he would make some headway with her.

He made it strong, black and very sweet, the way she used to like it. Then he tried again. "Sit up. Here's some coffee."

Reluctantly she stirred. Even with tousled hair and smudged mascara she was attractive. Dan wished he could climb back into bed with her, but there was too much to be done.

"Thanks," she muttered as she grasped the mug in her hands and took a sip. "Why don't you leave me here? I promise I'll stay until you get back."

"Sorry, I need your help."

"I knew I'd regret coming here," she said. "You haven't changed at all. You think because I agreed to get those explosives for you and because I slept with you, that you can order me about. Well you can't, I'm not getting involved in whatever you're mixed up in. I thought I had made that clear last time."

Dan shook his head. "You've got it wrong. I don't think that at all. But I still need your help."

"What for?" she asked.

"I have to get something out of a store, and I need you to exert your charms to distract the man in charge. I promise it won't take long, and there is no risk at all."

"And what makes you think I can do it?"

"Don't be daft. Wearing the outfit you wore last night would be enough to distract an army of men."

"No. I won't do it."

"Not even to help me get one over on Sinclair?"

"Sinclair, are you serious?"

"Yes. I've been trying to get him off my back for years without success. I'm pretty sure he's planning to double cross me and I intend beating him at his own game."

"I don't believe I'm hearing this."

"You will help won't you?" Dan pleaded.

"Yes, but only because I can't resist an opportunity of getting back at Sinclair. Tell me what you need done."

Dan smiled, he had her hooked. Now it would be easy, all he had to do was get into the store, unload the specially packed crates into the bay next to the ones he had delivered from Mallaig. As soon as he was sure Zandra had the foreman's attention he'd swap four of the crates from one bay to another. After that, he'd make a fuss to be sure that everyone saw him depart with an empty van. That way, he could get the second load collected from the store during the week, without rousing any suspicion. Sinclair wouldn't find out until later, by which time Dan planned to be well out of his reach. It was a pity he wouldn't be there to see the expression on Sinclair's face when he found out.

"Come on, tell me what you have in mind for Sinclair," Zandra said.

"You don't need to know any details. I promise you he will hate it. What we do need, is for you to get dressed, and quickly."

"Ok. But don't rush me too much."

Dan sat on the edge of the bed and watched her dress, until she suggested he'd be better employed finding her something to eat, and refilling her coffee. While he waited for the toast to pop up, he made a phone call, to check the van he had hired had been collected. It had. He went back to the bedroom to hurry Zandra up.

He was certain no one was following them when they left his flat. But he still kept watching. The van he had booked for the day was already parked outside the lock-up garage he had rented. He quickly unlocked it and with the help of the van driver loaded the ten large wooden crates into the hire van. He locked up the now empty garage, and pulled down the van's metal shutter and slid the catches into place. Then he gave Zandra a hand up into the cab of the van. He winked at her. "You know what to do when we get there?"

"Yes, of course I do," she replied.

Dan got the driver to drive round the block twice to make sure no one had followed them, before giving directions to the storage warehouse. They pulled up and Dan went into the office to inform them of his arrival. Zandra followed him. The warehouseman went round and slid the vast door open so the van could reverse right up to the building, towards the bay he had reserved for them. Once the van was inside he slid the door shut, then walked down with Dan and pointed out the area where they could unload.

Zandra came in on cue, calling from the office door, "Is there a ladies' toilet anywhere that I could use?"

The man looked flustered he obviously didn't get many female visitors to the warehouse, and none that had ever worn such provocative clothing. He started to call out directions, but Dan interrupted.

"You'd better show her. She has a hopeless sense of direction."

He had obeyed without question, leaving Dan and the van driver alone. They quickly unloaded the crates and then Dan selected the ones to be exchanged with the crates he had packed and stored previously. He checked to see if the warehouseman could see them, but he had not yet returned from his mission of mercy. Dan chuckled, Zandra always enjoyed leading a man on, though she didn't always know when to stop.

He and the van driver got back into the cab and hooted. His signal to Sandra the job was nearly over. She knew to take her time, so Dan climbed down and went into the office. Zandra was perched daintily on the edge of a desk displaying more leg than was actually necessary. She was clutching a chipped mug of steaming coffee and had evidently charmed the young man into completely forgetting his duties.

"I see you've made yourself comfortable." Dan said accusingly to her as he entered the office. The young man blushed and started fumbling with papers, trying to hide his embarrassment at being caught chatting up another man's girlfriend. "Get into the van," Dan added angrily. The poor man was getting more and more flustered as he searched for the docket that Dan had to sign. Then he found it and began looking around for a pen. Dan put him out of his misery, and produced one from his pocket, signed and went to get back into the van cab. He stopped for a second to look at his watch. It was missing. He called across to the van driver.

"Fergus, I've lost my watch. Can you open the back up for me so I look for it? It might have dropped off when we were unloading one of the crates I remember it catching on something."

Both of them moved to the back of the van, Zandra was already sitting in the driver's cab. The warehouseman followed them. The driver raised the tailgate and clambered into the back of the empty van. "Here it is!" he called, waving the missing watch in the air.

Dan feigned delight. He had known exactly where his watch would be found, because that was where he had planted it.

"I've found it," The driver said, as he jumped down. "I was worried we were going to have to search down at the bay. Sorry we've taken up so much of your time," he said. "You can open the gates and let us out now."

Dan looked nervously up and down the street as they pulled out. There was no sign of anyone in pursuit, and he sighed with relief.

Zandra was quiet until they were out of the van and back in his car.

"Are you going to tell me what all that was about?"

"No," he replied firmly. "You'll find out soon enough."

"In other words, if I want to find out, I have to hang about."

"Exactly."

"Well I might just do that," she replied with a smug look on her face.

Chapter 32

His mind drifted from one thing to another, but kept coming back to the fact he had something important to tell Jenny. What was it? Where was she? It was somehow connected with a letter. A letter that made him discharge himself from the hospital, even though Ellen tried to stop him. He closed his eyes tightly, and then he visualized the letter, it was the one Jenny had stuffed back into the pile on the kitchen table. Then his confusion ended. He remembered clearly how he had forced his sister to take him to the cottage, and persuaded her to open the letter and read it. He recollected her exact words as they argued.

"You know I hate doing this. It's an invasion of privacy," she said, as she shuffled through the pile, stopping when he called out.

"That's it."

"Are you sure?"

"Open it," he had instructed, frustrated at not being able to snatch it from her and open it himself. How could he with his hands totally swathed in bandages? Her hesitation had nearly driven him mad. There hadn't been a choice. He had to find Jenny, intrusion or not.

The sickening feeling of horror he felt as Ellen read the contents swept over him again, as he remembered her words.

"Jenny has an appointment for an abortion."

The truth hurt, but explained Jenny's reactions to his offer of help. She assumed he'd read the letter, and that's why she acted so strangely. She knew his feelings on the subject of abortion. It was something they had discussed at length one evening on the island. She would have known he would try to stop her. Then he remembered there had been the mysterious telephone call. Who was it from? Why had she seemed so afraid? Sending him to fetch Gavin had been her way of avoiding the issue or had her need to see him been sparked by the phone call?

He had snapped impatiently at his sister, "When? Where? We've got to stop her. Please don't waste time. Find out from Anne where the clinic is."

"No. First we have to phone them and get them to delay it," she answered, no longer reluctant to help. He was so relieved to have her on his side and taking this seriously. She called the clinic, explaining it was vital for him to speak to the doctor in charge before they operated on Jenny Marshall. She even held the phone for him while he explained the need for a delay. Then she had gone over to ask Anne for directions. One of the things he loved about Ellen was that he could depend on her in a crisis.

He had limped into the clinic as fast as his plastered foot would allow, stopping only to announce his arrival at the reception desk.

"Dr. Matthews is waiting for you in the room at the end of the corridor," the receptionist had informed him. She suggested he use one of the wheelchairs parked in the corner of the entrance. He gratefully accepted, though he wished he'd been in a position to use crutches as it would have made him much more mobile.

"Well, at least they were expecting me, so they must have waited. Let's hope I can persuade Jenny not to proceed," Jim said to Ellen as she wheeled him down the passage and opened the door for him saying, "I'm going to call Gavin, I'll come back, wait here for me."

"I don't have much choice, do I?" he replied.

Dr. Marshall was waiting for him. "You had better have a very good excuse for disrupting the days schedule by demanding we postpone Mrs. Marshall's termination. She was already under anaesthetic, waiting for us to proceed." His angry glare and aggressive tone put Jim on alert. This wasn't a man to cross.

He had never been through anything like this before to prepare him for the ordeal ahead. He could see the man facing him was not concerned about his appearance. His bedraggled unshaven face with its myriad of little cuts from the flying glass, and his hands cocooned in huge bandages and the plastered foot didn't appear to rouse even the slightest sympathy or curiosity from the man he confronted. This Doctor was more concerned for Jenny than anyone else, which had to be good. But instinct stopped him from explaining his personal involvement with Jenny. He had to argue this case on medical grounds alone, or he would get nowhere. His fingers throbbed, his ankle ached, and he had a blinding headache. These he ignored in his determination to argue his case on professional grounds. Steadily he outlined what little he knew of her medical history relating to the recent past since she had appeared on the island. He slightly exaggerated his concern over a few points, which he thought might sway this man into holding up the operation.

"I was aware of the amnesia, I must admit I was under the impression it was less severe. How can it affect her decision?"

"When she was found, she had been badly beaten and been drugged and was suffering severe withdrawal symptoms," Jim answered. "It could lead to complications with the anaesthetic."

"Why would that affect her decision, she wouldn't have known about the complications. Is there another reason why you think she shouldn't have an abortion?"

"I think her decision is based on the assumption the pregnancy occurred prior to her losing her memory. She's unaware I have proof to confirm the child was not conceived until later," Jim said. "Without this information she may regret her decision. That's why I want you to hold back?"

"She seemed to be so definite. I always counsel my patients well before agreeing to perform the operation, and she was the most positive one I've had for a long time," Dr. Matthews answered.

"Please, if it's a matter of costs or blame, I'll sign a release for you. I'll take full responsibility for everything, including payment if she decides to go ahead," offered Jim, aware that the doctor was mulling over all the complications, both legal and ethical, of going ahead or waiting.

"If I'm wrong, at least she can still proceed, but, if you continue it will be irreversible."

"Are you the father of this child?" he demanded.

Jim knew this answer would influence the decision, so he said in as calm a tone as he could muster. "The identity of the father is immaterial. Her mental well being is all that matters."

"All right, you win your argument, but with one condition," Matthews said.

"Anything," Jim replied hardly believing the man had capitulated so readily.

"You'll have to be present when I tell her."

That was it. That was all he had to do. Be there when she was told her operation had been postponed. "Fine," he answered, as his pain took over.

Where was she? Would they call him? He tried to sit up, the effort was too painful. He lay there thinking of the hundreds of things he wanted to tell her. The most important being, he loved her. Would she forgive him for stopping the termination? The longer he waited the more sure he became, that while abortions were something he considered to be totally unacceptable, if she insisted on going ahead, even though without a doubt it was his child, he would have to stand by her. He loved her too much to risk losing her.

His hands were hurting unbearably. The door opened and a friendly nurse appeared. Jim asked about Jenny.

"I don't think she'll wake for at least an hour. Dr. Matthews will be down before then. You might as well lie back and rest until he comes," she said as she adjusted his pillows, placing one on either side of him to rest his elbows on. The movement made him let out an involuntary gasp of pain.

"Don't worry, I'll go and get something to help with the pain," the nurse said as she disappeared.

The door reopened and Dr. Matthews strode in.

"I feel I owe you an apology," he said.

"What on earth for?" Jim asked, totally baffled by the change of attitude.

"My lack of belief in your story. I'm afraid I was inclined to think your motive might be personal."

"You mean, about the possibility it might be my child."

"Well yes, but I think I made a mistake."

"No, you didn't make a mistake. It is my child, but that isn't the reason why I wanted it stopped, every reason I gave you was true."

Dr. Matthews looked seriously at Jim. "You do realize that you've breached all the rules?"

"Right now, I don't care. Jenny's my only concern. If you think I've done wrong, then report me. I'm happy that I've acted in the best interests of the patient, regardless of who is in overall charge."

"Tell me why you dislike me so much," Matthews said.

"It's not personal, I simply hate what you do to earn a living," Jim replied. "You said I must be there when you tell her the abortion wasn't carried out," Jim added, trying to forget the agony of his hands.

"In view of what you have just said, I don't think your being there is such a good idea after all, I shall tell her myself. I'll let you know her reaction."

"I must go to her."

"Later. Your friend Inspector McKay has asked me to keep you here until he comes to talk to you. She's quite safe, nothing will happen to her. In fact, she's under armed guard. So relax. They'll give you something to ease the pain in your hands. Then you must rest."

The pain was becoming unbearable. Jim only faintly recollected the nurse reappearing and giving him an injection.

When he woke again Dr. Matthews loomed over him and informed him that Jenny had been told of the decision not to proceed and had taken the news very badly. "She seems to have withdrawn into herself. And when I suggested I get you to come and talk to her she made it very clear she didn't want to see you."

"Get my sister, Ellen to try and talk to her," Jim answered weakly, vaguely aware of more medication being administered.

Eventually the nurse reappeared, bustling about in a cheerful way. "Glad to see you're awake," she said, then became very apologetic. "I hope I didn't hurt you too much yesterday when I took the bandages off."

"I don't remember it," he answered. "How long have I been here?"

"Two days. Sorry I couldn't give you a shave because of all the cuts on your face. They're all healing nicely now. Sit up and I'll give you something to eat."

Jim found himself being propped up and spoon fed. It was such a frustrating experience being totally dependent on someone to feed him. He looked at the huge bandages covering his hands. He could imagine exactly what his hands must look like without them.

"Are they healing all right?" he asked.

"Beautifully, but you're going to have to be very careful not to bang them on anything. If you feel up to it I'll take you down to see Mrs. Marshall. I must warn you she isn't talking to anyone. The only person she'll allow near her is your sister, who thinks seeing you might make a difference to her state. I'll wheel you down later so you can see her."

He was shocked by Jenny's appearance. What hurt most was the way she lay cowering under the bedclothes. He tried to talk to her, but that made her burrow deeper under the covers.

Ellen came over and touched his shoulder tenderly. She looked tired. "Sorry, I thought it was worth a try. Let me wheel you back to your room." On the way she told him all he needed to know. "Dr. Matthews is very worried about her. She's been curled up like that since he told her he'd cancelled the operation."

"Has he fixed another date?"

"No. He says he can't while she's like this. She hasn't actually asked him to. In fact she hasn't spoken to anyone at all."

"What does Gavin have to say about it?"

"Nothing so far. He had to go up north. I gather he's been talking to Dr. Matthews about the possibility of Jenny going up there. And Matthews won't agree until she's calmer and he's talked to you about it."

Chapter 33

"You never did get round to explaining how your sergeant, Paula Dawson, discovered so quickly that the car belonged to Hill." Roland Hughes said.

"Oh I'm sorry, I forgot to explain. When I sent Paula off to check the registered addresses of the Mallaig vehicles, one of the owners said he'd been asked about his car before. Paula talked to him about the possible existence of another vehicle bearing the same plates, and left him her phone number and asked the owner to call him if there were any further enquiries. And of course there were. After the explosion the local police were on his doorstep in minutes thinking they had terrible news to break to someone, only to find the man and his car were intact. He told them about my enquiry and gave them Paula's number which is how she found out and called me.

"It was lucky we found out so soon, and that my chief had already allocated a team of men to work under you on the explosion at the cottage. Inspector Waverley of the Midlands division was quite pleased it's someone from outside their area, even if they did have the awful task of dealing with the wreckage."

"Not an enviable one," Gavin commented. "But I'm glad he's being helpful. You have filled him in on my problems?

"Yes, and he's agreed to assist if needed.

He and Roland Hughes had spent the last forty-eight hours in each others' company, they had covered a lot of miles and drunk several gallons of coffee, and were slowly reaching the point where they could almost mind read each other.

"You're not happy, are you? You feel something is wrong?" Roland queried.

Gavin nodded. They had forensic proof both the bomb at Jenny's cottage and the one that destroyed the blue car on the motorway had been made with the same type of explosive. It had so far been impossible to identify the driver because of the mutilation caused by the blast, and complication of the false number plates, but both Gavin and Roland agreed Ron Hill was the most likely candidate.

"I guess I won't be happy until I have proof that it was Hill in that car. I'll be glad when the search of his place is over."

It had been a hard drive in pouring rain all the way to Sterling. It was nearly nine when they got there. The flat caretaker had a hostile attitude towards them, partly because they had disturbed his evening, and because Gavin sensed he disliked the police. But a quick hint that there might be explosives stored in the flat resulted in his full co-operation. Suddenly the man became a willing informant, rattling off details of Hill as a resident, even recalled the last time he had seen him and what he had been wearing, and when his car had last been parked in its usual place. Then he eagerly handed Gavin the keys to the flat, and firmly declined the invitation for him to join them in the search.

Almost the first thing they found was the note. It was lying face down on the kitchen table, with the envelope next to it. The envelope was clearly addressed in childishly printed, thick black, felt-tip pen. It bore two words, "Hector Sinclair" and it was this name that captured Gavin's attention.

"Take a look at this," he called out.

Roland came and stood beside him as he carefully, using his pen, turned over the sheet of paper lying beside the envelope. The letter had been constructed by using words and letters cut from newspapers and pasted onto the page. It read, "I'll tell them about Gillespie if you don't pay up."

There was something wrong with the letter.

"No I'm not happy," Gavin replied moodily. "It's too perfect."

"I agree.

"No one in their right mind would leave something like this lying on the kitchen table."

"Plus, it's all too clean and tidy. It doesn't fit with whoever lived here. The lounge is filthy, I doubt if they've had a vacuum in there for at least six months. I vote we turn this place over and see if we can find something useful," Roland said as he began emptying the nearest drawer.

Their search was thorough but didn't take long. Hill was not a hoarder. And the flat was devoid of any documentation, personal or otherwise. There was a selection of well thumbed porn magazines scattered round the sagging settee, and dozens of empty beer cans littering every flat surface of the lounge, along with several supermarket carrier bags stuffed with more empties. The bedroom was a mess, the bed unmade, a piles of clothes all over the floor. Gavin noticed a heap of leather garments, similar to the ones that Jenny had been wearing, they were in a variety of sizes, some looked as if they had been worn, and some still had shop tags on them.

In the kitchen area there was a single black bin bag, filled with the cut out magazines and newspapers, glue, scissors and four of a pack of five envelopes. One fact stood out clearly: it was the only black bag in the flat. Also noticeable was that there wasn't another sheet of plain paper in the flat. Ron Hill was not a letter writer, nor was he the sort of person who remembered to buy refuse bags.

"Well," Gavin said, "it must have been planted here. Whoever wrote the letter can't have been too keen on Sinclair. I wonder who hates him enough to try to frame him."

"Someone who knew about Gillespie, someone who wanted Jenny out of the way, and who knew that Hill was going to be out, or dead, because they must have known the flat would be searched. Perhaps they got him to deliver the first bomb, and had calculated the distance he would do, before the one wired to his speedometer went off."

"Whoever it was must have had a key," added Gavin. "There's no sign of forced entry, perhaps we should check with the caretaker if anyone else has been here asking for the key."

"I'll go down and ask," Roland offered.

"Fine, I'll take another look round then I'll come down, and we can go back to the hotel."

Roland was looking extremely pleased with himself when Gavin came down, and announced, "The caretaker has given us a lead."

"What?"

"A perfect description of Dan Trench, turns out he was here on Saturday, he borrowed Hill's car."

"How come he's so sure?"

"Because, Trench parked in the wrong place and this guy is a stickler with regard to parking places."

"Well, that is interesting. Dan Trench seems to be the only person who we know had contact with all three," Gavin said.

"Exactly," Roland answered. "But what the hell do we do about the letter? Handing it in will put your boss Sinclair on alert and you'll never be able to prove his involvement."

"Use it to set a trap," Gavin replied smugly.

"How?"

"Give the original to forensic. Get a copy made and let Fowler find it. See what he does."

"But what if he lets Sinclair know?"

"It doesn't matter if he knows, so long as he thinks we don't. And it might push him to go after whoever set it up."

"True, it would also prove how trustworthy Fowler is."

"What I propose is that we tell Paula to chase up the Mallaig car lead, and get her to bring Fowler here, she can report what Fowler does."

"Do you think Fowler will cover up for Sinclair?"

"I'm not sure, but it will be very interesting to see the result," Gavin said thoughtfully. "Perhaps we should sleep on it."

"Best suggestion I've heard," Roland answered. "Always better to make that sort of plan early in the day."

Gavin looked at his watch. "I didn't realize it was so late. I had intended phoning the clinic to find out how Jenny and Jim are doing."

"Rubbish you only wanted to talk to Ellen," Roland said, then added hesitantly. "There's one thing that had occurred to me. It's only a very vague possibility."

"What?"

"Could Jenny have had anything to do with planting the bombs?"

"Jenny? You must be joking!" Gavin burst out. "She couldn't have."

"Well I don't entirely agree. If she was involved with the robberies and knows we've tied her into it, she could have set up that parcel at the cottage."

"It's ludicrous."

"No it isn't. Jim getting blasted might not have been intentional. She might have wanted to make us think she was in danger. She could also have organized for Hill to be killed. I'm not saying that she necessarily did it on her own, but perhaps she had Dan Trench's co-operation."

"No I refuse to accept it as a possibility," Gavin answered gruffly.

"You're quite entitled to disagree. It was only a suggestion. I never had a chance to get to know her so I'm hardly in a position to judge. Still I do think some sleep would do us both good. So I'll say goodnight now."

Gavin retired to his room also. It was a typical roadside hotel, characterless, clinical, and positively unwelcoming. He didn't care. The comments Roland made kept coming to mind. He couldn't believe Roland had been serious, the more he thought about it the more feasible the idea became. That and the problem of whether he wanted Sinclair to be involved in the investigation and be made aware of the letter kept Gavin awake.

One major decision was made during the night. He had to get Jenny back to the Mallaig house. He needed to find out what went on behind the dark green shutters. Roland's suggestion of her complicity with Trench was one he found hard to dismiss. Perhaps she was using her memory loss as a ruse to cover up her involvement. And if she were, he would expose her. He had made an early call to Ellen, who had told him that there was little change in Jenny's condition. She was in what was medically described as a catatonic state. She refused to communicate with anyone at all. Physically she was nearly back to normal, and had started eating without being forced, but refused to talk. Ellen had also reported, with relief that Jim was getting back to his normal difficult self, as bad a patient as ever, which was to her a very healthy sign.

Gavin put down the phone, and made a second call. This time to his friend who had originally advised him about amnesia cases. He had to find out if it would be dangerous to bring Jenny back to Mallaig. He quickly described Jenny, the situation he was in and the state she was in. His ideas were in line with Gavin's. If she was faking her mental state, no harm would come of taking her to Mallaig. And if the loss was genuine, the sooner something snapped her out of it the better. Gavin was happier. Now he could approach Dr. Matthews and perhaps get him to agree to release Jenny into Ellen and Jim's custody, then they could travel up together, and see her reaction to Mallaig.

"Good morning, Roland. I hope you slept well. I didn't. I was too busy trying to decide what to do about Sinclair."

"Come up with anything?"

"I want to go ahead as suggested," said Gavin. "I want you to get a copy of the letter made, also get them to make up a second bin bag just like the one we found. I'll arrange for Paula to take Fowler to the flat. I'll get her to send Fowler into the kitchen on his own. He will either remove the letter and envelope without saying anything to Paula, in which case we know where his loyalties lie, or he'll ask Paula what to do."

"What if he hides it?"

"Then we watch Sinclair like a hawk, to see what he does about it. Remember Sinclair will think that no one else knows about it."

"Fine, I'll go and get that organized, it will probably take a couple of hours, because forensic will want to go over the flat first. Where will you be?"

"I'll be here, I have several more calls to make, I'm going to try to get Jenny brought back to Scotland and take her to Mallaig. I'll get on to Paula and tell her what's going on."

The conversation with Paula yielded more than Gavin had expected. Paula told him about the activity at the storage depot where her friend Fergus worked. He described how Dan Trench had reserved a bay next to the load he had delivered from Mallaig, and how he had engineered for Fergus to be distracted while he was unloading, by getting him to direct a very attractive short skirted blond woman to the toilets. And how during that time he had unobtrusively exchanged four of the crates from the original batch with the crates he brought in."

"If this chap was so distracted by this woman, how did he know what Trench did?" Gavin queried.

"He switched on the night security video and recorded the whole thing," Paula answered cheerfully. "We have it in black and white."

"And Trench didn't take anything out of the store?"

"Nothing. In fact he even staged a scene to make sure Fergus saw there was nothing in the back of the van when he left."

"Perhaps we had better get some sort of homing device attached to those crates."

"Already done,"

Gavin then went on to explain what Paula should do when she took Fowler to the flat. He outlined how she should to react if Fowler asked for advice.

Chapter 34

"What the hell do you mean when you say the letter implicates me?" Sinclair almost screamed down the phone.

"The letter didn't actually name you. But the envelope lying next to it was addressed to you. The letter said, quote, 'I'll tell them about Gillespie if you don't pay up.' That's all. But, without the envelope there was nothing to connect you. That's why I only took the envelope. But I thought I ought to tell you."

"Who else saw it?" Sinclair snapped.

"No one. Paula Dawson and I were the first people to go to the flat. She went to check the lounge while I did the kitchen. It was lying on the table, staring me in the face the minute I walked in the door. I managed to remove the envelope with your name on before Paula came in."

"Was there anything else lying around?"

"Yes, a bag full of rubbish, mainly the magazines and papers; things that had been used to find the letters and words to make up the note," said Steven. "I don't think there was anything in it with your name on, but I wasn't able to go through it without Paula becoming suspicious, she was anxious to leave everything as it was for the forensic people."

"Yes I understand," Sinclair said, as he tried to calculate how much damage had been done.

"But why was it addressed to you? And what the hell do I do with it? I know I shouldn't have touched it, but I couldn't leave it there."

"No. You did the right thing. Hang onto it for the moment, I'd like to have a look at it," Sinclair said gritting his teeth.

He knew he had been incredibly lucky that Steven Fowler had been the person to find it. And that he had reacted the way he had. But where did he go from here? He could hardly admit to Steven that the accusation was true. He was responsible for ordering Gillespie's death. And that meant that the person who had left the letter had to be either Trench or Hill. And he could narrow the guilty still further because he had known Hill for years, and knew that he was virtually illiterate, there was no way he could have found all the words, let alone strung them together in such a neatly implicating fashion. It had to be the work of Dan Trench. The man had some hidden agenda or something must have gone drastically wrong. Dan's attitude had been different ever since he'd found out Gavin McKay had been watching the house at Mallaig. What a cock up, just because of a drunken accusation made by Gillespie. The filthy old drunk was not content with causing trouble when he was alive, but Sinclair had not expected him to be a problem once he was dead. The frustrating part was that he would never find out what made Gillespie a threat to his operation in the first place.

"What do you want me to do?" Steven asked.

"Nothing at the moment, but stick with Paula Dawson and see what else turns up. By the way, you never told me why you went to that address. What were you looking for?"

"Paula thinks the chap who lives there, might have been the man who was killed in the bomb explosion on the motorway. There wasn't much left to identify him. But the car was the one used by one of the men who they had been watching at Mallaig."

"Who?"

"Hill. Did you know him?"

"I know who you mean," he answered cautiously adding, "but only from the information on the files. Who gave Dawson the order to go there?"

"I think she got the call from the Midlands force, trying to find out why we had asked for information on the car number. It appears that it had false number-plates, and the owner of the real plates had told them that there had been a recent query about his car. They checked back and found out the query had come from our office."

"Did she tell anyone else what she was checking?"

"I don't think so. McKay is away still, and as Paula had done the initial search for information, she figured she should follow it up."

"Quite right. Now what I want you to do is to keep me informed. I need time to figure out who would try to set me up like that."

"Not McKay?" Steven questioned.

"No, this is someone who wants revenge. Revenge on the police and on me in particular."

"Do you know who?"

"A vague idea, but let's leave it at that. Call me if you find out anything else. And thanks again for the early warning, and the evasive action," Hector said as he slowly replaced the receiver on its cradle.

He took a few deep breaths to calm himself. He had doubted Steven's loyalty, well now he knew that

Steven was on his side. And he needed friends. He'd called in too many favours recently, leaving him vulnerable. It was over a week before the shipment was due. It was too late to cancel it. Trench presented the biggest danger. Fortunately he didn't know the exact time and place of the exchange. And now Hector knew that he shouldn't be told. If Trench did find out, Hector knew the information would be enough to put him in danger. Hector had no intention of being betrayed by Trench or anyone else. But then he smiled. He knew where Trench had stored the goods, so Trench was the one at risk.

Hector grabbed the newspaper. The article about the motorway bomb hadn't captured his interest before. He'd assumed it was a terrorist bomb and never considered it might affect his life. It was no longer front page news in fact it had been reduced to a three inch single column on the fifth page. One puzzling sentence linked the blast with a parcel bomb that went off in Devon. The matter was no longer being considered as a terrorist attack. He could feel panic rising at the mention of a second bomb in Devon.

What the hell was Trench playing at? Worse still he was worried that Gavin McKay's sudden decision to go on a golfing holiday in Devon was somehow connected? Hector dug out the previous weeks papers and scanned the articles on the two explosions. The graphic picture of the wreckage of the car strewn across the three lanes of the motorway made him nervous. If Trench was responsible, and he was sure he was, then he was in grave danger himself.

Chapter 35

The car wheels crunched on the gravel as it drew up outside the shuttered house. She shivered as she registered where they were. Why had they brought her here? What were they hoping to find out? She could feel the perspiration forming on her forehead, and her heart racing. She wanted to yell at them to go back.

She was shaking, losing control. Her hand flew out and grabbed hold of Jim's arm. But she was unable to speak.

"Gavin, stop!" Jim called out, then turned to her and said gently, in that calm voice she loved. "Jenny, take it easy, no one is going to hurt you."

"What's wrong?" Gavin asked as he switched off the engine.

"Look at the state she's in."

"It shows she recognizes the place."

"Maybe, but there's no need to be bullish about it."

"Sorry. We need to know what went on here." Gavin said.

"Back off Gavin, what's so special about this house anyway?" Jim asked.

"Jim, one man, and possibly two have died, and you very nearly lost your life in a bomb blast, that could have been meant for Jenny. Well the only thing that connects the dead man and Jenny is this house.

And if the only way I get her to talk is to shock her, then that's what I'll do. And no one can stop me."

"Why are you so sure I've been here before?" Jenny whispered.

"I have a witness," Gavin answered slightly less sharply.

Her mouth was dry. Nothing made sense, especially a witness.

She shivered. Her nightmare was becoming a reality. For weeks she had been trying to convince herself none of it was real. But Gavin would never joke about people dying. She would have to talk. There was no escape.

She forced herself to take deep breaths. She had to stay calm to face the truth. And face it now.

Gavin spoke quietly to her. "Jenny, will you help? I have to know what happened here, and you're the only person who can tell me."

She let go of Jim's arm. Her fingers tingled as the blood began to circulate again. Gavin kept his eyes firmly locked with hers.

"I'll try," she whispered opening the car door and stepping out.

Jim moved, but she put out a restraining hand, and backed away. The house seemed even more menacing now. Was it because she knew the sinister secrets hidden behind those dark green shutters? She needed time. Turning she looked down to the water and the boathouse. Steadily she walked towards it. Yes, she remembered it well. It had been her one glimmer of hope, her only chance of escape.

"That's where I found the boat," she informed Gavin who had followed her down to the water.

"I thought it might have been," he replied then pointed to a stone seat. "Shall we sit?"

Jenny nodded glad of the seat which faced out across the water.

"Had you done much sailing before?"

"No. But I didn't have much choice."

"Why?"

"I thought he'd come after me. I didn't know I'd killed him."

"What?"

Poor Gavin she thought. He doesn't believe me. But can I blame him. I feel too calm. It doesn't feel right to be confessing to having killed someone while sitting enjoying a beautiful view.

"Who? Who did you kill?" Gavin asked rather impatiently.

If only she knew the answer to that one. Who was he? She didn't even know his name. She only knew that she hated him. Perhaps she was glad that he was dead.

"Jenny, for your own sake you must answer me. Who did you kill?"

"I only wanted to stop him so I could get away. I hit him, but he kept coming at me.

"Who?"

"I don't know, I think he might have been called Ron."

"Sorry Jenny, let's get this straight. You think you killed a man?"

"Yes."

"You're not sure of his name?"

"No."

"How did you do it?"

"I hit him with a statue that I found on the table on the landing."

"Are you sure you killed him?"

"No. I don't know. Maybe. He tried to come after me. So I hit him again. He was bleeding. There was so much blood. He must have been dead. But I was so afraid. I had to get away," she said quickly, feeling detached from the whole proceedings. It was as if someone else was talking in her voice.

"And all this happened here, in this house?"

"Yes. But I didn't mean to kill him."

"No, I'm sure you didn't."

They sat in silence for a few minutes then Gavin said softly. "I want to talk to the others. Will you stay here?"

"Yes."

She felt a strange sense of relief now that she knew the dream that had haunted her was real. Sharing her secret left her more at peace than she had been for weeks.

"Start by telling me what your connection is with Dan Trench," Gavin said on his return.

"He brought me here."

"But he's not the man you think you killed?"

"No."

"Never mind. Try and explain why it took you three days to get from Devon to here."

"Oh. We were travelling by chance on the same train and stopped for a night in Gloucester and a night in Carlisle."

"So Dan Trench and you were lovers?"

"No. It wasn't like that. We were just friends. I met him at the booking office, quite by chance, and he suggested, as I was in no particular hurry that I should stop my journey in Gloucester and have dinner with him. I know he didn't expect anything more than my company for dinner. I thought there'd be no harm in agreeing with his plan, he was good fun, and I felt sure he'd behave decently."

"And?"

"It was fine. Then we did the same in Carlisle. It wasn't until after he got his car back that he changed."

"How?" Gavin queried.

"First he made a phone call, said he had to go to his house for something, and I could get to Comrie by coach. I was being silly, and insisted on staying with him, and wouldn't accept no for an answer. I pestered him so much he eventually agreed, saying it wouldn't take him long to sort out his business then he would take me to Comrie. It seems so obvious now, that he didn't really want me along."

"Perhaps he thought you were ready to sleep with him. And that's why he brought you here?"

"I don't know. Maybe he did. The house gave me the creeps then, and it still does. I didn't want to go in, and wandered down here to the water while I waited for him to open it up. I saw the boat house, and remember thinking it must be beautiful in the summer but so gloomy in winter. He called me in, I noticed that the car had gone, I assumed he'd put it in the garage. I offered to help take down some of the shutters, but he refused, saying that it would be dark soon and it wasn't worth it as we wouldn't be staying very long." She stopped, she was getting more flustered, but there was no choice, she had to keep on with her story.

"I just wasn't prepared for it, I couldn't believe my eyes, inside is the most exquisitely furnished house I have ever stepped into. I love paintings and antiques and it's like walking into a museum. In the hall there was nothing out of place. I must have stood rooted to the spot for about five minutes before he showed me into the lounge. That's even more spectacular." She noticed the look on Gavin's face, which told her he was getting impatient with her descriptions.

"He left me in the lounge, and went to make some calls, I could hear him arguing with someone, but not what it was about. I wasn't in the least bit interested. I was far too busy examining the contents of the room. There isn't one piece not of the right period, right down to the books on the shelves in the bookcase which were mainly original, leather-bound, first editions. And there was an unbelievable picture over the fireplace, a stunning oil painting, a Scottish landscape."

"Cut out the details please," interrupted Gavin.

"It's by the same artist as the painting in Ellen's lounge."

"Sorry. I shouldn't have interrupted, but please get on with what happened."

"Well, he came back with some tea for me. Then he disappeared again. He had promised to show me around so I didn't think he'd mind if I went and explored on my own. As soon as I went into the dining room, I recognized a piece of china that was identical to one I had examined in Gorton Manor. I counted about ten other items I could identify. I commented on the coincidence when he came back and he went quite odd. I was so excited at being able recognize the things. I paid little attention to him at all. I was so busy enthusiastically chattering on about visiting Gorton, and how I remembered there had been a robbery at Gorton Manor since then and I wondered what had been stolen." She shook her head slowly. "I was so stupid I should have guessed and kept my mouth shut. One look at him confirmed the fact they were all from Gorton Manor, and he was well aware of it. I didn't know what to do or say, I'd said too much already.

I knew then I was in trouble. He saw me as a threat. What could I do? I was so scared. I tried to convince myself he had a good excuse for owning stolen goods. The longer we stood there without him making any excuses, the more convinced I became he was fully aware of their provenance. I tried to pretend I thought he must have bought them not knowing they were stolen. I pleaded with him to take me back to the nearest town, I would make my own way from there and I swore I would never breathe a word to a soul about what I had seen.

I'm not sure, but I think Dan would have taken me. I'm certain he never intended to hurt me. But the other man appeared. I knew at once he'd overheard our conversation, and as a result I was in serious trouble."

She bit her lips in an attempt to keep control, but it was too much for her, tears began trickling down her cheeks.

Gavin sensed she had talked enough.

"Let's take a break. I think Ellen has some coffee for you. Perhaps you could tell her about the boat if you feel like talking. I'll be back in a minute." He signalled to Ellen to come and sit with her, and set off towards the house. It was only then she spotted they had forced open the door.

As she sat sipping the cup of coffee Ellen had handed her she recalled Gavin's words about Jim and a bomb blast. She had been so isolated in her own silent world she hadn't even wondered why he had been covered with bandages. Now it mattered.

"Is Jim going to be all right?" she asked. "I have been so wrapped up in my own problems to notice what has been going on. You must think I'm heartless.

"Not at all, you've had a lot to deal with."

"That's no excuse."

"I think he'll be fine, although it's going to take a while for his hands to heal."

"Tell me what happened."

Chapter 36

"Are you going to arrest her?" asked Roland Hughes.

"No," Gavin answered.

"But she confessed."

"I know, but there isn't a body, and I am sure it must have been Hill, and we know he left here alive."

"What about all the blood?"

"She said she hit him and he was covered with blood. It doesn't mean he died. Even if we do find a body, I'd have to think twice about arresting her. Has anyone got a photo of Ron Hill on them?" Gavin asked. "I'm certain that's who she thinks she killed."

No photo could be found.

"What do you want us to do?" asked Roland Hughes.

"Go through the house with a fine comb. There must be something here that will help to tie in some names. I'll go back and see if she's ready to tell more."

Gavin made his way back to the bench where Jenny was sitting quietly staring out at the water.

Ellen got up as he approached and said, "I've explained about the bomb that injured Jim. She's devastated."

"OK. Thanks, perhaps you should go and see what Jim is doing. I want to ask Jenny a few more questions."

As soon as Ellen had moved away, Jenny turned to face him.

"Did you find him?"

"No. There isn't anyone there."

"But I know he was there. He was lying on the landing. I know he was dead. Anyway, you said a man had died, and you had a witness."

"Hold on, Jenny. I had a witness that you had been to the house. Nothing more. The man I was talking about died after you had been found, and you certainly had nothing to do with his death, though he was somehow connected to this house."

"You don't believe me do you?"

"Yes I do. But I don't think you killed anyone. Perhaps you should tell me why you wanted to. What did he do?"

One look at her expression was enough to indicate her reluctance to answer.

"Would it be easier to talk to a woman?" She shook her head. "Never mind, tell me instead about the boat."

Her story unfolded, as she explained her knowledge of boats was minimal. She hadn't cared at the time, nor had she realized how strong the wind was. She knew she had to escape. She had grabbed sail bags, lifejackets, anything she could lay her hands on, and had stuffed them into the boat, then somehow got the boathouse doors open, and succeeded in getting the little outboard motor started.

"It was getting dark, the water was rougher than I bargained for, I had no idea which direction I was heading in. I soon discovered I had no choice. I had to go with the wind and the tide as I hadn't the strength to battle against them. I couldn't risk being blown back here. Distance was all that mattered. It took so much effort to steer the boat, the waves were getting so big, and some splashed over the side as it plummeted up and down. The cold numbed my hands on the tiller. Then the real pain began," she faltered, looking at Gavin for comfort and reassurance.

"Tell me about it."

"They had been keeping me drugged, and as they wore off the cravings began. I didn't know what to do. I couldn't go back, and I wasn't sure I could go on. I must have had a moment of sanity, because I put on a lifejacket. I even remember making a half hearted attempt to raise a sail but the wind was far too strong, and I wasn't too sure how to do it properly. One sail was blown overboard and I nearly went with it. Finally the engine spluttered to a halt, and I was at the mercy of the wind and the waves. It was so dark I could see nothing at all, so I huddled up under a tarpaulin in the bottom of the boat. I cried and screamed, but no one could possibly have heard me over the howling wind. I was woken by a crash. The mast had snapped and the boat was sinking. I grabbed at the first floating object to hand, and wound a piece of rope round my wrist so I could rest my head on it. That's all I can remember."

"Well it all fits with the coastguards theory, the tide patterns that week made it possible for a boat to have been swept out into the main current and then up to the island," Gavin explained, wondering how to broach the subject of the time spent in the house prior to her escape. She had mentioned being drugged, he was sure she wasn't ready to talk about it, and that a lot more happened that she was reluctant to divulge.

"Can you tell me what drugs they gave you?"

She shook her head.

"Did they hit you?"

She shuddered. Her fists clenched, and she gnawed at her thumb nail. Then quite unexpectedly she stood up. "Can we go?"

He knew then that he wouldn't get any more answers from her.

"OK. But I want you to come into the house first."

"I can't," she protested.

"Sorry, you have to."

She knew he wasn't going to give in, and reluctantly allowed herself to be guided towards the house.

"Where's all the good stuff gone?" she said looking startled by the stark appearance of the hall.

"Could you describe the things that are missing?"

"Yes, but you don't believe there is anything missing, do you?"

"Yes I do. And I want a full list from you, not this minute, we can get the details later," he replied. "What other rooms did you go into?"

"The lounge and the dining room," she said indicating the two doors on the left hand side of the hall.

"They've stripped out all the valuable stuff. It was so beautiful with all that furniture, and the books, and that lovely painting," she said on entering the first room. "Is the other room the same?"

"Yes. But what about the other rooms downstairs?"

"I never saw them."

"Well, let's go upstairs," Gavin said leading the way. Jim was sitting on the fifth step, looking extremely haggard, and as if he was in considerable pain and in need of a rest. They all needed to rest, but first he had to get Jenny up the stairs, in the hope of getting her to fill in the remainder of her story.

Jenny hesitated on the bottom step.

"Come on," he coaxed.

"No!" she replied with determination, her gaze fixed on the upper reaches.

Gavin wondered how he could persuade her, but before he'd had any inspiration, Jim spoke.

"Go on Jenny, there's no need to look at me as if I'm about to rape you."

There was a deathly hush. No one knew quite how to react to cover their embarrassment. Jim struggled to his feet.

Jenny didn't flicker.

It was Ellen who shattered the silence. "Jim, how could you say that," she said sharply.

"Sorry," he murmured apologetically. "I don't know why I said it. Jenny, I didn't mean it. Forgive me." He turned to Gavin for guidance, as to whether he should go up or down the stairs to get out of her way.

"It's all right Jim. It doesn't matter," Jenny whispered, as she forced herself on, up the stairs, passing him and going onto the landing.

As soon as they were alone, Gavin asked if Jim's comment had hurt her because it had been too close to the truth. She nodded and begged him not to say anything to Jim.

"I won't, if you tell me exactly what happened here" Gavin answered, hating himself for resorting to blackmail tactics. "You said earlier you didn't think Dan Trench intended hurting you. But he did, didn't he?"

She shook her head.

"The other man?" Gavin queried.

She nodded.

"What did he do?"

She struggled to answer his question. What the hell had been done to her he wondered. He had to be patient, she had suffered enough, she would break soon, and he'd get all the answers he wanted. It took a while for her to summon up the courage to start again, but she refused to face him as she spoke.

"He grabbed my arm and started yelling at me, accusing me of being a police spy, or working for an insurance company or a newspaper. He twisted my arm until it hurt. I begged him to stop. But he didn't listen instead he forced me up the stairs, and shoved me into that room and locked the door. I heard him ranting and raving and there was an almighty shouting match going on downstairs, but I couldn't quite hear what they were yelling. I was so cold. The room had very little furniture in it, just a bed and a dressing table." Then she seemed to lose her courage.

"What happened when they came back?" demanded Gavin. He waited for an answer and when none came he tried again. "Which one came back first? Was it Dan Trench?"

"No."

"What happened?"

"He'd been drinking, and suddenly he was hitting me and tearing at my clothes. I tried to fight back, but he forced me onto the bed. I couldn't stop him. Oh Gavin why do people do it?" she sobbed.

"I don't know," he answered quietly.

"Afterwards, Dan came, he tried to apologize." She was crying quietly, her shoulders tensed up and she struggled to carry on. Gavin reached out, touching her, but she flinched away, obviously unable to bear being touched as she recounted her story.

"Then the other man came back. I could tell he'd had more to drink. He stood in the doorway laughing," she stopped and wiped her tears with the back of her hand. "It was a horrible, vicious laugh, he threatened Dan, told him to go and..."

She stopped, stared into space as she searched for words to describe what he had done to her.

"And he forced himself on you?" Gavin asked assuming if he could get past that point, he might discover more.

"Yes."

"What happened to Dan Trench?" Gavin queried.

"I don't know, I think I heard a car leaving. After that the other guy hit me," Jenny managed to answer.

"Then what?"

"I think I fainted I can't really remember, he wasn't there when I woke up, I could barely move, every part of me was hurting. I thought I was going to die. One time when he came back, he had a syringe in his hand. I didn't want him to give it to me. I don't know what it was, but the effect was awful. I thought it would take the pain away, but it made each bruise and bump hurt more. I thought I'd go mad." She turned to Gavin, tears streaming down her face.

"Sometimes he'd sit and watch me, laughing at my pain. After that things aren't very clear. He kept coming back, sometimes to beat me, sometimes to give me another dose of whatever it was. I think there was food. I remember feeling so cold I was sure I would die, and then feeling so hot. I know after a time I wanted him to come back, I knew I was hooked, I needed a dose. At times I felt dreadful, but the good drifting dreams it induced wiped out the bad times. I no longer talked about getting out or fought against his physical demands, my reward was to be able to go to the bathroom."

Gavin listened as she related the events, it all fitted with her condition when Jim had found her. She had gone on to describe how a trip to the bathroom had been her only chance of escape. When the door opened, she had pushed passed him and grabbed the statue off the table on the landing, and hit him.

"I really thought I'd killed him. He kept moving so I hit him until he stopped. And then I ran."

"OK, we'll stop now," Gavin said kindly, he could see she had reached the point where further questioning would be cruel. "I'll get Ellen to come upstairs and sit with you until we're ready to go. Later on, you can give us a description of the antiques you saw downstairs."

Jenny nodded agreement.

"There is only one other thing I'd like to know. How long ago did you remember all this?"

"I'm not sure exactly, I thought it was all a bad nightmare, and then Dan Trench phoned me. I think that's when I began to realize it had actually happened."

"Do you remember when he phoned you?"

"No. Yes. It was very early in the morning. Jim was there, he came back to see me. I sent him to find you."

"Why, just to get rid of him, or because you really wanted to talk to me?"

"I can't remember. Both I think, and then I was too scared to stay. I was afraid of Dan Trench, and even more afraid of admitting what I'd done."

Chapter 37

Dan read and reread the reports of the car bomb in the paper. They hadn't named Hill as the dead man, but they had made a connection between the car bomb and the one in Devon. All he had found out from the earlier papers was that only one person had been injured in the Devon explosion, an unnamed man.

The plan had failed. Time to run.

Revenge on Sinclair would have to be scaled down. If he removed his crates from the store, Sinclair would end up in trouble, because he wouldn't have enough goods to exchange for the drugs. Guessing how the suppliers would react made him chuckle. They would go mad. Sinclair was going to find himself in serious trouble. So much trouble he wouldn't have time to search for someone as insignificant as Dan Trench.

The doorbell rang. Dan reluctantly rose to answer it. The last thing he needed at the moment was company. He peered through the spy-hole. Zandra was standing there, running her fingers through her soaking wet hair, trying to shake some water out of it.

"Hurry up and let me in," she yelled, as he fumbled with the lock. "Thank God you're in. I nearly drowned out there. Have you a towel I could use?" she said as she bustled past him to help herself to a towel from the bathroom. She slammed the door shut, and shouted out, "Any chance of a coffee?"

Dan felt as if a tornado had entered his life. He had been crazy to get involved with her again. He could sense if he didn't do something drastic she'd try moving in with him, which was the last thing he needed at the moment. He had to get shot of Sinclair first.

He filled the kettle, and switched it on. What the hell did she want? It must be important to have got her out in this weather, especially without an umbrella. Zandra had never been happy about getting her hair wet. In fact he could actually remember an occasion when she had refused to go out because of the rain. But something had her going, today of all days.

"What's up?" he enquired, as he poured the water into the mugs.

"What's up? Are you mad? That's what's up," she raged, stabbing her finger at the paper. "That bomb. You lied when you said you wanted the explosives for a safe cracking job. Now I'm in trouble with my source. He says the police are trying to pin it on him. Anyway why the hell did you have to do it?"

Dan suddenly had a brilliant idea.

"I didn't. It was Sinclair. He made me get them. I had no idea what he wanted them for."

"You're lying."

"No, I swear I'm not," he said, as he decided to play this angle for what it was worth. "In fact I'm worried for my own safety. I am going to have to disappear for a while. Will you help me?"

"Why the hell should I?"

"For old times' sake and a substantial sum of money."

"Oh Hell. What do you want done?" she answered.

"I need a van, I have to get those crates out of the store, and fast. Sinclair might try to get rid of me the same way he did Hill." Dan replied.

"Why would he do it?"

"Hill was getting too greedy. He must have tried to blackmail Sinclair. He had this new girlfriend, and she was a bit pushy, must have been putting pressure on him to get more out of Sinclair. I guess he overstepped the mark."

"Sinclair would never have left himself open to blackmail. Did Hill know something no one else knew?"

"I think he knew Sinclair was about to launch himself in the drugs market. There's a shipment due in sometime within the next seven days."

"Where do you fit in?" Zandra queried.

"I was the mug who found the antiques he intends to pay for the drugs with. And he got those by blackmailing me. And you know exactly how persuasive Sinclair can be."

"Yes, the bastard," she said, gleefully adding, "what can I do to upset his plans?"

"Well, first of all, we get the stuff out of the store. I've already sorted out the best pieces, so he will find what's left doesn't add up to the value he's expecting. Then we need to leave the country."

"Well what are we waiting for?" Zandra said. "Let's go, I know where we can get a van. Do you need anything else from here?"

Dan was surprised, he knew he had to act fast, but this was almost too fast. He had been sitting about doing nothing for weeks, and suddenly he realized what a waste of time it had been, he should have made his getaway as soon as the girl disappeared.

"Only a couple of things," he answered and went to shove them into a holdall. He made sure he had his passport and his driving licence. He knew he would have to get himself a new identity if he was to keep out of Sinclair's clutches, but they would do for the time being. He had a quick look round. All he saw was a few paperbacks and a stack of magazines. There was nothing in the flat that could be classed as a personal possession. He decided to leave his bunch of keys, he would never come back here, and he would never use the car again. Everything he had ever valued had been at Mallaig, which was now carefully packed in the crates at the store waiting to be collected.

"I'm ready when you are," he announced cheerfully. She had believed him that Sinclair was responsible for the bombs. He had her trust and he intended using it for all it was worth.

Chapter 38

The tension in Gavin's house could be measured by the lengthy silences, which were occasionally broken by the welcome sound of the telephone ringing.

In one corner of the room sat Jim. His quietness was probably a result of acute embarrassment, and guilt at his remark made to Jenny at the Mallaig house. That, coupled with his inability to do anything without assistance because of the dressings on his hands, made his presence very demanding, especially on Ellen who was bearing most of the strain. Gavin remembered how worried he had been about bringing Ellen to his house, never expecting her first visit would be quite like this. His ideas had been more romantically inclined, which for him was quite remarkable. She was here now, and seemed very comfortable. She had done wonders in the kitchen, and appeared to have no problem coping with feeding everyone using whatever ingredients she could find, including some he didn't even know he had, which were secreted away in the deepest recesses of his store cupboard.

Jenny meanwhile had been doing her best to show Jim she bore no grudge for what he'd said. Once she had realized her efforts were wasted she kept out of his way, and when she couldn't, she forced herself to be cheerful. Gavin admired her for this, the revelations she had given about her time at the Mallaig house had taken a lot out of her. There had been great relief when she identified Hill from a photo and learned he had not died at the house at Mallaig after her frenzied attack. Gavin could not totally overlook the fact that by her own admission she had publicly wished him dead, Roland's suggestion of complicity lingered. She had spent several hours with one of Roland Hughes men, going through the files that Gavin had taken from her cottage, helping to identify the items she remembered seeing at Gorton Manor which had been at Mallaig. She had also given such good descriptions of the other antiques she had seen, enabling them to tie in three more country house robberies to the same gang. Being helpful seemed to make her happier, and so very different to the withdrawn state she had been in after her visit to the clinic. Nothing seemed to upset her newfound calmness, not even when faced with hostility from Jim when she offered him a helping hand. She seemed to understand it was his helplessness he hated, not her. Gavin could understand how Jim felt, and was not sure how he would feel if he had been in the same unfortunate position.

But Gavin couldn't let Jim's behaviour alter his plans. He had no other solution; Jenny had to be protected, and there was only one place he could think of at short notice that would be perfect. And that was the island. It was the only place where they would not need police protection. He dreaded announcing his plans, but his mind was made up. All he had to do was convince them to accept his decision. He was sure Ellen would not put up a fight, but how Jim and Jenny would respond, remained to be seen.

One of the earlier calls had been from Roland Hughes. He and a few of his men were still following

Dan Trench, who had taken off that morning with his female companion. They had collected a van, then gone to the store and loaded up the crates from the second bay. The homing devices had made it easier for Roland and his men to keep close enough without the danger of being spotted. Gavin wished he knew what Trench was up to. All he knew so far was the pair were heading south. Gavin had decided he couldn't wait too long before they picked up Trench. They had enough reason to stop and search the van. If the contents contained any of the antiques Jenny had described as having been at the house at Mallaig they would have sufficient to detain him in custody. The more Gavin pondered the matter, the more certain he became that Trench was the only person who could provide the link between Sinclair and Gillespie. If the right pressure was exerted Trench would most likely give them all the information they needed.

Gavin hated being stuck waiting for the phone to ring. He hated not knowing when he could make the next move, or even what the move would be. He longed to find some solid evidence of Sinclair's involvement with the antique thefts, or with the bombings, anything so long as there was indisputable proof.

Ellen brought him in another cup of coffee. Gavin thanked her and motioned for her to sit down.

"Please help me," he said keeping his voice as low as he could. "They're not going to like what I have in mind, so I'm hoping you'll help convince them." He took a quick look round, Jim had heard the remark and was paying attention, Jenny had entered the room, and settling herself down in a chair by the fire, she looked up as if sensing she was expected to listen.

"I'll try," Ellen answered slightly hesitantly.

"I want you all to go back to the island."

"No!" Jim said firmly.

It was the reply he had anticipated from Jim, but Gavin was not deterred. "It's the only place I can guarantee Jenny will be safe. I can't afford the manpower to keep a twenty-four hour watch over her, and I'm certain she's still in danger."

"Why the hell can't she stay here? Jim snapped.

"Because, this is probably the lease safe place for her to stay. There's someone I work with who's involved with the Mallaig house, and the bombings. I don't know how dangerous he can be. Jenny is a key witness, and I don't want him to know she exists. I can't risk her life."

"I'll go," Ellen offered, "and Jim, unless you can find yourself a nursemaid in a hurry, you'll have to come with us." She looked across at Jenny. "You will come won't you?"

"I've caused enough trouble, I'll go wherever you suggest," Jenny said quietly. "I'm sorry if it means putting you all out."

"Sorry Gavin, I was being selfish," Jim said with a sigh. "I'll go. I hadn't realized Jenny was in danger still. I was only thinking how useless I'd be."

Gavin smiled, "Thanks, it's quite a relief to have you all agree. I shall get you taken over by the rescue service. I can get Dave Morgan to standby to check your hands before you go. I'll also get him to ensure you have enough dressings and any other medication you might need, all you have to do is give me a list."

The phone rang. It was Roland Hughes, who quickly told him Dan Trench appeared to be heading for the ferry terminal. Gavin issued the instruction to stop Trench at the first opportunity, and take him and the woman in for questioning. Roland agreed and hung up.

Gavin had a new sense of urgency. He wanted to be sure Jenny was safely out of the way, before any more information about Dan Trench came in. He wanted to be able to give catching Sinclair his full attention. He quickly put in a call to Alistair Duncan at his home, and between them arranged the transport, medical supplies, and some food. Alistair was more than happy to help when he knew Ellen was to be one of his passengers. He promised that he'd come and collect them from Gavin's house early in the morning.

Chapter 39

Gavin had ample time once Ellen had left for the island to formulate a plan. Arresting Dan Trench had provided confirmation of Sinclair's involvement. Trench had become very co-operative, especially after he had been led to believe his arrest had been ordered by Sinclair. Trench was aware connections between himself, Mallaig, Gillespie, Jenny, the stolen antiques, and the bombs had been made, but didn't know what proof they had. The fact that he had been in possession of stolen goods was sufficient to enable Roland to keep him locked up, pending further enquiries.

It was his girlfriend who broke down first. Once identified as Zandra Snow, the missing tutor of the classes Jenny had attended, Roland had a field day. He told her they knew about her activities, and had enough evidence on the house burglaries to put her inside for years, again hinting Sinclair was responsible for her arrest. It had started a flood of information. She swore Sinclair was the one who masterminded the robberies, and was blackmailing both herself and Trench. She told them he had something big planned which was coming off within the next week, which Dan had been trying to get out of, against Sinclair's wishes.

Trench when faced with this accusation had eventually confessed the stolen property in his possession had belonged to Sinclair as payment of a gambling debt. They had been destined as payment for a shipment of drugs Sinclair was purchasing.

The mention of drugs had opened a completely new dimension to the investigation. Gavin and Roland both agreed reinforcements were necessary; they could not risk letting a shipment through because of lack of manpower, nor could they risk letting Sinclair get off the hook. The main investigation was to be conducted by Roland Hughes with all paperwork being done through his department, thereby avoiding the complication of Sinclair's involvement. Gavin would concentrate on setting up Sinclair, by slipping him prearranged snippets of information, leaving all the details of phone taps, surveillance teams and co-ordination to Roland.

Both Sinclair's home phone and his office line were to be monitored. All Gavin had to do was pass on enough information to Sinclair to cause him anxiety. Then his reactions would be recorded.

The video of Dan Trench swapping the crates in the store was to be the catalyst. Gavin had to find a way of passing it on to Sinclair without him suspecting he was being watched. They had considered using Steven Fowler, but while he had proved his honesty when tested with the blackmail letter at Hill's flat, Gavin decided it would be better if the information came from a more open source. And what better way, than by Gavin returning from his holiday, finding out from Paula about the video, and immediately going to Sinclair and asking for the Mallaig investigation to be reopened.

Gavin found his house seemed strangely quiet, and empty. Everywhere he looked he could see the evidence of Ellen's recent visit. There were so many little signs, the curtains had been drawn back neatly, the dishes had been removed from the draining board and neatly stacked in the cupboard and the tea was in the caddy, not in its original packet. He put the kettle on, and decided instead of his usual tea bag immersed in a mug served up with the spoon in it, he would be civilized and make himself a pot. He found a tray, placed the teapot, sugar bowl, milk bottle and mug on it. He smiled to himself. Ellen would approve, though the milk bottle marred perfection.

The doorbell rang. Gavin hurried to answer it. Alistair Duncan stood grinning on the doorstep.

"Can I come in?" he asked. "I thought you could do with some company."

"Of course," Gavin answered, genuinely pleased to see him. "Did everything go all right this morning?"

"Yes, no problems at all, Dave Morgan checked over Jim's hands, they're healing very well I gather, but I have to confess I couldn't stomach watching him dress them. He says as long as Jim doesn't do anything foolish, in a couple of weeks they can remove the heavy dressings, and then he can begin to exercise his fingers gently. I think Jim will do what he's been told, he fully understands the dangers of ignoring the advice he's been given."

"That's a relief. I don't suppose he and Jenny were talking to each other?"

"Not much, I admit I did notice the tense atmosphere."

"An understatement if ever I heard one."

"Yes, but more interesting is what's up between you and Ellen?" Alistair said, adding quickly. "Don't deny it, I've known both of you for too long not to know there is something going on."

"The truth?"

"Yes."

"Nothing and everything," Gavin said with a sigh. "I seem to have had bad luck with timing. Something always crops up just when I've nearly plucked up the courage to declare my interest."

"Well I wouldn't worry too much, I have a suspicion she won't run out on you."

"Do you mean that honestly?"

"Yes, I'm serious, she has developed a glow that's been missing for years. Don't leave it too long."

"Don't worry, I won't." Gavin said firmly, as he set about making his guest welcome. They had a lot to talk about, and Gavin was glad to have someone with whom he could confide and reminisce.

The morning briefing went absolutely as planned. Gavin listened in turn to everyone's account of their activities during his absence, giving praise, and suggestions for further action where necessary. Finally he got to Paula.

Paula told them about the sudden interest in the car they had seen at Mallaig, and the possibility it was the same one that had been blown up on the motorway, and then how they had found the blackmail note at Hill's flat. Then she told them about the video her friend had made, showing Dan Trench swapping crates in the store. She said he'd only checked the film after Dan Trench had come back to collect the load. Seeing Dan back again reminded him about the video made of his previous visit.

Gavin had interrupted and suggested they watch the recording. As soon as the tape stopped, he announced he must show it to Sinclair. It would force him to authorize reopening the Mallaig house investigation.

Chapter 40

Sinclair's worst nightmare was coming true. Trench was trying to double cross him. The video had been enough to convince him of that. Was Trench going to try to blackmail him, using the stolen crates as leverage? Or worse, could he be planning to disappear with the stuff from the store? Knowing Zandra Snow had been with him the night he had switched the crates was a bad omen. Sinclair had crossed paths with her on several occasions and never enjoyed dealing with her, perhaps because he had never really succeeded in dominating her.

And then to add to his problems Gavin McKay was once more ferreting about trying to find a connection between Trench and Mallaig. Did the man never quit? What else did he know? Sinclair suspected McKay knew a great deal more than he was admitting. Had he come to ask permission to reopen the case because of protocol, or for more devious reasons? Sinclair couldn't be sure. It had taken a lot of control to hide his fear when McKay had played the video to him. He was left without choice. The Mallaig investigation had to become official. Somehow he had managed to answer yes, with an inward sigh of relief that Steven had made sure nothing linked him with the house at Mallaig.

One cheering suggestion about the operation came from McKay himself. Steven Fowler was to be assigned to watch the crates in the warehouse. Sinclair had been more than happy to agree.

After Gavin left his office Sinclair slumped into his chair, his heart pounding in panic. The frightening possibility that Trench had stolen part of the consignment of crates from the Mallaig house was far worse than even McKay could imagine. If Trench had left the consignment of antiques short of the value he had promised for the shipment, he'd be in big trouble. The full quota barely covered his debt. Attempting to pay with a load that was under-value would be suicidal.

Why had Trench gone to the trouble of substituting the crates? Unfortunately the answers that came to mind reeked of double dealing. Time was against him, he would have to check personally to discover what Trench had done. At least Steven might be in a position to help. But, if the shipment was short, the nightmare was only beginning. He had run out of places to get cash at short notice and it would take too long to find another backer.

Sinclair shivered, oblivious of the fact that the office was warmer than usual because the sun had been shining in for most of the morning. It was a shiver of fear. He had always known the deal was risky. Not just because of its size, or its complexity. The biggest danger came from the fact he would be setting up in opposition to existing dealers in the area. Some were known to him, some were even related by marriage, and nearly all of them had at one time or another been at his mercy, which was how he had made the contacts necessary to set up the deal. But if it went wrong, he could expect neither sympathy nor support from the people he had so blatantly planned to betray. If the shipment was short, as he suspected it was, he would have to pass on the deal, knowing the chance of ever getting into the drug dealing business would never be open to him again.

But first things first. Finding out what was left in the crates was top priority, which meant he must take an active part in the investigation, thereby avoiding surprises from McKay.

Gradually Sinclair began to calm down. He checked his commitments for the following few days, decided which he could postpone, and which he had to honour. Then he went down to see Gavin McKay to take control of the investigation.

Enthusiasm and co-operation from McKay came as quite a surprise. He had expected hostility knowing McKay's animosity was long held, never mind the addition of his being jealous at being overlooked for promotion.

"Tell me what you've organized so far," Sinclair said, after he'd been introduced to everyone in Gavin's department.

"Paula Dawson's friend Fergus, who supplied the video from the warehouse is due to take a three week holiday, and we've already negotiated for Steven to replace him while he's on leave," Gavin answered.

Sinclair could hardly hide his delight it couldn't have been organized better. He would be able to arrange with Steven to get in and open up the crates to see exactly what Trench had left in the store.

"When does he start?"

"They've asked for him to go over this afternoon, to learn the routine, looks as if he'll be in charge from tomorrow," Gavin replied.

It was tempting to ask about the night-time security arrangements, but Sinclair decided not to ask for too much detail, Steven Fowler ought to be able to fill him in once he had been to the store and been shown the ropes.

"Good," Sinclair said, before delving further. "Have forensic found anything worthwhile with the note found in Hill's flat? And has there been any further news about the explosive used to blow up the car?"

"Nothing on either, yet," Gavin answered, then added. "Would you like the Midlands Police to report direct to you?"

"Yes, that's a good idea," he said, again puzzled by the helpfulness Gavin was displaying.

He lingered for a while checking out what everyone was doing, and managed to text Steven the moment he was on his own before leaving the department. "Call in at the house this evening," he instructed.

Chapter 41

Gavin was delighted at how well Sinclair had responded. He had acted precisely as anticipated, but Gavin had to be careful not to become too complacent, a lot could go wrong. Secrecy was the key. Only Paula and Tom Jackson knew about the existence of Roland Hughes, and his team of detectives working in the background. Steven Fowler was also aware that Gavin was still investigating Sinclair's activities and any information he could pass on would be considered valuable. He had dutifully told Gavin of Sinclair's request for him to call at his house in the evening after he had been told of his assignment at the warehouse, and had asked for instructions as to how he should behave.

"Do exactly what he asks you to do. Don't even ask him why, just do it."

"But what if I know it's wrong?" Steven had asked, obviously terrified of the possible consequences of continuing to obey his uncle's instructions without question.

"As long as you don't actually endanger someone's life, then go ahead. I promise it won't go against you later. All I ask is for you to let Paula, or myself know what he wants you to do."

"How long for?" Steven queried.

"As long as necessary. Unless we have enough evidence to convict we won't make any move at all," Gavin answered. "And by that I mean evidence of serious crime, not some petty misdemeanour, is that clear enough?"

Steven nodded and said, "Perfectly."

Then the waiting game began. In anticipation of Sinclair's first move, surveillance cameras, and microphones had been installed in the warehouse. For added security Steven was not informed.

Steven, who had been rostered to cover the store on the Saturday evening, had been there for less than half an hour, when Hector Sinclair had appeared, making no effort to conceal his arrival. Once inside the premises he had poked about looking at the systems, and questioning Steven about the possibility of there being other security precautions in force. Steven had confidently told him he was the only person on watch, but could call for assistance at the press of a button, which would alert the rest of the team. Sinclair wanted more information about the internal security video system that had caught Trench doing his swap. Steven showed him the recording equipment, and explained the instructions the warehouse owner had given him earlier in the afternoon. Sinclair had prowled right round the enormous storage area. He examined the Mallaig crates with considerable interest. He then instructed Steven to switch off the recording device. Steven had made a token protest but obeyed.

"We have to open these crates, check the contents and reseal them. And be neat about it. Make sure nobody can tell we've opened them," Sinclair said. He produced a hammer, nails, and a tyre lever, which he handed to Steven. "You start on that one, lever off that section, be careful, don't damage the timber."

Steven set to work, and as soon as he had prised open one crate, Sinclair set him onto the next. It took several hours for them to open all the crates and for Sinclair to check the contents, and finally to reseal them. Once the job was done he instructed Steven to find a broom and sweep up the area where they'd worked.

Sinclair gave no explanation for his activities he simply reminded Steven that he should keep silent about what he'd done and instructed Steven to restart the video recorder. "If anyone queried the gap, say you had been demonstrating the tape to me and in the process rewound the tape to the beginning."

He patrolled the store once more, shook hands with Steven then departed.

Within minutes of his departure Steven had phoned Gavin and relayed the details of what had happened. Gavin was glad he'd called. It added further proof of his conviction Steven was totally trustworthy, but not to the point of telling him about the additional hidden cameras that had been installed.

Gavin was still not clear about what Sinclair had been looking for, but such an intense interest in the contents of the crates had to tie him into the Mallaig affair. It was just a matter of time before he made his next move, and Gavin intended being there when he did so.

The phone tap on Sinclair's office and private lines provided a great deal of interesting connections. Sinclair was desperately trying to raise large sums of money. He appeared to be calling in every outstanding favour owed to him, and his tactics were far from honourable. As the list of people he called mounted so did Gavin's desire to bring an end to Sinclair's corruption. Checking out the names on the list revealed the depth of his treachery. He was blackmailing most of the people he called, threatening to reopen cases which previously he had used his position to close down. The crimes ranged from petty theft, to murder.

"I can't understand how he got away with it for so long," Gavin said to Roland as he listened to the recordings of the phone calls.

"Well, his days are numbered, I'm as determined as you are to nail him," Roland replied.

"How much has he raised so far, assuming all those he's demanded money from pay up?"

"Nearly two hundred and forty thousand pounds and he hasn't finished yet."

"I wonder how much more he needs, and if he'll get it all by his Wednesday deadline? Trench taking off with those crates really did put his back to the wall."

"Couldn't he ask his wife, isn't she loaded?" Roland asked.

"Yes, unless of course she's lost it all at the races. She's a pretty heavy gambler, not to mention drinker."

"Where did her money come from originally?"

"Her father. He was a very successful bookie. When he died, the business went to the two brothers, and a large lump sum to Stella. Then she married an older man with a fortune, who died quite quickly and she got his fortune to add to her own. Then Sinclair moved in. I think he fancied living in the posh house, though I doubt it's been a perfect partnership, as far as I can make out they have absolutely nothing in common, except perhaps a love of money."

"What are we going to do? Let them all pay up? Or do we pick them up now?"

"We have to let them pay. He needs the cash to do the deal, and we need the deal to come off, firstly to catch Sinclair red handed, and secondly to keep that shipment of drugs off the street."

"It's crazy that we have to let it go so far, in order to catch him. Oh, before I forget, I've arranged for Trench's car and the van he used to pick up the crates to be left in the car park you suggested."

"Good, I'll arrange for them to be found tomorrow, it will make it seem the department is making some progress. We have to try to give the impression we're not sitting on our tail-ends doing nothing at all."

Chapter 42

Sinclair could feel the perspiration form on his upper lip. Why the hell had he ever let himself get into such a fix? He had managed to get the rest of the crates out of the store, thanks to Steven being in charge, and by using the same technique of swapping crates that Trench used, except this time he'd replaced the full ones with identical sized empty ones. The full crates were now in a lock up near the dock, ready for Thursday morning's delivery. He had also managed to raise over half the amount of cash needed to make up the deficit Trench had created when he absconded.

He still hadn't approached the family for help. They wouldn't take kindly to his request and hand over the money without knowing what he wanted it for. The only solution was to cut them into the deal. No doubt that they would demand a huge share, probably a lot more than he was willing to part with, but he was out of choices. If he failed to produce the money, the supplier would lynch him. Being in debt to the family was a considerably healthier alternative.

He had been ultra nice to Stella for the last five days, trying to ensure her support in the event of his needing help. He knew asking her outright for money would be useless. She would never give it to him without informing her brothers, and they would want to know why he needed funds so quickly. His best hope was to cut them into the deal and make it sound as if he had planned for them to be partners all along. No need for them to know he needed them to save his skin. He had carefully prepared his speech, but the tension while he waited for them to arrive was almost unbearable.

He tried to cheer himself up by plotting how he would finally get McKay off the Mallaig case. Trench had done an excellent job of disappearing. Perhaps it would be best if he wasn't found.

Once the shipment had been collected Sinclair would let Gavin get a search warrant for the crates in store, make him feel a fool for having spent so many man hours watching empty crates, and tarnish his impeccable reputation.

He heard the doorbell, and listened to Stella greeting his two brothers-in-law. He poured himself a stiff drink, which he downed in one gulp, quickly refilling his glass, and began to prepare drinks for the two men. Once they were seated he positioned himself in front of the fire, ready to launch into his proposal.

"I have a proposition to put to you. A profitable one," he added quietly. The two seated men stared at him with blank expressions. They seemed to be even more aggressive towards him than usual. "I've been given an opportunity to get in on a very large deal, and I agreed because I knew it would appeal to you. It requires a considerable amount of cash, but the rewards will be huge." They said nothing. Sinclair was left with no choice but to keep talking and outline the deal.

"What percentage did you have in mind for us?" one of the brothers asked when he'd finished outlining the plan.

"Thirty per cent," Sinclair answered with relief. They must be interested if they wanted to know their cut.

"Seventy five, or nothing," the other brother replied.

"That's ridiculous," spluttered Sinclair.

"No it isn't, and you know it. If we don't give you the money, you're in dead trouble. Do you think we didn't know what you were planning? If so, then you're even more of a fool than we thought."

"You fixed for Trench to do a bunk?"

"Oh no. But he was kind enough to let us know what you were up to before he vanished. He owed us a favour, and decided to clear his debt. We've been waiting for you to call us, and you certainly took your time about it. We're not too impressed you took so long. We know you only asked us because you couldn't raise enough cash elsewhere. In fact you could say it hurt our feelings, which is why we think seventy five per cent is a fair cut."

Sinclair knocked back the contents of his glass. What could he say? He hadn't been expecting them to be so well informed about his deal. He'd lost the edge, and knew he'd have to accept their offer. They had him well and truly trapped. He thought for a moment, perhaps he should try to up the percentage, just a fraction, if only to pretend he wasn't scared.

"Don't even think about arguing. We know exactly who you're dealing with, and he doesn't take kindly to being mucked about. If you argue, we'll walk out, and we'll make damn sure you can't raise the cash elsewhere. The only thing we stand to lose is the slightly dubious asset of a senior policeman in the family."

"OK you win, seventy-five percent. But you get to collect the goods."

"Not without you."

"What do you mean?"

"Do you expect us to trust you after you tried to cut in on our territory? No way. You have to be there and at every other delivery we ever have to give us a nice sense of security."

Chapter 43

Gavin and Roland sat huddled together in the cramped space inside the freight container they had commandeered on the dock front. Roland nudged Gavin and passed him a mug of coffee from his thermos flask.

"Anything happening?"

"No, not yet. We don't expect much to happen until after four. The boat won't be able to dock before then because of the tide."

"How many men have you got out there?" Gavin asked.

"Thirty, not counting the crew of the drug patrol boat. I think it should be enough."

"There's one thing I'm not happy about," Gavin said. "I still can't work out why Sinclair ordered Hill to plant the bomb at Jenny's. I can understand why he wanted Gillespie disposed of. And if Hill killed him, that would be enough to make him dangerous. But I have a feeling Trench is lying, and Sinclair didn't even know she existed."

"One man's word against another's," Roland answered.

"Look, car lights, someone's coming. We'd better shut up."

They silently watched as two cars drew up. Sinclair, the two Bairstow brothers, and three other men got out and went to the store they had hired a few days before. Then they began moving the crates out onto the jetty, ready for loading. The six men paced up and down, trying to keep themselves warm. One cupped his hands round the flame of a match as he lit a cigarette, the little red glow clearly visible from Gavin's vantage point.

Then Gavin heard the faint chug of an engine. The sound gradually getting louder and louder, then finally the engine noise stopped. Muffled voices echoed in the distance, followed by the sound of a heavy rope hitting the quay.

Two men disembarked, and began talking to Sinclair and the Bairstows. Then they called out to a third man on board, "OK, start loading."

"How long shall we wait?" asked Roland as he moved his weight from one leg to the other.

"Not much longer, Sinclair has to take possession before we move. They're bringing something off the boat. It looks like a briefcase. Sinclair has it. He's moving towards the car. Let's go."

There was a sudden blinding surge of light, as Roland hit the switch connected to an array of spotlights.

"This is the police," the voice on the tannoy boomed out. "Don't move. You're under arrest."

Sinclair spun round, obviously blinded by the lights, trying to make out who was calling out, and where the sound was coming from.

One of the Bairstows dived for cover behind the car, shouting out. "You bastard, I'll get you for this." He fired a shot at Sinclair. Sinclair dropped the case, and began to run. He was heading straight towards Gavin. A second shot was fired. Sinclair screamed and fell. He was about ten yards from safety, and Gavin could see clearly he'd been hit in the leg.

Without thinking of his own safety, Gavin dashed out and dragged Sinclair out of danger.

"Drop your weapon," A clear voice on the tannoy instructed. "We have you covered."

Bairstow threw the gun into water, and stood up slowly, placing his hands on the roof of the car behind which he had been taking cover.

"Move away from the car," the voice called. "Lie down on the ground with your hands and feet apart." The other men all obeyed instantly. Bairstow was the last to comply with the order.

The boat engine spluttered as someone tried to restart it. The drug patrol vessel drew up alongside the fishing boat and boarded it. The officers making their way cautiously below decks, reappearing quickly with the crew with their hands raised over their heads.

The successful operation was marred by the wounding of Sinclair.

"You were a fool to risk your life to save him," Roland said to Gavin after the ambulance crew had taken Sinclair away.

"Rubbish, you know as well as I do, that if I hadn't gone, you would have."

"Probably," admitted Roland.

"The difference is I really wanted him alive," Gavin said, "I want him to find out the hard way, that corruption doesn't pay."

"He'll do that all right with what we know about him."

"Yes, but let's make sure the paperwork is perfect. I don't want him getting off on any technicalities," Gavin said.

"Don't worry, I'll double check everything."

"How much was the haul?"

"We think the street value of the drugs would be in the region of half a million pounds. Plus the antiques that Trench had told us about, and the cash he raised to make up for what Trench stole."

"Thank God we stopped it when we did."

"Yes. What are you going to do about all Sinclair's enemies? He certainly seems to have accumulated more than his fair share over the years. Are you going to reopen all the files that you know he closed, in spite of his promises?

"I'm not sure if we'll bother with all of them, but certainly some will have to be looked into. That reminds me, we ought to send someone round to tell Steven Fowler what's happened. It's not fair to leave him sitting in that warehouse wondering when we're going to make a move. And I'd better get over to the hospital to see how badly Sinclair was wounded."

"And then I presume you'll hot foot it over to the island to see Ellen."

"That has distinct possibilities," Gavin answered happily.

Chapter 44

"It isn't working," Ellen said to Gavin over the transmitter. "They barely speak to each other."

"I'm sorry, but we had no choice. It was the only place where I knew she'd be safe. Anyway it's all over we've arrested Sinclair, and the others. She'll be fine now. I'm trying to get Alistair to bring me over to the island then I'll tell you all about it."

"Good. Because I don't think we can take the strain much longer."

"Dr. Matthews is putting pressure on me to find out if Jim has got her decision yet. He told me to tell Jim if he doesn't do it soon he'll have him up on a malpractice charge. Do you know if he's talked to her?"

"I don't think so," Ellen answered after getting a negative signal from Jim.

"Well for heaven sake make sure he does, and soon, because if she does want to go ahead I'll have to make arrangements immediately."

Jenny stood quietly in the doorway wondering what it was that Jim was supposed to do.

"What was that about?" she asked as soon as Ellen had finished the transmission.

"Nothing," Jim answered rather sharply.

"Jim, you have to get on with it," Ellen cut in. "You heard what Gavin said."

"Not now."

"When?"

"Don't interfere," he snapped back. "I'll deal with it later."

"For all our sakes, there's no point in putting it off."

"I'm going for a walk, I'll do it when I come back," he said as he limped over to the door.

Jenny knew he couldn't manage the handle yet, and instinctively reached out to open it for him. All she got in the way of thanks was a cursory nod as he left.

"Ellen, you've got to tell me. I can't bear to see you and Jim fighting, especially over something to do with me."

"I can't."

"It's something to do with my abortion, isn't it?"

Ellen said nothing.

"Please tell me," she begged. "I know he'll never forgive me. But I had to do it. You can understand that, can't you?" Jenny sobbed, tears streaming down her face.

"I think so," Ellen answered quietly

"I hate myself. I've tried to pretend that none of it happened, I've tried to block it all out." She wiped her tears away with the back of her hand. "But I can't. I should never have done it, and now Jim will never forgive me. I know he thinks it was his child and he hates me for what I did."

Ellen put her arm round Jenny. "No he doesn't. Go and talk to him. Tell him what you've just told me."

"I love him so much. I never wanted to hurt him. And now it's too late."

"No it isn't. He loves you too. And I know that even if you do decide to go ahead with the abortion, he'll still love you," Ellen said gently.

"What do you mean… if I go ahead with the abortion? It's too late. It's dead. I killed my child."

"No Jenny. No. You're wrong. It's not too late. Jim stopped it."

"He stopped it? What? How? I don't understand," she blurted out, "I don't believe this." She felt quite unable to cope with what Ellen was telling her.

"Your abortion. Jim went to the hospital and stopped it."

"Why didn't anyone tell me?"

"They did. Dr. Matthews told you himself. You behaved so oddly afterward he thought it was because you were angry. We tried to discuss it several times, but you always dived under the bedclothes and refused to talk. We thought that's why you were so tense around Jim. We assumed you were angry with him."

"I don't remember Dr. Matthews telling me. I only know I hated myself for what I'd done."

"Well, Jim has instructions to find out if you want to proceed with the abortion. Dr. Matthews didn't feel you were in a fit state to make the decision before Gavin dragged you back to Mallaig. Naturally Jim's not keen to organize it, and he's been putting off the evil day, hoping that you'll leave it too late for them to do it at all."

"I can't believe it," she sniffed and wiped her eyes. "You're telling me that I'm still pregnant!"

"Yes," answered Ellen putting her arm around her.

"It's so stupid, crying like this. But I'm so happy. I can't stop it," Jenny sobbed. "I've got to find Jim. Where do you think he is?"

"He might have gone to see Ned."

"No. I don't think so. He didn't look in the mood for talking. He'll have headed toward the ruined monastery," Jenny said, feeling calmer. Though I doubt he'll have the strength to get that far.

"You're probably right. I'd forgotten it was where he always used to go to be alone. Shall I come with you?"

"No. I'd rather go by myself," Jenny pulled on her coat and as she opened the door to leave, turned and said, "Thanks for telling me everything."

It didn't take long to catch up with Jim. He had stopped and perched on a large flat rock, sheltered from the wind not very far up the path. Jenny she was quite breathless when she reached him as she had run most of the way.

"Jim, we have to talk," she said as she flopped onto the rock beside him.

"Are you OK?" he asked.

"Yes, I'm fine, just a little out of breath," she panted.

"What's wrong?"

"Ellen told me about the abortion."

"She had no right to," he said angrily. "I suppose you ran up here to tell me you want to go ahead."

"No!"

Jim stared at her with a totally disbelieving look.

"Are you sure?" he stammered.

"Jim I'm so happy. I hated myself so much. And I thought you'd never forgive me for what I'd done. Thank you for stopping it."

"Sorry, I don't understand your change of mood."

"I didn't know."

"Know what?"

"That you stopped the abortion. I thought I'd killed my child. I've been so depressed and I hated myself for what I thought I'd done. When Ellen said I could have the baby I thought she was going crazy. But now I'm so happy. I'm sorry, I can't stop crying," she wiped her eyes with the back of her hand.

"You really thought you'd got rid of the baby?"

"Yes, and I thought you hated me because of it."

"I could never hate you. But I couldn't understand why you'd want to do it," he answered.

Jenny looked away, saying nothing.

"You were raped. Weren't you?" he said softly.

"Yes," she muttered wishing he hadn't asked. She didn't want to think about it anymore. But she could tell he wasn't going to give up.

"That's the reason?"

"It was one reason. The main one was I couldn't face having to tell the child when it grew up I'd killed its father," she replied quietly.

"You'd have been wrong. You didn't kill its father."

"I know. Gavin has finally convinced me of that."

"That's not what I meant. You didn't kill its father because you're looking at him now," Jim said firmly.

She took a deep breath. He had claimed that it was his child before. When? Then she remembered it had been at the cottage moments before that frightening call from Dan Trench that had sent her running.

"I don't care who you think you murdered. That child is mine," he said, then added almost as an afterthought. "I have proof."

"What?"

"My notes. The ones I wrote when we were stuck here on the island."

"Why should I believe them? You could easily have adjusted them to suit your needs."

"How?" he yelled, waving his bandaged hands at her. "Just tell me how. I haven't learnt to write with a pen wedged between my toes."

They stared at each other in silence for a moment.

"Sorry, I didn't mean to get angry," Jim said.

"No, I'm the one who should be apologising. I didn't mean to sound as if I didn't want you to be the father, I never allowed myself to consider it as a possibility before. Perhaps I knew that if I did, I would never have been able to go through with the abortion. Forgive me?"

"What for?"

"Nearly killing your child."

"I will, so long as you remember it is my child. Sorry. Our child."

She bent over and kissed him. "I'll remember."

"And one other favour, please," he asked.

"What?"

"Salvage my reputation."

"How?"

"Marry me."

She didn't know then whether to laugh or cry. In the space of an hour she had gone from depression, through confusion to elation, but right now she needed time to accept the facts before she could make any commitments.

"Jenny, I don't need an answer right now. All I want you to know is that I love you," he said, then added with a grin on his face, "and I can cope with the scandal, if that's what you want."

Jenny laughed, kissed him and said, "I promise I'll give you an answer soon."

The drone of a helicopter approaching the island gave her a respite.

"That's probably Gavin."

"Shall we go back?"

"Don't let's rush, I think Gavin and Ellen deserve a little time together."

"I think you're using them as an excuse to stay out here on your own with me," Jim an swered jokingly.

"You could be right," she said happily.

MHM Photograpy

Caro Ayre

A childhood in Kenya provided lasting memories of hot sun filled days, vibrant coloured birds and flowers, armies of insects, roaming wildlife in vast expanses of open spaces and warm waves lapping on silvery sands.

I now live in rural Somerset where family, gardening, painting and writing keep boredom at bay.

For more information about my writing go to:-
http://caroayre.wordpress.com/
Twitter @AyreC
Facebook- Caro Ayre Author
www.CaroAyre.co.uk

Feast of the Antlion
Caro Ayre

An action packed novel with a touch of romance set in Kenya.

Poachers, plane crashes, blackmail and murder are not what Sandra Harriman expected to face when she took control of a huge wildlife conservation project.

Sandra feels like an ant in an antlion's trap as she fights to protect her step children's inheritance.

Uncovering her dead husband's secrets leave her wondering who can be trusted

http://www.amazon.co.uk/dp/B006PZBXCI
http://www.amazon.com/dp/B006PZBXCI
ISBN 978-0-9572224-0-3

Breathless
Secrets tear a family apart
Caro Ayre

A family drama of coping with a life threatening illness

Clare has battled for sixteen years to keep Hannah healthy while Mike, her husband, has never accepted that their daughter has Cystic Fibrosis.

The reappearance of an old flame and exciting challenges set by her children complicate her bid for a fresh start. Repairing the fragile bond between her children and their father is an uphill struggle, but worth fighting for.

A donation to the Cystic Fibrosis Trust is made for every copy sold.

www.amazon.com/dp/B00DOFT5VI
www.amazon.co.uk/dp/B00DOFT5VI
ISBN 987-0-9572224-1-0

Lightning Source UK Ltd.
Milton Keynes UK
UKHW041244010520
362627UK00004B/687